For M

THANK YOU: Angus Wolfe-Murray, Caroline Dawnay, Billy Franks, Iain Ruxton, Piers Hawkins, Patricia Festorazzi, Andrew Torrance, Grant McLennan ('write somethin' funny'), assorted L,B sickos, and especially Mum & Dad, for instilling in me the reverence and gravity evident upon these pages.

Quite Ugly One Morning

Quite Ugly One Morning

Christopher Brookmyre

LITTLE, BROWN AND COMPANY

A *Little, Brown* Book

First published in Great Britain in 1996
by Little, Brown and Company

A CIP catalogue record for this book
is available from the British Library.

HARDBACK ISBN 0 316 87883 9
C FORMAT ISBN 0 316 87884 7

Typeset by Palimpsest Book Production Limited,
Polmont, Stirlingshire
Printed and bound in Great Britain by
Clays Ltd, St Ives plc

Little, Brown and Company (UK)
Brettenham House
Lancaster Place
London WC2E 7EN

ONE

'Jesus fuck.'

Inspector McGregor wished there was some kind of official crime scenario checklist, just so that he could have a quick glance and confirm that he *had* seen it all now. He hadn't sworn at a discovery for ages, perfecting instead a resigned, fatigued expression that said, 'Of course. How could I have possibly expected anything less?'

The kids had both moved out now. He was at college in Bristol and she was somewhere between Bombay and Bangkok, with a backpack, a dose of the runs and some nose-ringed English poof of a boyfriend. Amidst the unaccustomed calm and quiet, himself and the wife had remembered that they once actually used to like each other, and work had changed from being somewhere to escape to, to something he hurried home from.

He had done his bit for the force – worked hard, been dutiful, been honest, been dutifully dishonest when it was required of him; he was due his reward and very soon he would be getting it.

Islay. Quiet wee island, quiet wee polis station. No more of the junkie undead, no more teenage jellyhead stabbings, no more pissed-up rugby fans impaling themselves on the Scott Monument, no more tweed riots in Jenners, and, best of all, no more fucking Festival. Nothing more serious to contend with than illicit stills and the odd fight over cheating with someone else's sheep.

Bliss.

Christ. Who was he kidding? He just had to look at what was before him to realise that the day after he arrived, Islay would declare itself the latest independent state in the new Europe and take over Ulster's mantle as the UK's number one terrorist blackspot.

The varied bouquet of smells was a delightful courtesy detail. From the overture of fresh vomit whiff that greeted you at the foot of the close stairs, through the mustique of barely cold urine on the landing, to the tear-gas, fist-in-face guard-dog of guff that savaged anyone entering the flat, it just told you how much fun this case would be.

McGregor looked grimly down at his shoes and the ends of his trousers. The postman's voluminous spew had covered the wooden floor of the doorway from wall to wall, and extended too far down the hall for him to clear it with a jump. His two-footed splash had streaked his Docs, his ankles and the yellowing skirting board. Another six inches and he'd have made it, but he hadn't been able to get a run at it because of the piss, which had flooded the floor on the close side of the doorway, diked off from the tide of gastric refugees by a draught excluder.

The postman had noticed that the door was ajar and had knocked on it, then pushed it further open, leaning in to see whether the occupant was all right. Upon seeing what was within he had simultaneously thrown up and wet himself, the upper and lower halves of his body depositing their damning comments on the situation either side of the aperture.

'Postman must be built like the fuckin' Tardis,' McGregor muttered to himself, leaving vomity footprints on the floorboards as he trudged reluctantly down the hall. 'How could a skinny wee smout like that hold so much liquid?'

He had a quick look at the lumpy puddle behind him. Onion, rice, the odd cardamom pod. Curry, doubtless preceded by a minimum six pints of heavy. Not quite so appetising second time around.

He turned again to face into the flat, took a couple of short paces, then heard a splash and felt something splat against his calves.

'Sorry, sir. Long jump never was my speciality. Guess I'll be for the high jump now, eh? Ha ha ha.'

Ah yes, thought McGregor. Only now was it complete. Deep down he had suspected that it wasn't quite cataclysmically hellish enough yet, but now Skinner was here, and the final piece was in place. What this situation had needed, what it had been audibly crying out for, was a glaikit, baw-faced, irritating, clumsy, thick, ginger-heided bastard to turn up and start cracking duff jokes, and here was PC Gavin Skinner to answer the call.

He was not going to lose his temper. He felt that on a morning like this, it was only a short distance between snapping at Skinner and waking up in a soft room in Gogarburn, wearing a jumper with sleeves that fitted twice round the waist. He breathed in and out, closing his eyes for a short, beautiful second.

'Gavin, you're on spew-guarding duty,' he said calmly. 'Stay there. Guard the spew.'

'Do you want me to take down its details, sir?' Skinner asked loudly in his inimitable jiggle-headed way. 'Read it its rights maybe?'

'Yes, Gavin,' McGregor said wearily. 'All these things.'

Dear Lord, he thought, don't make me kill him today when I won't enjoy it.

McGregor ventured down the rest of the short hall to the doorless doorway at the end, which gave on to the living room. The room was at ninety degrees to the hall, a long, open area that ran the depth of the building, a partition wall having long since been consigned to a skip. Consequently, there were windows at either end. One of them was close-curtained, but through a gap McGregor could spy the crisp, cloudless blue sky and the lightly snow-dusted grass in the Square below. Through the other he could see the hazy, white-topped hills of Fife in the distance, the austere, dark blue calm of the Forth, and the snow-specked slate rooftops of Leith. In between there was a corpse in blood-drenched pyjama trousers, with most of its nose bitten off, two severed fingers stuffed up what remained of its nostrils, the rest of its face a swollen mass of bruising, and a wide gash around half the circumference of its neck. It was lying on the missing door, which sat at thirty degrees to the horizontal, propped up by the twisted metal frame of what had recently been a cheesy smoked-glass coffee table. The blood had run off the door and collected on the polished wood below, and might have lapped its way gently down to meet the postman's spew if much of it had not drained through a gap in the floorboards, from where it ran along an electrical flex into the main-door flat underneath, dripping off the end of the living room light-fitting. The police would find the unconscious Mrs Angus a few hours later amidst the damp fragments of a broken tea-set, and once revived she would swear never to let her clairvoyant sister-in-law bring the ouija board round again, before phoning a Catholic priest to come out and exorcise the place. And so what if she was C of S, when it came to this sort of thing, nothing less than a Tim would do.

3

Around the room's grotesque star attraction was a supporting cast of debris. Much of the floor was carpeted in scattered clothes, books and copies of the blue-covered British Medical Journal. There were huge, dark stains on the walls and floor around the kitchen door, shards of broken green glass and jagged bottle necks lying amidst the wine-soaked clothes and magazines. And there was a hatstand sticking out of the television screen, like a moderately impressive 3D effect.

McGregor looked on blankly and shook his head.

'So are we treating the death as suspicious, sir?' chimed Skinner cheerily from behind.

'Keep guarding the spew, Gavin.'

McGregor edged around some of the blood and leapt clear of the puddle, skidding slightly on a BMJ but managing to stay upright.

Splash.

'Aw, fuck's sake,' whined Skinner's indefatigably loud voice.

McGregor turned his head to see DC Dalziel step gingerly through the rest of the postman's puddle as Skinner picked at his bespeckled trousers, and enjoyed a brief smile.

Splash.

'Aw, Jesus, watch where you're . . .'

Callaghan.

'Naw, wait a wee . . . [splash] Aw, in the name of . . .'

Gow.

The three of them hopped over the blood one by one and spent a few moments taking in the sheer scope of the carnage and disruption.

'Hey, try not to make a mess you lot, eh?' said Skinner, with slightly less enthusiastic joviality than before.

The four cops stood staring at the corpse, then at each other, then back at the corpse, and eventually out of the windows. Between them they were never, ever lost for words, but this one had run them pretty close.

'It's eh . . .' started Callaghan strainedly, pulling at his chin.

McGregor slowly put a finger to his lips, and Callaghan nodded.

'The first one to say anything stupid gets full charge of this investigation, understood?'

'Yes, sir,' said Callaghan. Gow looked too ill to say much anyway. Dalziel just bit her lip and nodded.

4

McGregor looked again at the mutilated pyjama man.

'This,' he said, indicating the room in general, 'is what we experienced officers refer to officially as a fuckin' stoater. Observe and take notes, and consider yourselves highly privileged to be part of it.'

Callaghan lost his footing slightly as he tried not to step on any of the items scattered around the floor, and put his hand out to steady himself, grabbing a radiator behind an upturned armchair. Then his hand slid along it, causing him to fall backwards over the chair and rattle his head off the underside of a windowsill.

'Fuck's sake . . . look at this,' he mourned.

There was dried and drying sick all over the hot radiator and down the wall behind it, which went some way towards explaining the overpowering stench that filled the room. But as pyjama man was only a few hours cold, his decay couldn't be responsible for the other eye-watering odour that permeated the atmosphere.

McGregor gripped the mantelpiece and was leaning over to offer Callaghan a hand up over the upturned chair when he saw it, just edging the outskirts of his peripheral vision. He turned his head very slowly until he found himself three inches away from it at eye level, and hoped his discovery was demonstrative enough to prevent anyone from remarking on it.

Too late.

'Heh, there' a big keech on the mantelpiece, sir,' announced Skinner joyfully, having wandered up to the doorway.

For Gow it was just one human waste-product too many. As the chaotic room swam dizzily before him, he fleetingly considered that he wouldn't complain about policing the Huns' next visit if this particular chalice could be taken from his hands. McGregor caught his appealing and slightly scared look and glanced irritably at the door by way of excusing him, the Inspector reckoning that an alimentary contribution from the constabulary was pretty far down the list of things this situation needed right now.

They watched their white-faced colleague make an unsteady but fleet-footed exit and returned their gazes to the fireplace.

The turd was enormous. An unhealthy, evil black colour like a huge rum truffle with too much cocoa powder in the mixture. It sat proudly in the middle of the mantelpiece like a favourite ornament, an appropriate monarch of what it surveyed. Now that they had seen it, it seemed incredible that they could all have missed it at first, but in mitigation there were a few distractions about the place.

'Jesus, it's some size of loaf right enough,' remarked Callaghan, in tones that Dalziel found just the wrong side of admiring.

'Aye, it must have been a wrench for the proud father to leave it behind,' she said acidly.

'I suppose we'll need a sample,' Callaghan observed. 'There's a lab up at the RVI that can tell all sorts of stuff from just a wee lump of shite.'

'Maybe we should send Skinner there then,' muttered Dalziel. 'See what they can tell from him.'

'I heard that.'

'Naw, seriously,' Callaghan went on. 'They could even tell you what he had to eat.'

'We can tell what he had to eat from your sleeve,' Skinner observed.

'But we don't know which one's sick this is,' Callaghan retorted.

'We don't know which one's keech it is either.'

'Well I'd hardly imagine the deid bloke was in the habit of shiting on his own mantelpiece.'

'That's enough,' said McGregor, holding a hand up. 'We will need to get it examined. And the sick.'

'Bags not breaking this one to forensics,' said Dalziel.

'It'll be my pleasure,' said the Inspector, delighted at the thought of seeing someone else's day ruined as well.

'Forensics can lift the sample then,' said Callaghan.

'No, no,' said McGregor, smiling grimly to himself. 'I think a specimen as magnificent as this one should be preserved intact. Skinner,' he barked, turning round. 'This jobbie is state evidence and is officially under the jurisdiction of Lothian and Borders Police. Remove it, bag it and tag it.'

TWO

Parlabane came round slowly, his senses kicking in one at a time behind the steady, rhythmic throb of his headache, which for a few moments he had thought might be someone playing ambient trance through the wall.

Pound, pound, pound, pound.

Arse.

Different day, different city, same hangover.

Like a fortune teller in reverse, he struggled to peer through the haze and see what lay in his immediate past. At first he couldn't remember much, but was sure that the number 80 had been somehow very significant.

Then the smell hit him, and spun him into an accelerating panic. He sat up rapidly and winced, as his sudden movement brought a cymbal crash to the end of a bar in his head. That smell was miserably familiar and quite unmistakable. One hundred percent recycled materials. For best results, shake well before opening.

He felt a draught and saw that the window was open, which snapped a piece of the puzzle into place, but suggested the completed picture would not be pretty. He remembered getting up and opening it at some point during the night to let the smell out, and figured he must have spewed but been too incapacitated to clear it up at the time. The source of his panic was that he couldn't remember where he had thrown up, indeed couldn't recall the act at all, but was certain it couldn't have been anywhere sensible, because even an unflushed lavvy bowl of boak can't permeate a flat so comprehensively. Indeed, the smell was even stronger than before he had attempted to ventilate the place.

He quickly turned to face the other way, expecting to find a lumpy abstract etched on one side of the pillow, but it was clean. He whipped the duvet off, but there was no multicoloured surprise waiting beneath.

Where the hell was it?

Pukey come home.

Parlabane got up, which brought the snare drum into play

on top of the dull bass, but mere blinding pain could not be allowed to obstruct his quest. He wandered delicately around the flat, squinting as he entered the uncurtained kitchen, where the sun glinted painfully off the foil take-away cartons on the worktops.

'Thank fuck,' he mumbled, glancing at the greasy plate beside them. Looked like Chinese. Could have been Indian, but no matter. The main thing was that kebabs didn't come in foil cartons, so he couldn't have been *that* drunk.

Unfortunately, the smell was everywhere, and seemed to have invaded every room. There was no air freshener, but this was no great loss, as the stuff never really worked. Instead of replacing the smell of sick, it just mingled with it, and consequently he associated and confused the smell of each with the other.

He approached the open door of the darkened living room with genuine fear and a grim sense of fate. The stench was noticeably stronger as he got closer, and somewhere in the reaches of his memory he saw himself leaning over the back of a hideous green settee and serving up several quarts of second-hand soup. But somewhere else he pictured himself cleaning it up, picking slippery, fibrous pieces out of a deep-pile carpet in a pair of bright yellow rubber gloves, and figured it couldn't have been last night.

Walking into the living room, he was abruptly reminded that apart from the bed, the flat didn't actually have any furniture, and that the hideous green settee and the awful shag-pile carpet belonged to a photographer in London who had not regarded the episode as a good basis for starting a relationship, and had indeed – perhaps not entirely unreason- ably – never spoken to him again. This living room didn't have any kind of carpet to its name, and as its exposed floorboards were not of the trendy polished variety, he figured he would be picking skelfs out of his bare feet all afternoon.

Parlabane walked to the window and braced himself for the onslaught of light as he pulled back the curtains. What he saw made him open his squinted eyes wide with horror and dismay.

'Polis!' he breathed, and shut the curtains again hurriedly. 'Fuck.'

Not now, not already.

He spied out from between the curtains, looking at the

activity below. There were plenty of blue uniforms and the obligatory middle-aged man in a camel trenchcoat pointing at people, but, rather strangely, no cars.

Calm down, he told himself. Treaty or no treaty, extradition orders don't get served that fast.

And amidst the now rapid pounding in his skull, the thought finally crossed his mind that if they were here for him, they wouldn't be fannying about in the street.

He wandered down his hallway to the front door, from where he could hear the echo of voices in the spiralling close below. Through the spyhole he could see that no one was about on his landing, so he opened the door and ventured on tiptoe to the edge of the stairs, where the smell rose up to hit him like a surfacing submarine, afloat on a sea of sick.

More voices, the tapping of footsteps and an unidentifiable, intermittent squelching sound. Then a slam.

'Aaaw naaw.'

Maybe the wind in the close, maybe a draught through the open window in the bedroom, who cares. Something had closed his front door and left him on the landing in his boxers and a grubby T-shirt. He gave it a less-than-hopeful push in case it wasn't a slam-locker, but the gods were not smiling.

Mince.

Now, the rational course of action for any normal human being at this point would be to enlist the help of the conveniently present police in securing the services of a locksmith, or at least the services of few standard-issue Doc Martens. But even if he hadn't been reluctant to enter into any dialogue with Lothian and Borders' finest, he'd probably still have seen climbing in from another flat as the easiest solution.

Go with what you know, and all that.

There was no reply from the flat directly above, and a glance through the letterbox confirmed that the occupant wasn't merely standing behind the locked door, peering suspiciously through the spyhole at the scantily dressed nutter hopping from freezing foot to freezing foot on the landing outside. He tried the bell one more time, then admitted to himself that *he* wouldn't open his door to someone of his current appearance, with the phrase 'contributory negligence' still large in the public mind.

Bugger.

9

He padded his way back down the staircase, putting his tongue between his teeth to stop them from chattering, and, reaching the last turn before the landing where the voices were coming from, glanced down to make sure his dick wasn't hanging out of his shorts. First impressions last, however shallow and unfair that may seem.

Parlabane peeked around the wall to see the back of a policeman's head going down the stairs in front of him, leaving the open door to the flat beneath his own unguarded. This was, apparently, the centre of attention and the source of the smell, and a lethal combination of desperation and professional curiosity drew him towards it. The polis wouldn't leave the flat empty like that for more than a matter of moments, so he would have to be quick; just nip in, get out the back window sharpish and climb up into his bedroom.

He darted from the stairs through the doorway and involuntarily stopped as his bare feet made contact with a jarringly unfamiliar surface.

Lovely. Liquid Axminster.

He noticed the streaks on the wall and the open door, then spotted the foot-dragged trail on the floor, leading along the hallway. His eyes followed it to the room at the end, where a half-naked dead man with two truncated digits up his wrecked nose stared horrifiedly at him from his position of repose on what looked like a broken-down door.

Parlabane walked, entranced, towards the body, his field of vision widening to take in the peripheral debris as he approached the living room, a distant part of his mind contemplating the mystery of how the stuff underfoot could have such effectively lubricant and adhesive qualities at the same time.

The other man didn't seem troubled by such trivial philosophical diversions, but his expression suggested he had a lot on his mind nonetheless.

'Sorry to hear it, Jim,' Parlabane muttered, looking aghast at the havoc that had been wreaked upon the man's person and – presumably – belongings. He took in the deep, wide and apparently fatal wound to the man's neck, then glanced down at each of the mutilated hands which had provided the unconventional nasal stoppers.

Parlabane had seen a few bodies in his time, some murdered more imaginatively than others, but this was something of a creative masterpiece, with hints of inspired improvisation. Surveying the attendant chaos, he pitied the poor bastard polisman that had to figure this one out, a thought which brought the belated consideration that this was not the wisest place to be discovered right now. He decided to head back out, reckoning locking himself out of his flat an easier thing to explain than what he was doing wandering around a murder scene with very few clothes on.

As he prepared to lunge across the flat's bilious moat, he heard voices and footsteps in the close below, and spun back on one heel, dismayingly brushing one of the wall's loftier damp daubs with his sleeve.

Tits.

He tiptoed round the puddle of blood and picked his way across the cluttered floor towards the back window, hoping it wouldn't be paint-stuck. He paused momentarily, deciding whether to go around or over an upturned bookcase, when he became aware of movement to his right. He turned his head slowly and reluctantly to see a suede-headed woman in a dark green suit stare inquiringly at him from the entrance to the flat's kitchen.

Parlabane gulped.

'I'm sleepwalking?' he offered, with an appellant, not-very-optimistic, please-take-pity smile.

She shook her head apologetically and held up an ID badge.

Parlabane decided to go for the direct and truthful approach.

'Look, I've locked myself out of my flat upstairs. The window's open directly above. Could you possibly just let me climb up there, pretend you didn't see me, and then you can get on with whatever's going on down here, and I can get on with my hangover?'

Dalziel looked at him with a pained expression of dilemma.

'Well, here's the problem,' she said. 'There's been a brutal murder in here this morning, so we're looking for a brutal murder-*er*, and under such circumstances we tend to broaden our definitions of what constitutes "suspicious". Unfortunately that covers half-dressed, vomit-streaked men attempting to leave the crime scene by the back window. I mean, ordinarily . . .'

'Yeah,' conceded Parlabane, holding his hands up. 'You really are caught on the horns.'

11

THREE

'Jesus, don't you heat this place?'

'Well, our usual suspects tend to be more sensibly dressed. You know: trousers, shoes . . .'

'Stripy jumper, mask, sack marked "SWAG"?'

'That kinna thing, yeah.'

Parlabane shivered and pulled at the jaggy sweater they had given him, his T-shirt having been binned despite his protests because its smell reminded everyone of the inside of that bloody flat. He had agreed to come along quietly to avoid or at least defer being formally arrested, but they hadn't allowed him to attempt to enter his home and had taken him to the station in his partial state of dress. He grudgingly gave them permission to force an entry and search the place, trying not to dwell too long on the irony, but they hadn't managed to get in by the time he was led away by Dalziel and Callaghan.

To Parlabane's incredulous horror, the police station was fifty yards away on the opposite side of the square, a local feature McLean had neglected to mention when he gave him the keys. Still, fugitive beggars couldn't be choosers.

They had walked him across the snow-spattered grass, past the inevitable gawking onlookers and what he instinctively (but just too late) recognised as a press photographer, who got half-a-dozen frames in before Parlabane's face was obscured by a fist and an erect middle finger. By the time they reached the front desk, his feet were soup-free but purple with the cold. A pale and visibly trembling postman was led out of the door as they came in.

Parlabane had been allowed to wash and been issued with the jaggy jumper, then led to an interview room where he sat for close to an hour before Inspector McGregor turned up with Dalziel, briefly rolling his eyes when he saw the shambles that was before him.

'Bad morning?' Parlabane inquired.

McGregor widened his eyes and exhaled, nodding.

'A dead body in pyjama trousers in a wrecked flat awash

with blood and boak, and a huge jobbie on the mantelpiece for garnish.'

Parlabane gaped.

'I didn't notice a jobbie myself.'

'No, it had been removed for tests before you showed up.'

'What, you removed a jobbie before you removed the corpse?'

'You didn't smell this jobbie.'

'I'm not so sure about that.'

'Anyway, a short time later one of my officers discovers a barely dressed man wandering around the murder scene with the declared intention of climbing out the window. Now, I understand you have already agreed that we were not being over-zealous in considering this suspicious. So can you possibly explain what you were doing there?'

'Yes,' Parlabane said, trying to sound as calm and reasonable as his chattering teeth would allow. 'As I told DC Dalziel at the time, I was locked out of my flat and I was attempting to climb back in.'

'Well, that seems logical enough, Mr Parlabane, but let me just ask you a couple of things. Did you know the occupant of the flat downstairs . . . what's his name?'

'You tell me.'

'OK . . . Ponsonby. Dr Jeremy Ponsonby.'

'Not at all. Never seen him before.'

'And how long have you lived at that address?'

'Oh, a good thirty-six hours.'

'And where did you stay before that?'

'Sweetzer Ave.'

McGregor tried to place it. 'West End?'

'West Hollywood.'

McGregor nodded. 'Right. So it would be fair to say that you didn't have the run of Dr Ponsonby's premises, and that were he not dead, he might have minded a wee bit if you walked in unannounced and used his back window to gain access to your flat?'

'Pretty fair, yeah.'

'So here's my problem, Mr Parlabane,' he said, patiently but tiredly. 'Most people, even when they are locked out and underdressed, tend not to just walk into someone else's property, even if the door is wide open. But just supposing they did, just for talking's sake. Most people would be put off

13

by a strong smell of spew and by the large puddle of it at the door. But again, just for talking's sake, let's pretend that's not the case. Most people would have quite a strong reaction to a mutilated corpse. Some might faint. Some might throw up. Some might run out screaming and calling for the police.'

He looked Parlabane fiercely in the eye. 'Very, very few would be sufficiently unperturbed as to continue going about their plan of climbing out the window to get back into their flat. Most might consider, shall we say, that matters had overtaken them. That there were greater things afoot than their need to get back into their home.'

Parlabane nodded, understandingly.

McGregor continued. 'I suppose what I'm really trying to say is that I consider your behaviour to have been . . . unusual. Exceptional, even. So I have to ask myself two questions: A, why you ventured into Dr Ponsonby's flat, and B, why his condition failed to give you the screaming heebie-jeebies.'

Parlabane sat back in his chair, hugging himself with the over-long sleeves of his jaggy jumper. His hangover had not abated through his new predicament, and he felt that large quantities of Irn-Bru, fried food and sleep were the only things that could save him. Between Parlabane and those things was McGregor, a man so clearly resigned to the inevitable unpleasantness and frustration of this case that he would probably sit patiently probing Parlabane well into the middle of the next century if he felt he had to.

Frank, uncomplicated honesty was a dangerous gambit with police anywhere, as you risked blowing their minds, with ugly consequences for all concerned. However, as McGregor was already looking bored in anticipation of a tedious fib, Parlabane decided to chance it.

'All right. A, Curiosity. B, Dr Whatsisface was not the first murder victim I've ever seen. I'm assuming you've ruled out suicide by this point.'

McGregor smiled. It wasn't a big smile, but it was definitely there, and in it Parlabane could see relief, Irn-Bru, fried food and sleep. McGregor made a beckoning gesture with his right hand, encouraging Parlabane to elaborate.

'I am, I will freely admit, a dedicatedly professional nosy bastard,' he said with a sigh. 'I'm a journalist, and I'm afraid I find it difficult to walk past an open door, never mind an

14

unguarded crime scene. It's like a reflex, an uncontrollable instinct.'

'Like a fly to a shite?' asked Dalziel.

'Well, I'll admit that groups of cops tend to attract my attention, so if I'm the fly . . .'

'We're the insecticide, Mr Parlabane,' said McGregor firmly. 'So having had a look around, why didn't you go back out the door?'

'I heard someone coming up the stairs, and I didn't think it would look good to be found trespassing on a crime scene. After all, I didn't want to end up in the police station in my underwear, freezing my bollocks off, being questioned about what the hell I was doing by polis who I'm sure have more important things to be getting on with right now.'

'Quite.'

There was a knock at the door, and Callaghan stuck his head round to beckon McGregor outside for discussion.

'Do you reckon he believes me?' Parlabane asked Dalziel once they were alone.

'Why are you asking me whether *he* believes you? Why aren't you asking me whether I believe you?'

'I already know you believe me.'

Dalziel laughed, as if she couldn't help it, and shook her head. She had softly curved features but a rather sharp nose, upon which Parlabane spotted a tiny dimple where he was sure a stud sat when she was off-duty.

'OK,' she said. 'You got me. But I'm just the DC, and instinctively believing you could be the kind of mistake I have to learn from as I climb the ranks.'

'But it's not instinctive,' he said, shamelessly going into charming/flirtatious mode, forgetful of his ridiculous appearance. 'You believe me because if I had anything to do with the murder, it would be both unlikely and improbably stupid for me to wander back into the scene of the crime while it's crawling with police officers.'

'Ah, but the dog does return to its own vomit,' she said, pointing at him with a pen.

'Let me assure you, none of that vomit was mine. In fact, I was looking for mine just before I locked myself out, but my subsequent discoveries have cast doubt on whether there was anything to find.'

15

'What?'

'Don't ask. So what do you figure to the late Dr P?'

'Back off, scoop. I'm hardly going to reveal the facts of an on-going investigation to a self-confessed hack. Given what's already happened today, I think it would be . . . imprudent, to say the least, to encourage your involvement in this case.'

'Believe me, Ms Dalziel, *nothing* could encourage me to get involved in this case. I've seen the mess, remember, I've smelt the smells, and I don't envy you this one whatsoever. But how can I keep my eyes peeled if I don't know what to look for?'

'What do you mean by that?' she asked, now more serious.

'You know fine.'

Dalziel stared sternly and hard across the table at Parlabane, who felt he was doing enormously well to be commanding the slightest modicum of respect in his current condition.

'Are they sharp eyes?' she finally asked.

He gave her a wry grin.

'I'd say your guy was dead less than nine hours when I saw him this morning,' he stated. 'Going by the mess on the floor and the mess on his face, it's safe to assume he struggled heavily with his assailant before succumbing. He was tied up before his throat was cut, as he bled exactly where he was found, then whatever was used to restrain him was removed. The messiness of the severing suggests his fingers were bitten off rather than sliced with whatever cut his throat. And as he lost specifically the index fingers of *both* hands, I'd guess they were bitten off while he was restrained rather than during the struggle, maybe even after the fatal wound. It would also be my guess that they were bitten off in retribution, that the good doctor accounted for one of his killer's index fingers earlier in the battle.'

Dalziel made a poor job of trying not to look impressed

'All right scoop,' she said. 'Sticking with the premise that you had nothing to do with this and aren't giving me these things from first-hand knowledge, tell me where you were while you reckon this was going on.'

'Asleep upstairs.'

'What, you slept through all the racket this fight, murder and interior flat demolition must have made?'

'Ms Dalziel, believe me, I *have* slept through an earthquake. You might have more luck with whoever lives in the main-door flat below.'

16

'Her name's Mrs Angus. She's a widow, lives alone, and doesn't wear her hearing aid to bed.'

'Of course. So nobody heard anything. Did anyone see anything?'

'No one's come forward so far.'

'I'm not talking about the public.'

Dalziel winced as she realised what was coming.

Parlabane smirked. He tried not to, but it was too good.

'You mean someone got murdered across the street from this station and not one flatfoot noticed anything suspicious?'

'Go on, lap it up,' she muttered impatiently.

'I'm sorry,' Parlabane said, smothering a laugh. He wondered how many times he had heard frustrated cops ask whether people go around with their eyes shut, how come nobody ever notices a bloody thing . . .

'So what's the story?' he asked.

'Way too early to say, although it seems a safe bet it wasn't premeditated. As a lot of the mess couldn't have been made by a fight, McGregor reckons it was a burglary gone wrong.'

'But you don't.'

'I didn't say that.'

'Oh, but you did.'

At that point, McGregor came back into the room, and all was quiet.

'Right, Mr Parlabane,' he said with a strangely light, almost cheerful tone. 'We've been through your flat and belongings. We tried to mess the place up as is standard procedure, but as you don't seem to own very much it was a bit of a poor effort, I'm afraid. DC Callaghan went through your wallet and has confirmed your identity, occupation and – from the ticket stubs – your recent arrival from Los Angeles. He probably also removed a small sum of money but there's not much either of us can do about that.'

He handed Parlabane the keys to his flat.

'They didn't force the door, in the end. Someone followed your lead and climbed in from Dr Ponsonby's place. You're free to go when you wish, but I'd ask you not to stray too far for a few days – it's just that if we draw a total blank on this one, we'll need someone to fit up for it, and you're the obvious choice.'

*   *   *

17

'What are you so bloody happy about?' Dalziel asked as Parlabane shuffled out of the room.

'It took a second climber to get into Mr Parlabane's flat,' McGregor replied contentedly. 'The first one fell in the attempt and broke his ankle.'

Dalziel didn't need to ask who it was.

FOUR

Stephen Lime lay back in his bath and farted contentedly to himself. If he pressed his chubby legs together just the right way, he could send the bubbles rolling along beneath him until they emerged between his ankles near the taps. And if he got his timing right he could let some of the next volley emerge between his knees at the same time, twin currents disturbing the calm surface eighteen inches apart.

He was not, he was convinced, fat. Poor people were fat. Stupid people were fat. He was a man of imposing stature. Like a great oak, the wider rings of girth were evidence of health, strength and vitality.

He smiled to himself.

It was all coming together, the orchestra of his business plans finished their cacophonic tuning and now playing in concert, conducted expertly by his baton. To plan, to organise, to execute and to reap from such complex and multifarious components as he was doing required a talent that was no less than exceptional. And exceptional abilities deserve exceptional reward. He wasn't in the half-a-million-plus-twice-that-in-share-options bracket, far from it, but the success of his present enterprises was proof, to himself at least, that he was of that calibre. And talent like that does not go unrecognised for long.

These insect pipsqueaks who were always questioning the salaries of top British management were not only ignorant, but bigoted and bitter if they couldn't – or simply wouldn't – appreciate the priceless brilliance that it bought. Cheap at twice the price.

He had been furious when he saw footage of those select committee hearings on the news that time. Malignant, unworthy and ungraciously envious worms, sneering little bastards and tub-thumping luddites. He knew you had to watch what you said these days, and that they were elected members and all, but there was still something patently very wrong when the finest of Englishmen could be spoken to like that by blacks and Jews.

And why weren't they scrutinising the fact that some bunch of layabouts could pick up millions just for strumming three chords and going without shampoo for six months at a time? Or that there were northern scruff earning more than he was simply for kicking a ball around a patch of grass in front of hordes of other neanderthals.

But not for long. The cash was piling up, and the floodgates were about to open; within a couple of years he might be making more per annum than his father did in his whole life.

However, what meant most now was not the money, but the sense of achievement, and there was no fitter crown to it all than the Trust being on the verge of going into the black for the first time.

His father had taught him well, given him the basics. A climate of job security is a climate for stagnation. In management, you are the benefactor who has granted the worker a job; it is you who is putting food on his table and clothing his grubby litter – and for that he owes you diligent service. That kind of thing. Truths that you couldn't stick your head above the parapets and openly declare in these topsy-turvy times, but truths nonetheless.

No man works harder for you than your money, his father had always said, and had made sure he got an assured, worthwhile but unspectacular return on every last brown penny he invested anywhere. A valuable lesson to the young Stephen, possibly the most important he ever learned, with the attendant warning that risk and reward were inseparably proportionate.

But what had distinguished Stephen Lime, what had afforded him the opportunities to soar above heights his father had never imagined, was that he had been the one with the vision to realise that there was an exception to the rule – that there *was* something you could invest in which guaranteed vast returns for negligible risk.

It was called the Conservative and Unionist Party of Great Britain.

Obviously it was not just a simple matter of pouring in ostentatious contributions and being awarded lucrative contracts, although that did happen at a more upscale level than he was operating on, and usually carried the obligation to employ one of the appropriate senior minister's useless

20

offspring. No. It was a question of having still more vision to see where the returns would appear, strategically placing oneself to reap their benefits to the full.

Stephen had served his management apprenticeship under his father's tutelage, been given control of the old man's biscuit business in his early twenties after he and his university had discovered a mutual incompatibility. He knew the old man had clearly seen the bigger picture when he encouraged him to seek a post with another firm, obviously appreciating that the sudden high-gradient plummet into debt of BakeLime Biscuits was merely a teething problem of a doubtlessly brilliant long-term strategy.

Out on his own in the real world, his on-going investment worked a little like a nest egg or even a trust fund, helping him make a proper start in the business world through contacts and management appointments. Observing his superiors, he knew he had a lot to learn, but was sharp enough to see the qualities that made them so invaluable. They could see the wood for the trees, were not distracted by trivia and kept their eye on the bigger picture. They knew the fact that the last three companies whose boards you served on went rapidly and resoundingly bankrupt did not reflect on your management abilities or your suitability for a vacant post. Eddies in the currency markets, union skullduggery, interest rate fluctuations – these such unstable factors were what knocked companies for six *in spite of* first-class leadership and visionary business strategy.

He watched the men above him bravely rise, phoenix-like, from the ashes of a closed concern, to take the reins elsewhere with an optimistic smile and a fatter pay-packet.

And, as he reassuringly discovered, many of them had invested too.

Never forgetting his father's words, he put most of his money to work, and in the family tradition, backed favourites at low odds, watching his personal assets slowly but steadily multiply.

Above all, he was patient, always aware that he was still on a learning curve, gathering the knowledge that would serve him when the right opportunity presented itself and when he was ready to take it.

*　　*　　*

When opportunity knocked, it did so fairly quietly, so much so that it took a while for him to hear and to recognise.

It was vital to the direction the government was taking the NHS that the right people had their hands on the helms of the nascent Trusts, and his reliable political sympathies plus a healthy annual tax-deductable charitable contribution made him ideal material for a quango post. He was appointed to the board of St George's NHS Trust in his native Romford, 30K a year to attend a few meetings a week, very much the kind of occasional, mid-level dividend he had expected from his on-going investment.

But when he took up his position and looked a little closer, he could not believe the magnitude of the opportunities that lay before him. The government were slicing up the biggest public pie in British history and he would be well placed to fill his plate.

The National Health Service was an aberration, no other way to describe it. It was such an affront to Conservative values and ideology that he was sure Thatcher would have happily closed the whole thing and grudgingly paid for the humane putting down of anyone who got ill but couldn't afford private healthcare. It had a terrifying, massive, insatiable appetite for public funds, chewing up and swallowing billions of pounds every year; but unlike other greedy mouths at the public tit – defence being a shining example – precious little of it found its way into the pockets of Party members and contributors. It was just one huge, amorphous, unanswerable entity, running its own ship, its spending dictated almost entirely by patients' healthcare needs. No familiar faces at the top with the power to award hefty contracts; indeed, precious little in the way of external contracts at all. No six-figure executive posts with company Beamie.

The only way to score from it was perhaps to buy into one of the big drug firms, but anyone could do that, and as purchases were all in accordance with doctors' prescriptive practices, there wasn't even an easy way to manipulate the market. It just swallowed up public money and circulated it within itself until it needed more.

Nightmare.

Aberration.

The basic fact of the matter was that if public spending

could not be avoided, it should at least be spent in the private sector.

But then came the NHS reforms and the dawn of the Trusts, and the picture got suddenly and dramatically brighter.

Stephen Lime made great play of resigning two part-time, higher-paying consultancies to concentrate on his duties with St George's Trust, and dramatically increased that year's tax-deductable charitable donation, thereby subtly indicating to the right people that he was claiming his long-term investor's bonus. And after less than nine months on the St George's board, he was appointed Chief Executive of the Midlothian NHS Trust in Edinburgh.

Then he really went to work.

But this evening he was relaxing, having a good soak before getting ready for dinner, and waiting patiently for the phone call that would confirm the removal of one last small obstacle from his path.

He had his portable on a table by the bath, having carved a space out for it among his self-multiplying aftershave collection. He picked it up, enjoying the feel, the weight of it in his hand, and yes, he would probably admit, willing it to ring.

Strange that such a small and relatively inexpensive item could give him so much reassurance, but there was no denying it, his portable always made him feel good. Smooth, compact, sleekly black, satisfyingly heavy, he always thought of it as his light-sabre. Few could guess from its appearance what power this harmless-looking little electronic object could wield in his skilled hands.

There was a knock at the door which startled him momentarily and gave him a nasty fright as the phone slipped from his right hand but nestled itself between his left forearm and a fold of fat on his stomach, barely a centimetre above the water.

'Mr Lime?' It was Mrs Branigan, the housekeeper.

'Yes, Theresa?'

'The newspaper is here.'

'Thank you, Theresa.'

Lovely. As such a busy man he seldom got time either to enjoy more than a brief shower a couple of mornings per week or a decent read at the paper, so when he did have the opportunity he loved to combine a good bath with a glance at the local rag. And perhaps there might be a brief reference to what he needed to know, although chances were it might not be discovered for another day or so. He looked down over the side of the bath to see his copy of the *Evening Capital* sliding under the bathroom door, dried his hand with a towel and leaned over to grab it.

Farting once more as he sat up, he unfolded the unwieldy broadsheet to reveal the top half of the front page, read the headline and shat in the bath.

FIVE

'Yeah, but a fucking polis station Duncan, for Christ's sake.'

'Aw, come on, Jack. You didn't exactly give me much notice. I don't think I did too badly.'

'I'm not ungrateful Duncan, and I'm not complaining about the flat. I'm just saying you could have warned me.'

Parlabane sat with his friend, Duncan McLean, on high stools at the bar of the Barony on Broughton Street, Parlabane sipping a tomato juice with Worcester, Tabasco and quite definitely *no* vodka. It was late afternoon, the sun bathing the wooden surroundings in a slow-fading glow.

'And as for this, fuck's sake.'

He flipped over the *Evening Capital* from the sports section at the back so that his picture was staring up from the front page under the headline: MAN HELD AFTER RITUAL SLAYING, with the strap: GORY FIND: *Police question half-naked suspect over Maybury Square bloodbath.*

'"Half-naked suspect"? What are the sub-editors on at that bloody place?'

Parlabane distastefully examined the photograph again, his profile visible next to the back of Dalziel's head, which she had turned away from the camera in sharper anticipation. If he looked very closely he could make out the smudges of spew on the sleeve of his T-shirt as well.

'I'm supposed to be turning up there to get some shifts in a few days,' he said bemusedly, his companion trying not very hard to suppress a laugh.

'Well, Jack, I did tell the news editor you'd fill the front page in no time.'

'Oh, very fucking amusing. And what's this: "Police believe the murder may have been the result of a burglary-gone-wrong – although as both the victim and the suspect were found in states of undress, they have not ruled out a sexual motive." I fucking hate when they do that. I have *never* done that.'

'Done what?'

'Say that something has not been ruled out when you know

fine that no one ever ruled it in. And I would just like to stress that I was not a suspect. I volunteered to assist the police with their inquiries.'

He stared angrily at the byline again. 'Who the fuck's Finlay Price?'

Duncan shook his head and sighed. 'You don't like it up you, do you, Jack?'

'What, is this you finally propositioning me, Duncan?'

'No, I'm just thinking about your unfettered glee as you stuck it to all those people on all those front pages when we worked together through in the West. The words "taste" and "own medicine" keep inexplicably popping into my head.'

'Yes, but *they* all did it. Those fuckers were all guilty. I wasn't.'

Duncan spluttered a mouthful of his Guinness back into the glass and put it down on the bartop, wiping his mouth.

Parlabane put a hand up in a gesture of backing off.

'All right,' he said. 'I'll take it like a man. But Christ, you could enjoy it all a little less.'

Duncan folded up the newspaper and handed it to one of the bar staff who put it back on the rack by the door, next to the *Evening News*, *Daily Record* and *Shavers Weekly*, a self-styled pisshead fanzine which enjoyed greater editorial clarity than any of its neighbours.

'Forget about it,' he said. 'Come on, have a pint, chill out. You're back in the old country. Haven't you seen the beer adverts?'

Parlabane shook his head distractedly.

'Somebody tried to kill me, Dunc. Chilling out is going to be a protracted process.'

Duncan gaped. 'Last night? Here?'

'No, in LA. That was the emergency. That was why I came home in such a hurry.'

'Jesus, sorry, Jack. I had no idea.'

Parlabane sipped at his tomato juice and looked around the pub, the motes of dust and smoke swirling in the dying rays through the big window at the front. He was catching his breath for the first time in seventy-two hours, eight time zones and Christ knew how many thousand miles. The Barony was beautifully placid, comfortingly calm, inescapably Edinburgh. Shining, polished pump handles priolling along the bar, open fire being stoked up in anticipation of a cold but clear night, single malts glinting in pale gold on their shelves. He couldn't imagine anything less LA; in the difference there was distance, in the distance there was safety. The cops, the spew and the dead guy were just temporary inconveniences. He had survived.

'You know, we must have joked about it a dozen times, remember?' Parlabane said. 'Someone trying to light me up for sniffing too close to something. It was kind of an ego-trip fantasy that I never for a moment believed in. I received a few veiled and not-so-veiled threats in London, but . . .' He shook his head.

'Do you know who it was, what it was about?'

He shook his head again and stared into space.

'You don't want to talk about this, do you?' Duncan asked, putting a big hand between his friend's shoulders.

Parlabane smiled. 'Your move into sports reporting hasn't blunted your keen powers of journalistic observation, McLean.'

Duncan ordered another pint and protestingly asked for a second tomato juice for Parlabane.

'So, the cop-shop aside, is the flat all right?'

'Well, not counting the slaughtered bloke in the Hammer House of Vomit downstairs and the knife-wielding, finger-munching psychopathic jobbieman on the loose, it's fine. How long have I got it?'

'At least a month, then really until my pal finds a buyer, which might prove difficult after this morning's events.'

'Not at all. Just have to phrase the ad properly. "High-profile city-centre residence", something like that. "Historical significance." Certainly a significant address in the history of Dr Ponsonby.'

By about seven-thirty the place was filling up with the evening regulars, the post-work swift halves and cathartic office bitching-therapy groups having come and gone over a bustling ninety minutes. Parlabane had stuck advisedly to the tomato juices and watched with accustomed awe as his big friend punished the Guinnesses with little detrimental effect on his mind or body. Didn't the bugger ever go for a pish? His bladder capacity must put supertankers to shame.

Duncan exchanged waves and nods of acknowledgement with several of the steadily arriving drinkers, and seemed to be on familiar terms with all the bar staff. Parlabane reckoned his friend must be wasting a fortune on mortgage payments on his New Town flat, as he quite clearly lived here.

'All right, Jen?'

'Hi, Dunky,' came a female voice from behind Parlabane, the woman passing her respects as she waited for her change and for her pint of Eighty Shilling to settle. Parlabane was side-on to the bar, facing Duncan, and so without turning round inquisitively, he was unable to make out more than the edge of a woollen cap and a strong but delicious whiff of perfume. From the corner of his eye he was aware of her taking a long, slow pull at her pint, then heard her sigh with satisfaction.

'Tough day?' Duncan said to her over Parlabane's head.

'You don't want to know,' she said breathily, then reached for the life-giving heavy again.

'So who's your pal, big man?' she said, moving around Parlabane on his left just as he turned right to introduce himself.

'Sorry, Jen, this is Jack,' Duncan was saying as Parlabane turned back round, his much-practised, usually affected (but not today), weather-weary-but-winning smile giving way to blank disbelief when he realised who he was being introduced to.

'Jack, this is Je . . .'

'DC Dalziel,' Parlabane stated, looking very sternly at Duncan.

'I'd consider it a magnanimous gesture if you'd call me Jenny,' she said, offering a hand.

Parlabane gripped the outstretched fingers and couldn't help but laugh. 'Jack,' he smiled. 'Grab a stool.'

That morning, Dalziel had seemed to be dressed with severity of impact in mind, but tonight she was a bright kaleidoscope of reckless and frequently conflicting colours, apart from the black woollen cap atop her closely-cropped head. A tiny diamond indeed glinted on one side of her nose as he had predicted, and although it was one of the few such ornaments that he didn't find clumsy and unattractive, it still made him slightly squeamish. Parlabane almost passed out with pain when he accidentally plucked a nose-hair. The thought of ramming a needle through there was like chewing tin foil.

'It's not his fault. I never told him what I do for a living,' Jenny explained.

'Well what the hell do you guys talk about in here?'

'Not everyone is quite as job-obsessed as you, Jack,' Duncan said in defence.

'We talk about football, for instance,' Jenny offered.

'Oh, you talk about football with un-job-obsessed Duncan, the football reporter?'

'You have to forgive him, Jen,' Duncan said, getting up. 'I'm afraid he tends to get a bit nippy after being arrested in his Y-fronts.'

'I was *not* arrested. And they were *not* Y-fronts. Where are you going?'

Duncan quickly finished off his pint. 'Excuse me a wee minute. I just spotted someone through the window. I'm off to see a man about a man.'

Through the glass they saw him cross the road and head into the Buzz Bar of the Blue Moon Cafe opposite.

'Call of nature,' Jenny muttered.

'Hmm?'

'Le Gay Café.'

'Oh, is it.'

'Used to be the Pink Triangle. Weren't the Eighties a time of subtlety.'

'Is that why you never told him you were a cop?'

'He never asked.'

'That's not the point.'

'And that's none of your business.'

Parlabane held his hands up. 'Fair enough.'

He sipped at his tomato juice and winced slightly. The barman had been sufficiently liberal with the Tabasco that it burnt the palate more than straight whisky.

'I'll grant you, off-duty you don't look like a cop.'

'I'll consider that a compliment.'

'Yes, but then are you off-duty?'

'Don't get paranoid, Mr . . . Jack. I'm not checking you out.'

'Bet you pulled my file though, didn't you?'

She gave a mischievous grin. 'Of course. Standard procedure. Two court appearances for charges of breaking and entering. No convictions, thanks to no material evidence. Did you do them?'

29

He smiled. 'What, are you wearing a wire?'

'Well, as I'm not about to bare my chest to you you'll have to take my word for it that I'm not.'

'I trust you. Yes and no. Yes I entered, but I never break and I never take.'

'You never broke, you mean. Those two times, the *only* times.'

'Of course.'

'I mean, it's not like you're the kind of person who is so experienced at such criminality that – if you locked yourself out, say – you would try and climb in from someone else's flat rather than ask the police for help.'

She finished her pint and gestured in a familiar fashion to the young woman behind the bar for a refill.

'So what were you looking for?'

'Nothing. And I *was* trying to get back into . . .'

'Not today. I meant when you "entered but did not break"?'

'Documentation, usually. Records, files. I never remove the stuff, just shoot copies. Proof. Evidence. Helps stand up your story, keeps the libel lawyers at bay.'

'Not exemplary journalistic practice.'

'I didn't say I was an exemplary journalist. Although unlike most these days I prefer to find a real story rather than create one from an out-of-context quote or a grotesque exaggeration.'

'Aye, you're a real hero. Spare me the sermon, scoop. How do you explain where these documents came from when you write your story?'

'They were "leaked". They "fell into our hands". These phrases sound familiar?'

Dalziel shook her head. 'You know, if we acquired evidence that way, you're precisely the sort of person who would be leading the outcry about it.'

'Now you can spare me the sermon,' Parlabane said. 'You *do* acquire evidence like that. How often have "stolen" documents been "anonymously" delivered into police hands, then turned out to be "surprisingly useful" to a current investigation?'

'I have no idea what you are talking about,' she said, accepting her drink from the barmaid with a nod. 'That sounds far too resourceful and imaginative for our lot.'

'Hmmm,' he said, lifting the drink he hadn't noticed her

30

ordering for him. 'Well, let's just say I've met some cops in my time who were *extremely* resourceful and imaginative. Cheers, by the way.'

'Slange.' She drank a foamy mouthful from her glass.

'You know a few cops, don't you?' Dalziel said.

'What makes you say that?'

'Anyone so familiar with murdered stiffs is either a doctor, a cop or someone a cop knows well enough to allow him into a crime scene.'

'Or a serial killer. Or someone who habitually trespasses on crime scenes.'

'Someone who just habitually trespassed on crime scenes wouldn't be able to deduce what you did from thirty seconds of staring at a body.'

'I scored?'

'Well, the PM hasn't been completed yet, but you got the ETD right. When they cleaned the blood off down at the mortuary they found rope burns around the waist and under the armpits. And we found another finger amongst all the crap on the floor.'

'Find any hairs above the mantelpiece?' Parlabane asked.

'Where?'

'I heard your killer took a dump up there. If he banged his head on the ceiling, there might be hairs in the cornicing.'

'If he banged his head on the ceiling he'd be seven feet tall.'

'Yeah, so he'd be easier to spot. You'd know his approximate height and hair colour, as well as his maximum number of fingers. Find anything else interesting?'

'Hypodermic needle.'

'Literal needle in a metaphoric haystack. Impressive. Syringe?'

'No. No syringes in the flat at all. So we reckon that means the needle didn't belong to the doctor. McGregor's increasingly married to the burglary-gone-wrong theory. Needle equals junkie, junkie equals uncontrolled, random, potentially explosive burglar. And these days there's a lot of attacks on doctors by junkies looking for drugs. But I'm reserving judgment until I know more about Ponsonby. Naughty doctors do sometimes deal drugs. Drug deals sometimes go very wrong . . .'

'Lovely girl, Jenny,' Duncan said. 'I'd never have guessed she was in the police in a billion years.'

31

'Apparently not. But against my better judgment I do like her. If I could overcome the threat to my masculinity of her being about four inches taller than me, I think I could quite fancy her. Do you think it would be unwise for me to get involved with an officer of the law?'

'I don't think it would be wise for you to get involved with anyone I know. I've seen how your relationships develop, remember. Anyway, you're not really Jen's type. Believe me, I know at least that much about her.'

'Oh come on, Duncan, that's unfair,' Parlabane protested, trying to sound hurt. 'I've done a lot of growing up in the last few years – even more in the last few days. I'm slightly more sensible and a *lot* more sensitive. These days I'd be prepared to change things about myself to attract the right woman.'

Duncan arched an eyebrow. 'Yeah? Could you grow tits?'

Parlabane closed his eyes. 'Fuck.'

'Sorry, Jack. I tried to be gentle but you weren't picking me up. I thought as I didn't tip you off about the police station I should at least let you know that.'

Parlabane stood up and slapped Duncan on the back.

'Naw, you're all right, big yin.'

'Where are you going?'

'Home. It's been a very long day and I'd quite like to forget that most of it ever happened. You don't know a good smack dealer, do you?'

SIX

Sarah had expected to feel more scared. Her hand trembled slightly as she gently, slowly, quietly turned the key in the lock, but it wasn't the thought of being caught, intruded upon that was bothering her. In fact it was the disorientating emotional numbness of the days since his death that she was seeking to dispel with whatever she found within; a feeling of plain old terror would at least be a feeling.

There seemed nothing to make sense of, as if the final reel was missing. It was not a dramatic crescendo or a devastating dénouement. Neither did it feel like a sudden tragedy or a never-expected blow.

The feeling was far worse than of anticlimax; it was one of abortion. Someone had ripped the pages from the back, taped over the last half-hour.

She hadn't loved him for years, but she hadn't hated him so much for a wee while either. She needed to feel something for him, one way or the other, but there was just a gap, a question mark. Perhaps in his flat there would be some trace of his presence that she could latch on to; she had long since exorcised it from her own. The police had refused her request to be allowed into the premises, but she still had the keys Jeremy had left with her in case he ever lost his own set. The cops had said she could come back when they were finished there, but she feared they would somehow neutralise the place.

She pushed the door open and stepped between the crime-scene-warning tapes. The smell of disinfectant filled her nose immediately and her eyes filled with tears as she wondered blindly at what it might be covering up, the physical, visceral reality of her ex-husband's murder hitting her for a vivid, horrific moment.

Sarah closed the door silently and let her eyes grow accustomed to the dark, the hallway illuminated solely by the play of streetlights coming in the living room window. The living room door was off its hinges, propped up against the wall a few feet from where it should hang.

Ironically, the place looked like Jeremy was about to move out. His books and papers and even clothes were all arranged in piles on the floor, items of furniture racked up on top of and against each other along one wall. Most of the floor was bare, and despite the half-light she could still make out a large, dark stain and guess wincingly at what had made it.

She looked down at it but it didn't precipitate any floods of emotion. She now knew nothing in here could disturb her more than the imagination of what had been cloaked by that disinfectant.

'Oh, Jeremy. You've really screwed it up this time,' she found herself mumbling.

At the time she had been glad Jeremy's father had been asked to formally identify the body, but as events unfolded she had felt increasingly excluded from the whole affair. She had gone to his parents' house in Morningside because she didn't really know of anyone else she could talk to about it. They had been civil enough, but she couldn't miss their underlying question of 'what the hell does anything concerning our son have to do with you any more?' She had divorced him, hadn't she? What did she care if he was dead?

The police didn't seem to think she had any right to know what was going on at all, and what they did tell her just added to the numb sense of nothingness. Killed by some malnourished-looking *Trainspotting* character the police had picked up and charged, with a history of smack and aggravated burglary. Just chance. Plain old bad luck.

She felt there had to be more to it, but had seen enough random tragedy to know that there was no reason why there should be. Why should there be a big answer for her when no one had been able to give one to all the bereaved spouses, parents and children she saw every week?

As divorces go, it had been a pretty clean break. She had forgiven but had learned to protect herself too much to forget. For a long time she still felt something for him, even if it was only pity, but that was always mixed with the kind of relief a sailor must feel when he looks back from the lifeboat at his ship going down.

Perhaps what had so thrown her about Jeremy's death was that someone had pre-empted the climax of his inevitable self-destruction.

She was right. There was little trace of Jeremy left in the flat.

34

For a start, the whole place looked too tidy. Even the debris was in neat little piles, splintered wood separated from broken ceramics. She squatted on the floor next to an orderly section of glass shards which she recognised as from the revolting coffee table Jeremy's parents had given them, one of the things she had gladly let him keep when they split.

Then she found herself doing a double-take; she had seen something uninterestingly familiar and looked away for the half-second it took to realise that it was familiar from an entirely different context. It was a small plastic ampoule, empty and without a label, stuck in between two fragments of glass. It was possible that the police had ignored it or even that it was awaiting inspection along with all the other items ranged around the room, but there seemed a good chance that they had missed it altogether. Now that she had seen it, she couldn't just leave it, as what if they had missed it or ignored it and it turned out to be important? However, she realised that there was no way she could tell them about it without letting them know she had been in the flat.

She carefully removed it and popped it into the pouch at the front of her bag. She would get it analysed herself and then own up if it turned out to be anything interesting.

Sarah tiptoed back to the front door and peeped through the spyhole to make sure there was no one on the landing. She held her breath and listened for noises in the close, but there was nothing. Then she opened the door, climbed back through the tapes and closed it again, turning the key and releasing it so that the lock didn't slam.

'Find what you were looking for?'

Sarah's stomach made a valiant escape bid but was foiled by her rapidly expanding lungs as she gasped and turned around to see who had spoken.

There was a man standing on the staircase, blocking off her route out of the close. He looked early thirties, about 5' 7" – her height – and of slim build, dressed in jeans, a black polo-neck and a biker-style leather jacket. He had a shock of fair hair falling over his forehead, and darkish skin that suggested regular exposure to the sun rather than a fortnight's tan. She figured all that was missing was a skinny roll-up in the mouth and a notebook of dreadful beat poetry in his right hand.

Her first instinct was to kick the shit out of him for creeping up on a lone woman at night, but she thought she had better establish first whether or not he was a cop.

'Why, who the fuck are you?' she offered.

'I'm someone else who has trouble reading "keep out" signs,' said Parlabane. 'There's a polisman heading over here right now. Do you fancy coming upstairs for a cup of tea or would you rather bump into him on your way out of the close?'

There was a tingle in Parlabane's nose. It was a familiar one, but no less enjoyable for it, and it made him feel like he was off the canvas again. It was created by sticking the said nose where it didn't belong; better yet, where someone specifically didn't want it.

He hadn't lied to Jenny. After seeing the carnage in Ponsonby's flat, he genuinely didn't have any intention of getting involved in the investigation, any more than passing on anything he might happen across. Throwing a decent cop a few titbits was always worthwhile, especially when you were new in town, and Jenny had instantly struck him as a lot more than just a decent cop. The calm, assured and even intrigued manner in which she had reacted to finding him in Ponsonby's place had told him from the off that she wasn't standard-issue.

At first he was too jet-lagged, hung-over and shaken up by the LA thing to think about anything more than getting himself out of being arrested, but as he spoke to Jenny later, he began to realise what had been wrong with the picture.

He had seen plenty of McGregors. Decent men made cynical through the constant disappointment of discovering what human beings are really capable of, numbing themselves so that nothing shocked them, nothing surprised them. Problem was, as a result they became too credulous of atrocity; they were prepared to believe anything as long as it sounded authentically sordid. They had lifted some scrote of a junkie in Leith who had a string of burglary convictions and a history of violence. McGregor would have no problem believing the wee runt was capable of doing it, and if the evidence didn't fit, he'd be off looking for another such smackhead housebreaker.

But Jenny had been looking for something else, and having had time to think more calmly about what he had seen, Parlabane thought he knew why.

*　　*　　*

His first and most probably last shift at the *Evening Capital* had not gone well. When Duncan accompanied him into the newsroom, one hack had jumped over his desk and darted out of the door, and the news editor had backed up against a pillar and warned: 'I've already called security. They'll be here any minute.'

'Donald, this is Jack Parlabane,' Duncan had said, bewildered. 'He's here for a shift, remember?'

The visibly sweating news editor looked back and forth between Duncan and Parlabane, nervous and confused. 'But I thought . . .'

'I was the guy you stitched up on the front page the other day? Small world, huh?'

For Donald McCreedie, it ranked among his least comfortable moments in journalism, right up there with the time in Portsmouth when he splashed the front page with an exposé of an adulterous affair between a top local councillor and a pictured mystery woman, who turned out to be the proprietor's wife. It was all true, but that didn't make his sacking any easier to take.

'Er . . . em . . . welcome aboard, I suppose. Em . . . no hard feelings, eh?'

Parlabane stared at him for a long time without saying anything.

'Look, eh . . . why don't you eh . . . sort of . . . sit here maybe?'

Parlabane picked up a dictionary and started thumbing through it. McCreedie looked on in gaping fear.

'There,' he said, pointing to the word 'suspect'. 'Read and remember.'

As a freelance, from out of town and low on local contacts, he was unsurprised to be stuck at a desk all day, landed with exactly the sort of busywork the staffers hated doing. The knowledge that transferring funds from his bank in LA might take a couple of days and that this was a fast way of getting some ready cash kept his professional ego in check, but he was still relieved no one seemed to know who he was.

However, the feeling of being a shark getting fed plankton was starting to get to him, and the editorial style of the paper was grating on his nerves like sandpaper. It seemed to be a mixture of blue-rinsed moral disapproval and parochial couthiness, mixed with a paranoid, negative preoccupation with all things Glaswegian, an animosity which it mistakenly believed to be enthusiastically reciprocal. He didn't know how to break it to them. 'Hey guys, sorry, but through in the West, you know . . . we don't actually *worry* too much about Edinburgh . . . you know, like, *ever* . . .'

And the more copy he read, the more annoyed he got about the fact that he had been the high-profile subject of it the other day. Finlay Price, the little bastard who had written it, snuck back in quietly after a while, a slimy wee shite with greasy hair and big damp patches under his arms. Parlabane clocked him immediately as a national tabloid wannabe; this gig was just his audition. He wasn't interested in what the real story was, just what would make the loudest splash below his byline.

Price had taken what the police had told him and gone straight to work on it; the thought that there might be more to discover would never occur to him. His job wasn't to find things out, his job was to 'make' stories. Some innuendo here, some association there and *voilà*: you had fifteen pars on the front page that suggested much but actually told you fuck-all.

The success of popular reporting since the Eighties had lain in the practice of massively increasing the ratio of column inches to facts. Facts were both expensive and time-consuming to procure, so you had to use them as sparingly as possible.

On last night's final edition front page, Price had the junkie burglar found guilty by the end of the standfirst. Listening to him on the phone and watching him talk to people around the office, Parlabane was in almost awed disbelief that someone could have so little doubt that the police had the right man. But if they let the junkie go and arrested a different bloke tomorrow, Price would work on the premise that the new suspect was one hundred per cent guilty too. What Parlabane found so hard to understand was the guy's lack of a need to get his own perspective, to look for anything deeper in the story than 'Gory murder – police seek baddie – police catch baddie – baddie goes to jail'.

Watching this fucking moron work had him climbing the walls, desperate to get out and get his teeth into finding the real story behind the Ponsonby murder.

The final edition's front page was going to lead on a story about the police confiscating a stash of hard-core tapes from a video store in Leith. Just the sort of morally indignant tale to have them snorting over their scones in Murrayfield.

COPS SEIZE PORN was the gleeful banner headline planned in on the chief sub's computer monitor, but McCreedie, the deputy editor and the hack who had faithfully jotted down the police statement – sorry, written the story – were gathered round trying to improve on it.

Parlabane was wandering relievedly towards the exit, his shift mercifully over, when McCreedie called him across to their gathering.

'Can you think of a better headline for this?' he asked.

Parlabane leaned over and read the story on the screen, then stood with his brow furrowed for a few moments as they looked expectantly at him.

'I've got it,' he finally said. 'How about: DRACONIAN CENSORSHIP CONTINUES, with a strap saying: *Sexual repression maintains sad climate of dangerous ignorance*? No? Just a thought. Good night.'

From his window that evening he had seen the woman remonstrating with the police, and had made out enough of the conversation to understand that she wanted into Ponsonby's flat. He made sure he got a good look at her face and clothes, and scribbled down *Girlfriend?* on his notepad.

He was still suffering from jet-lag, and was finding it very hard to get to sleep before about three in the morning as his body got used to the time difference. Staring at the ceiling had lost its appeal after a couple of hours, and he had got up and out of habit wandered into the living room, forgetting that he didn't have a TV. Instead he found himself looking out of the window at the Square, his eye occasionally caught by the meanderings of drunks heading down Elm Row. Then he saw the woman from earlier on, looking back and forth – but inexperiencedly not up – to check no one was watching her. She disappeared out of view and into the close. He got dressed.

Twenty minutes later he was making her coffee in his kitchen.

It was a total lie about the policeman.

SEVEN

Darren Mortlake was in the huff. He was feeling unappreci-
ated, taken for granted and unfairly chastised. He had shown
initiative, proven his ability to adapt under pressure, and
bollocks, he had got the job done. But it hadn't been enough,
apparently. That bearded wanker Lime had been furious,
talking to him like he was some stupid kid, ranting away
down the phone and telling him – no, ordering him – to stay
put in this fucking awful guest house until he had decided
what to do about it.

It was at times like this he wished he had just killed the
cunt that night. Christ, plead guilty to a reduced plea of
manslaughter, keep his nose clean inside and he might have
been out by now.

But the real reason Darren was in such a bad mood, he
knew, was that he *had* screwed up, and because he had
screwed up he had had to listen to the little hairy fat bastard's
whingeings without being able to give him an earful back.

He had been quite proud of the way he had improvised
in a tricky situation, and had managed to kid himself for a
while that Lime might even be impressed. He had 'thought
on his feet to protect the investment'. A 'successful damage limitation exercise', he would say. Lime liked words
like that.

But there had been no getting away from the one crucial
error.

Lime had given him the cash and told him to get someone
else this time, 'put the contract out to tender'. His job had
been simply to find 'an independent operator' to 'neutralise
a potential liability'. They 'could not afford high exposure on
this transaction', and Darren had to assume 'a less pro-active
role' and 'take the job out-of-house'.

What? Did the cunt think Darren was in some nationwide
guild of criminals, that he could put an ad in the news-
letter and find a good operator up in fucking Jockland, just
like that?

Darren had assured Lime that he had found someone with

the appropriate skills, pocketed the dosh and decided to do it himself after all. Lime wouldn't be any the wiser.

It was supposed to look like suicide. Lime had given him the syringe and the stuff to pass on to the 'sub-contractor', with the instruction that there should be no mess whatsoever, or 'the second instalment of the remuneration' would be withheld.

No mess.

The words had popped in and out of Darren's head in Lime's nasally little voice all throughout the battle in the flat.

He had got in silently through the first-floor window at the back, despite the shoulder-strap from his little plastic satchel catching unseen on a piping bracket and almost strangling him. He had contorted his huge frame to try and wriggle out of it, his feet resting on another pipe below him. He twisted his neck and his head popped free suddenly, rattling painfully off the stone by the window-frame. At least it hadn't hit wood or glass, as there might have been more sound than just the quiet, dull thud which preceded the steady flow of blood into his right eye.

He wiped it with his sleeve and clambered in. He had dripped some blood on the window-sill inside, but no matter. Once the job was done he could clean up after himself.

He removed the ropes from the satchel and crept stealthily into the bedroom, where the 'liability' was asleep on his stomach, head turned away towards the wall. He had planned to restrain him before the injection, but he didn't think his ropes would fit around the double bed and there was no headboard to tie him to either. Besides, he might leave ropemarks, and that would just get the Filth interested. Best to just stick him right away, get the stuff into him and if he wakes up, hold him down until it takes effect.

He held the syringe delicately in his left hand and leaned over, having selected a spot on the liability's arm. However, as he was about to penetrate, another little rivulet found its way into his eye, and he instinctively brought his hand up to wipe it, ramming the needle into his forehead and breaking off the syringe.

He failed to stifle a yelp, and it was enough to waken the liability, who looked on in bewildered terror for a moment, quickly decided he wasn't dreaming and darted for the door. Darren leapt blindly after him, catching his foot and tripping him up so that he spilled into the hallway, kicking out at Darren's face. The liability got his leg free and scrambled into the living room as Darren pulled the needle out of his forehead and wiped more blood from his eye.

He heard the living room door slam and the turning of a key in its lock. With enormous relief he saw that there was a telephone on a small table in the hallway, and he picked it up to hear whether the liability might be calling the Filth from another extension. Just a dialling tone.

He backed up the full length of the hallway, took a run and lunged shoulder-first into the living room door, which crashed splintering through on to the wooden floor with him on top of it.

No mess.

The liability was on top of him instantly, pummelling at him with some sort of metal ornament, like a cast of a race horse going over a jump. He rolled over to throw the liability off, and lashed out with a heavy right fist, which smashed into the plate of glass on top of a coffee table very similar to the one in his mum's house in Dagenham, breaking it into huge shards. His fist emerged like an over-ripe plum, purple and gushing juice from several lacerations.

No mess.

He saw the liability sprawling next to him on the floor, looking to get some purchase with his fucking race horse again. He let him stagger almost to his feet, waiting for that half-balanced moment, then suddenly sprang up and charged, running him across the floor until they rammed a bookcase, sliding it a few degrees out from against the wall and spilling its titles on to the floor. Darren punched the liability in the stomach, doubling him over, then threw him to the ground and toppled the bookcase over towards him. However, the liability rolled reflexively out of the way, so Darren leapt upon him and they struggled about the floor in an angry tangle of limbs.

Darren found his good hand trapped somewhere amidst the two heaving bodies, but could feel facial features with his pulped one. He reached around, seeking out the eyes with his straining fingers. The face was slippery under his hand due to blood and sweat, and the liability's writhing made it impossible to get a grip on anything. His pinky slipped into a hole which he guessed to be a nostril, then it happened.

42

He felt a searing, tearing, grinding pain as the liability clamped his jaws closed on his index finger, biting with mortal determination. Darren screamed and tried to pull himself away, but just couldn't get the finger free. Then with a mighty lunge he rolled himself clear, his hand whipping out from his opponent's face with a sudden recoil. The liability must have finally opened his fucking mouth, which was inevitable if he wanted to breathe, as Darren had still had a finger up the cunt's nose.

Then he saw the liability spit something out, and looked in alarm at his hand.

He had bitten his finger off. The Jock cunt had bitten his finger off. Next to his thumb there was just a messy stump with little stringy bits and a throbbing, pumping spurt of blood like a burst water pipe.

Right. That was it.

He leapt at the liability once more in a blazing torrent of rage, getting hold of one of his ankles and punching his bollocks once with his free fist. Unfortunately it was the recently ravaged one, and the pain on contact was blinding. He got his elbow into the liability's groin instead, and started pumping at it until the bastard was paralysed, then got hold of his ears and sank his teeth into his nose, shaking his head and worrying at it, at which point the liability passed out.

He stood up and scanned the wreckage – the door, the table, the bookcase – and the noseless, blood-spattered wreck lying unconscious in front of the fireplace.

He reckoned the Filth might not think it was a suicide now.

The room's condition reminded him of many such sites in his teen years, breaking into places just for fun, wrecking the joint and taking their cash and booze. Maybe the Filth would think so too. He could empty out a few drawers, make it look like he had really been through the place.

Then he had his flash of inspiration, his moment of genius. Make it weird.

Confuse the Filth. Get the bastards guessing.

He moved the liability on to the door and tied him to it securely with the ropes, then propped the whole arrangement up on the remains of the table.

'Right you cunt,' he said.

Taking his knife from the satchel, he quickly and practicedly cut the liability's throat, which brought him round and initially started him screaming until he cut through the vocal chords, after which he just sort of gurgled. Darren placed a hand over the dying man's mouth because the gurgling noise was annoying him, then remembering what had happened earlier, he stuffed a rolled-up magazine in there instead, and held the door in position from behind as the liability struggled against his bonds.

Gradually the struggling calmed and Darren stood away, sighing with exhaustion.

What next, he thought, then remembered. When he trashed a place in his youth he usually liked to shit on the floor somewhere, a nice centrepiece to the surprise the poor suckers were coming home to. It wasn't a unique calling card, everyone did it. The Filth knew that too. So if he left a turd they'd be sure it was a burglary – might even reckon he was laying the finishing touch when the victim had come home and surprised him. Only thing was, where to put it? If he had just squatted down on the floor in here, there's no way the Filth would believe the thing could be intact after the battle that had pretty obviously taken place.

Then he noticed the space in the middle of the mantelpiece where that fucking race-horse statue thing must have stood.

By the time he had climbed back down, the liability was dead. He looked with satisfaction at the bloody throat, the ravaged nose, but glancing at the stump where his index finger should be he felt another wave of anger, and grabbed at the liability's right hand, gnashing and chewing at the index finger until the bone was exposed and he could snap it off.

Make it weird, he remembered.

He stuck the finger up one of the liability's nostrils. Then he repeated the drill with the other hand.

Right. Done.

His anger extinguished, his rage calmed, he simultaneously caught a whiff of his turd and a taste of the liability's flesh, and vomited copiously over the radiator.

Darren diligently ferried a few armfuls of clothes from the bedroom and scattered them liberally about the floor, then conscientiously upturned most of the remaining items of furniture, and as an after-thought, rammed the hatstand through the telly.

He took his purple shellsuit out from the satchel, pulled it on over his bloodstained clothes, shoved the ropes, knife and syringe into it, and headed out of the front door, which he left unlatched.

No mess.

EIGHT

'So, did you find what you were looking for?'

They stood on opposite sides of Parlabane's one hundred per cent furniture-free kitchen, waiting for the kettle to boil.

'You know, before I even think about answering that question, I think I should get a reply to the "Who the fuck are you" one.'

Sarah felt the confidence of being behind a mask. There was always an unreality to the sudden death of someone you knew, this time doubly so due to it having been murder. There was a feeling of the rules having been suspended, a grace period during which you were someone else until you were ready to resume being yourself and accept the responsibilities ahead. The shock, the jolt gave a hazy sense of control having been lost, and the appearance of a mysterious stranger together with the promise of other knowledge had drawn her, like an open door on a train pulling away from the platform, headed for an unknown destination.

'Sorry,' said Parlabane. 'My name's Jack. Jack Parlabane.'

'I didn't ask your name, I asked who the fuck are you. I feel pretty sure you're not a cop, and I came up here in the fervent hope that you're not just a nosy neighbour.'

Parlabane chucked his jacket on the worktop and spooned powder into a suspiciously murky cafetière.

'I could be the killer. Didn't that occur to you?'

Sarah sniffed dismissively. 'No you couldn't. From what I gather, the killer got the better of Jeremy after a real ruck. Nothing personal, but you don't look up to it. You'd have to be a lot bigger, a lot stronger and probably a lot fitter. So one more time, who the fuck . . .'

'I'm a journalist.'

Sarah rolled her eyes. His intriguingly mercurial look had just become probing and seedy. Reality was starting to precipitate in a sordid grey.

'Fuck your coffee. I'll take my chances with the police.'

Jesus, thought Parlabane as she made to leave, Rupert Murdoch had a lot to answer for.

'Wait,' he called after her. 'Two things you ought to know. One, I'm not that sort of journalist.'

She kept walking down his hall. 'What sort of journalist is "that sort of journalist"?' she muttered.

'The sort it would be wise to walk out on without hearing what he had to say.'

She stopped with her hand on the lock.

'I'm not after you for a story,' he assured her, hands in the air. 'At least, not the kind of story you're worried about.'

'All right. Milk, no sugar.'

She walked back to the kitchen behind him. He was actually a couple of inches shorter than she had first thought, his initially menacing stance lending him stature. He looked very light-framed but not skinny, like a lightweight boxer, and the black leather belt fastened tight round his waist seemed to pull the denim neatly around his well-formed buttocks. An endless parade of flabby arses presented to the surgeons for abscess removal had taught her great appreciation of a nice bum when she saw one.

'What's your connection to the late doctor?' he asked, pushing down the plunger on the dark liquid. 'Ex-wife, ex-girlfriend?'

'Ex-wife. How did you guess?'

'Well, no offence, we all grieve in different ways, but you're not quite crying buckets over there.'

'Cried my last tears over Jeremy a long time back. We broke up more than a year and a half ago.'

Parlabane handed her a mug of steaming coffee.

'Afraid it's UHT. No fridge yet.'

'That's fine,' she said and took a few sips.

She sighed and put the mug down on the worktop.

'Sarah,' she said. 'My name's Sarah.'

Parlabane nodded acknowledgement over the brim of his mug. They stood quietly drinking for a few moments, exchanging brief, assuring smiles, aware of the almost bizarre awkwardness of their situation. Sarah looked younger than Parlabane, about twenty-seven, twenty-eight, he figured. He instinctively began piecing her together. Young to be divorced, divorced from a doctor . . . chances were she was a doctor too. Female doctors had the highest divorce rates of any profession in the country. English accent with Scottish inflections meant she probably studied up here – Edinburgh or St Andrews –

met the ill-fated Dr P and stayed on. He couldn't be sure though. From what he could remember, Edinburgh was full of natives who spoke with that anonymous, Home Counties BBC accentless English accent, and who got very shirty and upset when you asked where they were from down south. To them, theirs *was* a Scottish accent, just a more refined one than the rather rough and coarse vernacular favoured by the lumpen proletariat. In Parlabane's more militantly Glaswegian moments, this pissed him off no end.

Sarah had fine, wispy, shoulder-length red hair, worn straight, framing lightly freckled pale skin which bore no make-up. She was in black jeans and a black, blazer-style jacket, on top of a white cotton button-up blouse, the kind it had taken Parlabane years to discipline himself not to try and peek through.

'So have the cops had you in yet? Fishing for background on your ex?'

'Briefly. Miserable-looking sod called McGregor and a big drink of water named Gow. But either I couldn't tell them much or they weren't asking the right questions. Probably thought they would get better information from his current girlfriend.'

'Who's that?'

'Oh, some nineteen-year-old nurse with blonde hair and big tits, someone happy to suck his cock metaphorically as well as literally.'

'Was she anything to do . . .'

'With the divorce?' Sarah laughed. 'Oh God, no.'

'Then why so bitter?'

'Disappointment, really. The embarrassment of having been married to someone who has turned out to be . . . oh, never mind. You don't know doctors much, do you?'

'Guess not. Apples are an important part of my daily diet.'

'Wise man. And trust me, meeting them in a social capacity is often worse than having to meet them in their professional capacity.'

Parlabane looked her in the eye. 'And what about meeting them in a just-trespassed-on-the-ex-husband's-murder-scene capacity?'

She took her time swallowing a mouthful of coffee, playing calm but buying a moment to silently recoil.

'You're very perceptive. You should be a journalist.'

'Maybe some day. So the nurse . . . they weren't living together, so how long . . . ?'

'Couldn't tell you precisely. More than six months, I know that. It's a familiar scenario, suits someone like Jeremy down to the ground. Worshipful girlie he can pick up and play with when he wants to, then put back down when he's finished. And believe me, she'd have put up with it, no matter how long it stayed that way. There's legions of young nurses in that position. White Coat Syndrome, their peers call it. Ego-massage and fuck-therapy for the dashing young doctor, lying back and thinking of some suburban two-kids-and-a-volvo dream he's going to make come true. Sad cows.

'The cops won't have got much out of her. Jeremy would never have let her close enough. She won't know a great deal more about him than that he drinks in Montmartre's, plays rugby on free Saturday mornings and says "Oh Jesus" a lot when he comes.'

'Present tense,' Parlabane said.

Sarah made a self-dismissive waving gesture. 'I know, I know. A change of tense in talking about him could be the only practical difference his murder makes to my life. It's not easy to get used to the fact that he's dead. The change would obviously have had a more profound impact if we were still together, but as I only saw him occasionally . . . I don't know, I never felt like I missed him, so I was very much used to him being out of my life already.'

'So if you were used to him being out of your life, what were you looking for downstairs? Family heirloom? He still owe you money?'

She smiled sadly to herself, thoughts Parlabane could but guess at.

'Oh, he owed me plenty of money, but that was written off way back. I suppose I was looking for an ending. I had got Jeremy out of my life and out of my head, but deep down there's still a lot of loose ends, questions I intended to seek answers for when a lot more water had passed under the bridge. Maybe a few more years down the line I thought I would be able to look at him and know a bit more about what went wrong between us.

'But on the other hand his death somehow didn't surprise

49

me, and that's what makes it feel even emptier. As if I should have known. As if I *did* know it was coming but just didn't anticipate precisely when or how. But that's probably because, if you like, he was already "dead" to me in a way. I'm not known for great psychic awareness. Oh, I don't know. Maybe I just wanted to say goodbye.'

'Where'd you get the keys?'

'He gave them to me. Foisted them upon me in fact. He was always losing keys when we lived together. Often turned up on a ward or outside a theatre looking for mine after finding himself locked out. So once he was out on his own, if he lost his keys he was stuffed. He asked me to keep a set at my flat that he could collect as a back-up. It was really just a ploy, an excuse to show up, a way of keeping my door open in case he needed something else. I know that because although he was bound to have kept locking himself out, he never once came round for them.'

Sarah put her mug down, emptied but still slightly steaming. By her folded arms, Parlabane knew it wasn't just the coffee that was finished.

'So what's your role in all this?' she asked. 'I'm assuming you're after more than the "dead doctor's sex secrets", so what's the story? And come to think of it, you said "two things" earlier and never told me the second.'

Parlabane put his own finished mug down and took a deep breath.

'Can I trust you?' he asked quietly.

'I have absolutely no idea,' she said. 'That's your call.'

'All right, scratch that. I'm *going* to trust you. I saw the place downstairs, before the police had cleared up. I saw the wreckage. I saw the body.'

He swallowed, nervously. He was about to turn her world upside down, black into white, light into dark, and she had no idea what was coming. He knew it was not entirely fair to share out such a burden without really waiting to be asked, but he needed her help and the best way to get it was to make her need his.

'I believe your ex-husband was murdered.'

She closed her eyes for half a second, then opened them to reveal a bemused stare.

'I don't want to injure your professional pride here,' she said, 'but I don't think you're going to be able to claim that

50

as an exclusive. I think maybe even the Lothian and Borders have scooped you on this one.'

Fuck.

Sometimes he wished a sub-editor could give his speech a once-over before it was issued.

'I'm not finished,' he said, trying to dig himself out. 'I mean I have reason to think *he*, specifically Jeremy Ponsonby, was murdered because someone wanted him dead.'

Sarah's eyes remained fixed, cold, on his own. She hadn't run out screaming and she wasn't looking at him like he was nuts. This was both a good sign and a bad sign. Good because it meant she thought he might be right. Bad for exactly the same reason.

'Keep talking,' she said.

'I don't know how much you've been told about how he was murdered and I don't know how much you want to hear.'

'Trust me, I'm not easily shocked.'

'Fine. All right, he was badly bruised and had had his nose and both index fingers bitten off. Messy, gory, horrible and weird as fuck. But he was killed by having his throat cut. Plain and simple. Now nobody has found the murder weapon, and I doubt anyone ever will, but they're certainly not going to turn up some kitchen knife missing from your ex-husband's flat. I've had the misfortune of seeing more than one cut throat, and this one was done by someone who took pride in their work, wielding an implement designed with just such a purpose in mind. It was a clean, deep, practised cut with an extremely sharp and probably pretty large blade. No hacking, no slashing.

'Whoever killed your ex-husband has killed plenty of people before, and although the recession has hit us all, I find it hard to believe someone of his skills is having to supplement his income with burglary.'

Sarah squinted as if at too-bright light, too much information coming in at once.

A question came along to buy her time to assimilate.

'But if he's so efficient, what about the mess, what about the fight?' she asked.

'I said he was efficient at cutting throats. Getting hold of Dr Ponsonby's must have proven more difficult than he anticipated.'

'And where did you see all these cut throats?'

'A live-action version of the *Journal of Wound Care*. AKA Los Angeles. I worked there as a reporter for the best part of two years.'

'But why didn't the police notice this? Why only you, or are you just Mr Hot-shot.'

'The police saw a burglary. They saw a chaotic mess. They saw a giant turd on the mantelpiece. Whether they also saw what I saw . . . they still have to pursue the more obvious line of investigation. That's incumbent upon them. I mean, yes, there is a possibility that the killer was a burglar who got very lucky with a kitchen knife. I can afford to look into the other possibility and be wrong. They can't. I've got a contact on their side. I'll tell her what I think. She can then tell McGregor if she buys it. From there it's his call.'

'One of them saw it though, I'm sure,' Parlabane said. 'The contact, DC Jenny Dalziel. She wasn't buying the burglary story, anyway. She suspects there might be more to know about the man himself. You're the expert. What do you say?'

She held up a small, transparent-plastic tube.

'Yeah, I'd say there might be more to know.'

NINE

'Removing evidence from a sealed police crime scene. You're showing prodigious potential. So what is it?'

'It's a plastic drug ampoule. NHS standard. The label's been removed. I can get it analysed to find out what was in it.'

'Jenny Dalziel mentioned that naughty doctors have been known to deal drugs, but that looks to me more a receptacle for prescribed rather than proscribed substances. What's the deal? He was a doctor. Don't you have these things around?'

Sarah shook her head. 'Not at home, you don't. You get glass ampoules which you have to chuck straight in the sin bin – the sharps bucket – when you've emptied them. The plastic ones can just go in any bin, but you still wouldn't stick one in your pocket or anything. The lack of a label is very suspicious. I want to know what this was and what he was doing with it at home.'

'The police found a needle but no syringe, so they figured the missing syringe was taken by the killer. What if the ampoule was his too?'

'Then he's no junkie,' she said. 'Smackheads don't shoot up mid-burglary, I don't imagine. And heroin doesn't come in these.'

'So what's your angle on all this, Jack. Is it just a good story? Is that all it takes to get you involved?'

They were sitting on the bare floor in the living room, their backs to opposite walls, drinking more coffee. The room was lit by streetlights from the open-curtained window, as the only alternative was the bare bulb hanging from the centre of the ceiling, which was a little oppressive and hurt the eyes at this time of night. It was almost pleasantly conspiratorial. They had grown tired of standing in the kitchen, and although the living room had no furniture either, it felt a more natural place to squat down.

Sarah was interested, concerned, maybe even excited, but too tired to exhibit strong symptoms of any of the above. She stared across at Parlabane in the half-light, that shock of fair hair occasionally falling over his eyes in a way that seemed to be irritating him too much for it to be an affectation.

He had scored high marks for not saying, 'Oh, I didn't think you had to be a doctor to do that' when she said she was an anaesthetist, and had trumped it by failing to remark at all when she told him her surname, which made her professional title Dr Slaughter.

He seemed sharp, attentive and perceptive; he listened not only to what she was saying, but what she was telling him. However, when he stared at her with those mischievous hazel eyes, she had an uncomfortable feeling of being robbed. She had no idea who he was, where he came from, what was in his past, which had made it strangely easier to talk to him initially, but there was an inescapable feeling that he was hiding something.

'Is a good story not enough?' he asked. 'It's my raison d'être, remember.'

'I don't know,' she stated flatly. 'I'm not sure who you're asking. Is a good story not enough to explain your involvement to me, or not enough to explain your involvement to yourself?'

Parlabane shook his head and smiled, hiding.

'Now that's a whole other mystery,' he said.

But Sarah wouldn't back off.

'Oh no. You don't get to be the stranger with a past here. You're asking me to trust you, but I don't know anything about you. You're sitting here in a flat without furniture, for God's sake. What are you actually doing here?'

'I'm here because it wasn't wise to stay in LA any more.'

'And why were you in LA?'

'Because it wasn't wise to stay in London any more.'

'And what were you doing in London?'

'Wasting my time.'

Sarah smiled, but it was not a happy smile. 'You know, every day I find myself running round in circles with a patient because there's something they don't want to tell me. But I get it out of them eventually through tedious perseverance. I have to. It's my job. I'd imagine yours is a lot like that too.'

Parlabane nodded.

'Then you of all people should be giving me a fucking straight answer.'

It was a very fair point.

So he told her.

'My grandfather always maintained that where there was muck, there was brass,' Parlabane said. 'If you're not afraid to get your hands dirty and put your back into your work, you'll get a fair reward. However, throughout the tenure of our present government, I discovered a valuable reciprocal to be true: where there's lots of brass, there's usually muck, and I've made a career out of looking for it.

'As Michael Portillo fearlessly said, in this country, as opposed to those wog-ridden foreign sties – I'm paraphrasing here, although only slightly – if you win a contract, it's not because your brother is a government minister or you blatantly bribed an official. Of course not. That would be corruption. In this country, you win contracts because you are "one of us", you went to the right school, give money to the right party, and have awarded an executive post to a member of the cabinet's family, or have promised a seat on the board to the appropriate minister when he resigns to spend more time with his bankers.

'We don't have anything as vulgar or primitive as a bribe. It's a matter of trust. For every action, there's an equal and opposite reaction. For every contract, there's a kickback. It's more noble, more gentlemanly. A matter of mutual understanding. And very, very British.'

Sarah stared across, unimpressed. 'Once again, hot-shot, this much I know. Not an exclusive. Cut to the chase.'

'Fair enough. I got a bit of a reputation for myself through in Glasgow, sniffing out scams, investigating dodgy deals. But what I really wanted was to go after the big game down south, and I was head-hunted by one of the big broadsheet Sundays. I thought it would either make my career or turn out to be the worst move south by a promising young Scot since Charlie Nicholas. In the end it was both.'

'What went wrong? Did the stories dry up?'

'No, quite the opposite. It took me very little time to establish my contacts and get stuck in. I seemed to be notching up another big-splash story every month or so. I wasn't operating as autonomously as in Glasgow, so I was often following up a lead from the head of the investigative team, with back-up and resources like I had never imagined. Up north I usually had to fish around on my own, chasing down a few blind alleys before I found something worth really going after, and even then I was pretty much a one-man show.

'I felt like the star striker justifying his big transfer fee by enthusiastically flogging my guts out, turning on all the style and getting results. And like the star striker, I had been brought in to finish off the chances being created by the rest of the team. I was so hungry for it that I barely stopped to look around myself for the best part of a year. Or maybe I was believing in my own myth too much to want to see what must have been in front of me all the time.'

'You were being used,' Sarah stated with a dry smile.

Parlabane sighed. 'It's a sight easier to notice from the outside looking in. I stumbled across something, just as a small follow-up on a big story I had done. There was a very unpleasant land deal going down in East Anglia somewhere . . . I can't even remember the name of the shithole. Lots of public protest over the proposed use of the site, industrialisation of what had been a public park that the council had suspiciously let fall into dereliction, that kind of thing. I was doing a hatchet-job on the environmental record of the chemical company that was trying to buy the land. I even found out that one of the local authority planning players had an undisclosed interest in the company concerned.

'Thought I was Mr fucking Green Hero. Expose the polluters, local authority throws out proposal, land stays a park. I could see it all. Christmas card from Jonathon Porritt, environmental journalist of the year award and probably the fucking Nobel prize thrown in.

'And it worked. The planning department guy resigned, the plan got junked. But the land didn't stay a park. It was sold instead to Woodford's, a major housebuilder whose proposals were considered more palatable by the locals, still worrying over what might have been. They were building a whole load of yuppie flats with a tiny new swing-park thrown in to sweeten the neighbourhood residents.

'I did some checking, looking for another link between the authority and this time Woodford's. Instead I found that the chairman of Woodford's was a close business associate of my newspaper's proprietor and owned a sizable share of the controlling media group.

'I checked back on all of my big splashes, and every time

I had buried someone, there was an anonymous winner, someone in the background quietly doing very nicely thank you from the fall-out from my story. In most cases I could establish the link with the proprietor, but where I couldn't it was even more interesting, as clearly no one else knew of a connection between these figures.'

'And what did you do with what you found?'

'Nothing, at first. I kept it all quiet and then waited for my next major assignment. Then instead of investigating what I was supposed to, I sought out the intended beneficiaries and dug some dirt on them instead. I filed the story and appended my resignation to the end of it, then went to the pub for a couple of pints.

'When I got home I found my flat burgled. The place had been torn apart, and every computer disk, every file, every folder, every notepad taken. In fact, they even gutted the fucking computer itself.

'I called the police immediately, but as soon as I had put the phone back down I was struck by a paranoid but understandable thought. Anyone organised enough to break in and steal all my research as quickly as that would not be beyond stitching me up as well, and an old favourite was planting class-A drugs then tipping off the police. Except I had called the police for them.'

'Setting your own time-bomb.'

'Well, let's just say it was the world's fastest and most high-stakes game of hunt-the-thimble. Colombian dry white, recent vintage, big package, stuffed out of sight underneath my reservoir water tank. It was a lot of stuff – I took it as a back-handed compliment that the proprietor was shelling out so much to get me sent down.'

'What did you do with it?'

'Climbed up on to the roof of the building with it and put it under a bird's nest. It's probably still there.'

'And that's why you left London?'

'Not entirely. My decision was made easier when the cops arrived. It wasn't some Operation Bumble Bee soco and a flatfoot. Half-a-dozen beat bobbies and two trenchcoats. And they didn't do a convincing impression of investigating a burglary. One of the trenchcoats made a B-line for the watertank, a rather idiosyncratic place to start any new investigation, I'm sure you'll agree.'

Sarah pretended to dither, then nodded, mock-reluctantly.

'He rammed his hand under the tank without even looking, and got a disappointing surprise.'

'No drugs.'

'Well, partly that, and partly that when he rapidly brought his hand out there was a mousetrap attached to three of his fingers.

'He told me my card was marked, but we both knew I'd foxed them that time. However, I wasn't waiting about for the rematch if the bad guys had bent cops on their team.

'I made a call to an ex-colleague in LA who had once approached me about doing a stint out there as a crime reporter, giving an outsider's perspective on the kinds of atrocities Angelinos had come to accept. I was out there in a matter of days.'

'And who did you upset out there? The Cripps?'

Parlabane laughed. 'No. I played it straight for a long time. I had some fun, made some very good contacts on the LAPD, one of whom I owe . . .' he looked briefly, blankly out of the window . . . 'a lot.

'I saw lots of crime scenes, lots of bodies, wrote lots of worthy prose about the decreasing value of human life, the too-high price of America's gun culture. Pissed off the NRA on a regular basis. Learned that you don't need a southern accent and a pick-up truck to be a redneck. You also don't need a brain to be a gun-owner.

'But the old *reportage* thing could only take me so far. My instinctive, fundamental, primal need to cause trouble inevitably kicked in. I still kept my head down, let the cops put the two and twos together when I followed up a murder. But I suppose I noticed a pattern emerging among certain of the resulting fours, and I believed there might be a motive to a number of apparently motiveless killings. I had nothing concrete to go on, just a gut feeling, the kind that used to serve me in Glasgow before I got duped into being hand-fed in London. I had very little, not even a theory. Just the feeling I get when I'm sure there's something wrong with the picture. I was just fishing around, but I had no idea how deep I was casting, which makes investigating either very hard or very risky. When you ask someone a question, you don't know who he's going to run off and tell about it.

'And in LA the baddies don't burgle your apartment and

plant some marching powder. As is common with Americans, they tend to be a bit more direct.'

'Someone tried to kill you?'

'Someone *paid* someone to kill me. You wanted to know what my angle was here? Wasn't a good story enough? Well, you've got it now. Someone I didn't even know paid to have me killed. Just like that. A simple business transaction. And someone who had never even met me was prepared to murder me just for money. Believe me, you can't even begin to imagine how angry that makes me.

'So I know I can't get to whoever was responsible in LA, but I'm prepared to make do with a couple of surrogates.'

TEN

Maybe it would all blow over.

Maybe the cro-magnon moron had actually pulled it off. Maybe the sheer, breathtaking stupidity of his actions had indeed thrown the police off the scent. They had no witnesses, no descriptions, and they did seem to have believed that it had been a burglar who had killed Ponsonby. In fact, they had brought one in for questioning, according to the paper.

Still, they had to sit it out for the time being, and that bloodthirsty oaf would have to stay where he was until the coast was definitely clear. His initial thought was to get him the hell out of the city, back to Dagenham on the first train, but the thought that things might be about to get tricky and complicated meant that it was best to have Darren at his immediate disposal.

He couldn't afford any more slip-ups, any more risks. Killing Ponsonby was supposed to tie up the last loose end, but it also had the potential to unravel and fray the whole thing.

So near and yet so far.

The visionless, the ignorant, the blinkered – the clinical staff and the general public, basically – had said it was madness, that it was entirely wrong to place the Trusts in the hands of people with no medical experience. What could people who had run biscuit factories and textile firms possibly know about running hospitals, they asked. This isn't about profit and loss, but about medical care, they bleated.

They just couldn't see, could they. It was people who had medical experience who were precisely the wrong candidates for NHS senior management, as they brought along so much obstructive sentimental baggage. They didn't have the experience to deal in hard facts and harsh realities, and couldn't help letting their hearts rule their cheque-books. For God's sake, what kind of doctor had any knowledge of real decision-making?

But now they would be forced to see, now they would be forced to sit up and take notice, because the Midlothian NHS

Trust – 'We've got a heart in the Heart' © – was about to go into the black.

When he had first arrived, the situation had seemed so horrifying and desperate that he thought for a moment he had been stitched up, and was almost about to ring the bank and find out whether his Party contribution cheque had bounced for some reason. To secure Trust status, as was very much the norm, the hospitals' books had been cooked so complicatedly that Delia Smith would have been proud of the recipe. Debts and liabilities had been hidden, or their impact deferred, just waiting to loudly declare themselves throughout his first year in charge.

However, a closer look at the figures revealed to him the massive potential for improvement, as well as for the private endeavours he had envisaged.

The first important action was to declare the Trust's true financial position, as it wasn't as though Trust status would be withdrawn by the health ministry once the truth was known, and it meant that any savings he managed to make would be more visible.

There had to be radical change. Right away he purchased a small fleet of company Mercedes, to attract the right calibre of management staff to undertake the stiff measures needed to turn the place around. There was the inevitable whining about why such perks weren't required to attract the right calibre of doctors, but it was such a juvenile comparison. You had to think of the responsibility that would be in the hands of these people, for a start. If you wanted people who could handle that responsibility, you had to show them that they would be valued as much as if they worked in industry or in the City. And what the moaners didn't appreciate was the commitment and loyalty that such perks engendered in staff, things impossible to put a price on.

The Trust covered the massive, city-centre Royal Victoria Infirmary and a small geriatric hospital, the George Romanes. The administration department was based at the RVI, and was a run-down, shambling basement, totally unsuitable for its intended purpose.

On a first tour of the sprawling, gothic monstrosity that was the RVI, Stephen Lime was most taken by the light and city-wide view afforded by the massive windows in the East wing, and within a month had moved the administration department there, closing two wards and moving the others to where admin had previously been. However, it couldn't just be a matter of moving all that tawdry old Seventies office furniture up the stairs. Top-quality administrators had to feel they were working in a top-quality department. Massive refurbishment had to be undertaken immediately, and when it came to something as important to the hospital as that, no expense could be spared. New carpeting, proper wall-coverings, pot plants, a marble floor for the atrium lobby, new PCs, new desks, new chairs, new filing system, the works. Because when you really came right down to it, people's lives were depending on the work done in there.

Of course, savings desperately had to be made, and his successes in that field followed recovery from a major early setback. He had looked at the pay and conditions of all domestic and auxiliary staff, and the cumulative cost of their employment. Ideally, if he had a blank slate, he would have put their whole field out to tender, bringing in private firms who could do the job for half the current outlay, with some of the spend quietly trickling back to him from the chosen contractors as a mark of appreciation. However, the reality was that he was saddled with this unwanted, overpaid workforce. Then the idea hit him, so simple he really hadn't been able to see it for looking at it. When the hospital became a Trust, these people's employer effectively folded, which in other circumstances would have made them all redundant. The Midlothian NHS Trust – 'We've got a heart in the Heart' © – had continued their employment on the same terms and conditions. This was insane.

The plan was simple. He would announce that they had indeed been effectively made redundant, but were generously being re-employed by a new company, Midlothian NHS Domestic. However, the new company, to remain viable and competitive in the marketplace, could not pay them what they had earned before, so wages would be cut by an average of twenty-five per cent. And as new employees, they would have to work at least a year before they had any holiday entitlement.

It was genius. The trust was about to save millions per annum at a stroke.

Unfortunately, about a week before he was due to make the big announcement, the kilty media exploded with indignation over one of his counterparts in Glasgow attempting to pull off a similar coup. There was strike action, widespread condemnation, and even the Department of Health spokesmen wheeled out were disappointingly limp-wristed about the whole affair. The Glasgow thing went down in flames and he quietly wiped all trace of his own plans from the records.

On the plus side, one cloud on the horizon, the New Deal for Junior Doctors, did turn out to be a blessing in disguise. The talk of an across-the-board, statutory reduction in junior doctors' hours had been fairly terrifying, as the only way of bringing it about seemed unavoidably to employ more of the buggers.

However, this proved to be far from the case. His administrators were soon able to assure him that juniors' rotas could be reduced with no increase in staffing whatsoever, by putting them on-call on fewer nights, but having them cover more wards per doctor. It would concentrate their workload, making their on-call nights busier and more stressful, but what the hell, they weren't paying the bastards to sleep.

They also explained that what had to be reduced was not the number of hours the juniors actually worked, but merely the number of hours they were officially contracted to work. With no tangible alteration to the total workload, this meant in practice that – to get the job done properly – the doctors would still have to work well over the new limits and thus the hours they were contracted for, *they just wouldn't get paid for it*. The Trust could then let the media report – as was happening across the land – that no junior doctor in its employ was working beyond the new legal limits – and could save money into the bargain!

Some of the stuff he had found in the books was terrifying. There was an instance of £57,000 having been spent in one month on *one patient*. When he investigated further, it turned out the cash had gone on some extortionate drugs for a cancer-sufferer who had died a few months later anyway. In a time when resources had to be pro-actively channelled according to needs and merits, this amounted to a shocking misappropriation of funds. In fact there were *millions* being spent each year on expensive treatments for terminal cancer patients.

Then there was the George Romanes Hospital, a whole group of buildings full of coffin-dodgers with nothing specifically wrong with them other than age, haemorrhaging funds to give some old grannies a few more years of drooling and incontinence. But that wasn't even the half of it, as the GRH's bedspace was massively congested with long-stay geriatric cases, screaming, shrieking dements, some of whom had been there for over a decade.

It was all very daunting at first, but he quickly saw that money could be saved, and money could be made. It just took the vision to see it and the nerve, damn it, the *balls* to carry it off.

The smell was really beginning to get to Darren, and he was sure Mrs Kinross was becoming suspicious. It was getting on for a few days now, and he had spent most of the time in this fucking crappy little guest house room, waiting for Lime to either give him the all-clear or at least give him something to be getting on with. He had taken the odd walk round the block to get away from it for a while, but that made it seem all the more pungent when he had to go back in.

He had tried to open the window, but not only was it freezing cold and raining, but this fucking Jock city seemed to have a permanent gale blowing through it. The only other alternative had been soaking hankies in Brut and putting them over his nose and mouth, which worked for a while, but was giving him a sore throat.

He would have to do something. The last time he had returned from a trip into the fresh air, he had noticed the smell from halfway down the stairs on his way back in. She was a batty old trout, but she might still put two and two together if she was given enough time.

He hadn't even meant it, really. He had been half asleep at the time, but to be perfectly honest he really fucking hated dogs. Bane of his existence when he was a burglar, and he had never forgiven the cunts for the bother they had caused him. Two separate stretches inside and fuck knew how many bites and scratches.

On the other hand, he might not have learned to handle his knife so well had it not been for the dogs. He had tried to avoid screwing places that had them, but when he found he'd made a mistake – or a place looked just too tasty to pass over – he made his first procedure to slaughter the fucking mutt. He made a special cuff out of two plastic shin-guards he shoplifted from a sports store, and wore that over his right wrist like a falconing glove. When the mutt went for him, he would let it sink its teeth into that, then whip the blade up under its exposed neck.

It had been the morning after the job, lying there sore and knackered, having had a frustratingly restless night. He had drifted in and out of a light sleep, and started having this horrible dream that the stump of his severed finger was being swarmed over and eaten by ants and maggots. He had opened one cloudy eye to see that his arm was hanging off the end of the bed, and the ravaged stump was being solicitously licked by Ruffle, the landlady's miserable little white Scottie.

In semi-conscious malice he had slowly reached under the pillow for his knife, then leaned over and stuck it between the fluffy little twat's eyes. Then he had rolled over and slept peacefully for six more hours.

The thought of infection struck him belatedly when he awoke, and in the absence of Dettol or any other recognisable antiseptic, he had to make do with sticking the stump into a cup of bathroom bleach. The pain brought tears to his eyes and made him doubly glad he had killed the yappy little mutt.

That afternoon, through the window on to the back garden, he had heard Mrs Kinross ask her neighbours with increasing anxiety whether they had seen Ruffle. He had kept the room locked when he was in or out, but he knew she would be wanting in to clean the place at some point that day, so he had bought a canvas sportsbag, placed the deceased Ruffle in it and gone out looking for a skip to dump it in.

He had walked for bloody miles and seen nothing but narrow-mouthed litter bins, and on a couple of quiet streets had attempted to stuff the bag through the gap when no one was looking, but the fucking thing just wouldn't fit.

He had thought about leaving it in a garden or a park, but with the luck he had been having lately, some cunt would see him dump it and come forward with a description when the contents were discovered. He had read about American serial killers getting caught because they were picked up for speeding. He did not want to be the first hit man to get caught because he was picked up for having a dead dog in a sports bag.

In the end he had to bring the fucking thing back to the guest house and stick it on top of the wardrobe, where the old cow wouldn't disturb it.

However, with Lime hopping about on hot coals after this doctor business, it was looking like he might have to stay in this place for at least a few more days, and he just couldn't cope with the smell any longer, or the danger that Mrs Kinross might want to come in and find out what was causing it.

Bollocks.

He took the bag down and, covering his mouth and nose with another Brut-soaked hanky, pulled open the zipper. Ruffle was stinking and very stiff, but he was still acceptably fluffy, apart from the big bloodstain over his muzzle. He zipped the bag up again. What would the old bat know about dead dogs.

Darren was woken by the alarm on his digital watch at three in the morning. His initial response was to roll over and go back to sleep, but upon turning away from the wall, he got a couple of nostrils full of the reason he really had to get up.

He opened the back window and climbed down quietly with the Ruffle bag slung over his shoulder. It was a clear night and there was a big moon, but there was no real choice but to go ahead with it. He hopped over the hedge into the garden next door and placed Ruffle out of sight between a row of conifers and the dry stone wall at the back. Then as an inspired afterthought, he removed a large boulder from the top of the wall and placed it on top of Ruffle's head.

Accidental death.

Darren climbed back into his room and went back under the scratchy blankets with his clothes on, so that he would be warm enough with the window open to finally clear the place of that pong.

In the morning he awoke to find the room breezy and fresh, apart from the smell of dead dog wafting through the open window from next door's garden.

ELEVEN

This Parlabane was quite definitely trouble. She just had to look at him to see rules being bent, control slipping gracefully away, lengthy and tortuously complicated explanations to senior officers and a run-in with McGregor that would make the one over her most recent haircut seem a fond memory. He seemed to combine an air of conscientious honesty with a blatant, mischievous untrustworthiness, and the resultant effect was like hypnosis. He commanded your attention with knowledge and facts, but you felt you couldn't take your eyes off him anyway because you feared what he might get up to. He dealt in truth like a drug, but you got the impression that he was cutting every score with about ten per cent bullshit.

And for all these reasons she was very glad he had appeared. He might well precipitate chaos and devastation, see her booted off the force and even drown her in a sea of flames, but at least whatever happened, it wouldn't be boring.

She liked the way he had been so unflustered and unapologetic about either her finding him in Ponsonby's flat or the fact that he had slept through such an obviously noisy and prolonged murder. Mind you, she had felt slightly hypocritical about scorning his failure to hear or see anything, as at the time of the killing she had actually been about fifty yards away in a flat in Annandale Street, having a delightfully squishy time with a shy and bespectacled young law student called Angela, who had lost her spectacles, shyness and eventually clothing after some extraordinarily good hash.

It had been a memorable evening all round, really, the frustrating rarity of which was why she kept her profession quiet among her social group. Parlabane had asked what the hell they talked about, and it was true she and Duncan usually did talk about the Hibees when they bumped into each other in the Barony, but she had to admit that she had always steered the conversation away from anything that might bring work into it. She didn't know Duncan incredibly well, only from the pub and the Blue Moon, but she figured he had picked up on her reluctance to mention what she did and been content never to ask.

It often felt like a guilty secret, but the bare fact was that it was not easy to get laid when everyone knew you were a cop, with the sole exception of a one-night stand with an Aberdonian pillow princess who had a uniform fetish. In fact, the only thing more difficult was getting some blow. It was a depressing fact that in the past, when no one would admit to knowing who they could score off, she had had to rely on knowledge accumulated through the job. Of course, the big fear was the embarrassment factor of being present on duty when they busted someone she regularly bought from, but mercifully it had only happened once, and he clearly valued her custom sufficiently to keep his mouth shut throughout.

The Angela thing was promising, and she knew that she would have to tell her soon, but the timing was critical. Too early and she might run off screaming, thinking she was being set up as part of a rather extreme undercover operation. Too late and you risked the question: 'Why couldn't you trust me with this?', or, worse, her finding out herself and asking the same question, but in a much angrier tone of voice.

When Parlabane had called but refused to come to the station, she asked him to meet her in the Blue Moon, partly because the Barony's real ales would have offered a great temptation to drink on duty, and partly because she hoped it might give her an edge – Parlabane was Duncan's friend, but still, many straight men were less cockily assured in the context of a gay bar, pointlessly terrified that their usual attention-seeking behaviour would attract a string of burly, unwanted suitors.

No such luck. Parlabane had breezed in looking tired and vaguely rumpled, as if he had been neither into bed nor out of his clothes the night before, but showed no discomfiture about his surroundings whatsoever. He ordered an espresso, turned down her offer of a roll-up and sat back in his chair, pushing his hair back, yawning and opening his eyes wide as if the waking was not his natural state.

'PM results through then?' he asked.

'I thought you had things to tell me, scoop, not questions to ask.'

'Yeah. I'm just checking how much you've seen of this week's exciting episode. Pro job, huh?'

'Yes, our pathologists are all highly trained and fully qualified.'

But she knew what he was saying, and he could see that too.

'Nice to still see quality craftsmanship in this day and age,' he said.

'Pathologist was impressed too,' Jenny remarked. 'And he believed such a standard of work required the finest of tools. How do you know all this?'

'I told you the other day. I've seen a lot of such craftsmanship. I've seen the less refined amateur work too, enough to spot the difference.'

'Why didn't you say this before?'

'Well, I wouldn't want to prejudice an investigation with spurious speculation.'

'No, of course not.'

'Plus I reckoned you suspected it too and I wanted to see if you drew the same conclusion without me introducing the idea.'

'That's better. Any other pieces of brilliant deduction you're holding back?'

Parlabane sipped at his hot espresso and nodded.

'It was too messy for me to be sure, but did the pathologist say whether the cut was right-to-left or left-to-right?'

'Right-to-left.'

'Then your boy's a Southpaw. Right-to-left would make it a left-handed job.'

Jenny shook her head. 'You don't know whether he was in front of or behind Ponsonby when he did it.'

'Well, I know this guy did wreck the place, but I doubt his fondness for mess would extend to getting sprayed with blood when the blade hit the carotid. It poses problems with anonymity on your way home. People sometimes remember that about you. "Yes, officer, he had black hair, sallow complexion, ear-ring . . . oh yes, and he was drenched in blood." He tied the guy to a door, propped him up then went behind and . . .'

Parlabane had another sip at his coffee.

'That finger came from his right hand, didn't it,' he said.

'Yes.'

'So the finger confirms it. I'm sure he lost it before he made the cut and it would have detracted from the quality of his work if he wasn't left-handed.'

'OK, scoop, very clever. But here's the problem. If this guy's such a professional, why the barney? How did he end up wrecking the joint and losing a finger struggling with Ponsonby? There's a lot of ne'er-do-wells handy with a blade in this city who might bring one along as insurance when they're screwing a house. How can we be sure that isn't the explanation?'

Parlabane grinned that utterly unnerving grin. 'I wasn't, entirely, until about five minutes before I called you.'

'Why do I get this feeling things are about to take a sharp turn for the worse here?'

'The needle,' he said, ignoring her mumblings.

'What about it?'

'Get it analysed? Apart from blood traces, I mean.'

'Of course.'

'Potassium chloride.'

Jenny's eyes widened in increasingly worried surprise. 'What, have you got a fucking spy camera following me? Have you bugged the station? How the bloody hell did you know that?'

Parlabane just smiled. 'I'm sorry, but as a journalist I can't reveal my sources.'

Jenny glowered threateningly.

'Unless, of course, I get a guarantee that it goes no further than you and that no action is taken regarding the removal from Ponsonby's flat of an object found discarded amidst a pile of broken glass.'

'I haven't heard a thing you've said all day,' she said, her expression mellowing. 'I'm not even aware that you're sitting near me in this cafe.'

'Good enough. Right. The source is the ex-wife. She had a key, she took a look around, she found a drug ampoule your boys had missed. She got it analysed – she's a doctor too. Potassium chloride. Induces a heart attack in a matter of seconds, and leaves no trace in the body whatsoever.'

Parlabane sat upright in his chair.

'I think what happened in Ponsonby's flat was plan B,' he said. 'Plan A would have been much less messy and just as effective. But something went wrong, and your boy had to improvise. Hence him not going for the big blade from the kick-off. Hence the free-form furniture rearrangement.'

Parlabane downed the rest of the rich, black but rapidly cooling espresso.

'So,' Jenny said, 'you're saying someone wanted him killed but didn't want it to look like murder.'

'He'd just have been found dead. PM would establish heart attack but there would have been no further explanation. Ex-wife says it would even have been a plausible method of suicide for a doctor. Killer could have wiped his prints from the syringe and stuck it in Ponsonby's hand. Either way you've got a dead doctor and no apparent reason to suspect foul play.'

'All of which rather rules out my initial drug-dealing idea,' Jenny stated. 'Hits in the drug world are usually intended to leave no doubt in anyone's mind that the victim was purposefully murdered. If someone had Ponsonby killed, they weren't intending to send anyone a message by it.'

'Just a wee, quiet murder at home.'

Jenny rubbed a hand across her stubbly head.

'So tell me, scoop. Why was the ex-wife snooping about? What did she suspect?'

'Nothing. I was the one who introduced the idea that her ex-husband was killed. She was just sort of paying her last respects.'

'Pish,' Jenny snapped. 'You have funerals for that sort of thing, Jack. If someone had Ponsonby shafted it was because he was into something they didn't like. She must have sniffed something, even if only vaguely.'

'Possibly. I don't see her telling you anything, though.'

'How could I ask her when we never had this conversation? But she might tell you, perhaps. I mean, she must have taken an instant shine to you to entrust you so quickly with what she has so far.'

'Maybe that's just part of my journalistic talent,' Parlabane said dryly.

Jenny snorted. 'No, believe me, Jack. She likes you. I mean, I've known you a few days longer than she has and I don't fucking trust you.'

'Yeah, but you're paid not to trust me.'

'I wouldn't trust you in my spare time either.'

Parlabane laughed.

'So what are you doing here?' he asked.

'Need and trust are different things, scoop. I've checked out your background and I know how far you're prepared to go to get to the bottom of a good story. It sounds like you're on to something, but we both know you're better placed to follow it up at this stage. So anything you offer I'll gladly accept. The bigger mystery is what you want from me.'

'I regard it as my civic duty to assist the police in any way I can,' he said. 'I also find it comforting to know that a cop owes me favours.'

Jenny shook her head. 'I'll do what I can, Jack, but no promises. I can't turn a blind eye if you decide to get up to something naughty.'

That unsettling smile, more misanthropic than ever before.

'Don't worry, Jenny. If I decide to get up to something naughty, you can look with both eyes wide open through a space telescope, but you won't see me.'

Jenny said nothing. She was sure she'd enjoy putting it to the test, but she had a worrying feeling he might be right.

TWELVE

Sarah wanted to marry Parlabane.

This was, of course, after she had recovered from a brief moment of (initially) fright and (secondly) wanting to kill him. Wanting to kill him was a reaction many people frequently had to Parlabane, although it had only been recently that anyone had attempted to put it into practice.

It was some vague time of night, that on-call temporal displacement vortex that she got trapped in after one a.m. and before five, when the hours disappear and the minutes stretch like strings of albumen. The evening had dissolved into white walls and theatre greens, time suspended and warped by the cumbersome labours of an infuriating, moustachioed Dutch orthopaedic surgeon named Joost van der Elst, or 'Joost a couple of hours' as the anaesthetists called him in reference to the time he took to carry out even the most minor manipulation.

The atmosphere had not been pleasant. Joost wasn't the most sensitive of orthopods, which was a bit like saying he wasn't the most sober of alcoholics or truthful of pathological liars, and Sarah was still furious with him over an incident that morning when he had refused to let her administer any analgesia to a patient undergoing a coccygeal manipulation. The girl was seventeen, scared and crying loudly and tearfully in pain, but the local anaesthetic would have taken ten minutes to work and Joost had a lunchtime ring-smooching session with a consultant that he didn't want to be late for. He had to get his finger out of the patient's arse and his lips to the consultant's by twelve, as Sarah later explained to one of her colleagues.

So when Joost turned up (half-an-hour late) for the evening list of familiarly dubious 'emergency' ops, most of which could comfortably have waited until the next morning or even the next month, but which the orthopods wanted out of the way, Sarah was not in a tolerant mood. The first patient was seventy-nine with a fractured neck of femur, and Sarah wanted to make sure he was well under before letting Joost loose on him with his bag of DIY home improvement tools. Joost had frowningly popped his head round the door of the anaesthetic room twice in the ten minutes since he had actually condescended to show up, and then on his third visit asked Sarah if he could have a word.

'Dr Slaughter, I have several patients to attend to this evening,' he said flatly in an accent that suggested he had learned English from watching Max von Sydow movies. 'We cannot afford such a wait for all of them. We will be here all night. Why is this patient not ready? How long will he be?'

Surgeons chronically misunderstood the role of the anaesthetist. They thought he or she was there in an auxiliary, subservient capacity, to gas the patient and keep the awkward bugger quiet and still while they worked their little miracles. The anaesthetist saw his/her role instead as keeping the patient (a) alive and (b) comfortable while the surgeon did his/her best to ensure otherwise.

Sarah bit her tongue, took a deep breath and explained that the patient was old, frail, dehydrated, had a history of ischaemic heart disease and had been insufficiently prepared for theatre by the orthopaedic house officer. Consequently, he would not be ready for another fifteen minutes. Joost left the room.

Two minutes later his head was back round the door, and then again a whole ninety seconds after that. Sarah stopped what she was doing and slowly turned around, then walked to where Joost was loitering in the doorway.

She grabbed him around the upper arm and led him roughly over to the patient.

'Mr van der Elst, while we're waiting – patiently – for this anaesthetic agent to take effect, why don't I demonstrate how one of our most vital monitoring systems works,' she said. The simmering Joost looked uninterestedly at the various machines surrounding the trolley, then noticed that Sarah was pointing beyond all of them to the wall, where a large white clock was mounted.

'You see that dial right there? We anaesthetists use that to measure time. I'll explain how you read it. The patient will be ready in another ten minutes. You see that big hand pointing at the number one? Well, when that reaches the number three, that means the patient is ready. Understand?'

Joost just stared furiously at her.

'Understand?' she asked again, more sternly.

He nodded curtly.

'Good. Now fuck off and let me do my job.'

After that, she was convinced Joost was going even slower than usual just to annoy both her and the Operating Department Assistant, who had so visibly enjoyed her outburst.

The canteen had long since closed by the time she had got the last patient round in Recovery, and the vending machine had swallowed the last of her cash in exchange for a grinding noise and no chocolate on her way back to the on-call room.

She opened the door and found that the light was on, which was less surprising than the fact that Parlabane was sitting on the edge of the lumpy bed next to a large, flat cardboard box.

That moment accounted for the fright part.

The realisation that he must have broken in was responsible for the wanting to kill him part, along with everything else that had happened today, with a special mention going to having only had an apple to eat since breakfast and being hopelessly hungry.

Parlabane flipped open the box to reveal a huge and lavishly decorated pizza.

That was where the marrying part fitted in.

Sarah was munching through her second slice before the questions of how he had got in and what he was doing there regained sufficient importance.

Parlabane held up a mangled paper clip.

'It's not much of a lock.' He showed her a small black canvas wallet, the kind she had once kept her surgical instruments in back in first year at university. It contained a number of metal slivers and what looked like bent or awkwardly serrated steel nail files.

'This is the heavy artillery,' Parlabane explained. 'I got in with a pop gun.'

'You just picked the lock?'

'Well, I had to circumvent the doctors' on-call accommodation security systems first, which required the elaborate operation of asking someone where it was and walking straight in.'

'No kidding. We keep finding tramps and all sorts wandering about or even kipping down in the corridors. We've all complained about the risks but with the Trust's money so tight, priority must obviously go to important things like new corporate logos and pot plants in the admin block.'

Parlabane reached for another slice of pizza. 'Now that's unfair,' he said, swallowing a well-chewed mouthful. 'It's inevitable that there's going to be no cash for security when they've obviously blown it all on your accommodation.'

Sarah shook her head. 'That's not even funny.'

She had a brief look at her immediate surroundings: the blistered and decades-peeled paint on the ceiling, the damp patches on the wallpaper, the sticky and threadbare carpet, the chipboard nailed to the frame in lieu of one window pane which a colleague confirmed had now been in place for four years. Sarah usually shut it all out of her mind and thought only of getting into the shower as soon as she got home, but occasionally the squalor of it could still depress her afresh.

'So where did you learn to pick locks?'

'I can't tell you.'

'Of course you can tell me. I'm a doctor.'

Parlabane laughed.

'No, I mean I can't tell you where exactly because I was on a train from Glasgow to London at the time. I was down for an interview. Not a job interview, a me-talking-to-someone-important interview. I had this wee padlock on my travel bag, and we had just reached Motherwell when I remembered I had left the key for it on my bedside table and forgotten to pick it up when the taxi peeped its horn outside. I had a paper clip and a scheduled five – actually eight – hours with nothing else to do – my book was in the bloody bag. I picked the lock and was so proud of myself for managing it that I decided – with time on my hands – to have another go, prove that it wasn't a fluke. I got so into tinkering about with it that I opened and shut it about a hundred times and forgot about the bloody book altogether.

'For the return journey I bought a doorlock and a screwdriver, and spent the journey taking it apart, examining the mechanism, picking it with the back off and then picking it fully assembled. After that if I didn't have anything particularly good or important to read I used to buy a different lock for every long train journey.'

'Remind me not to give you my address.'

Sarah finished off her slice and washed it down with a

76

mouthful from one of the Irn-Bru cans Parlabane had also brought. 'I felt like Abraham Lincoln tonight – thought I was never getting out of that theatre. Contrary to what you might have heard, not all surgeons are bastards. Some of them are slow bastards.' She lifted another slice. 'You have no idea how much this is appreciated. I can't be the first doctor you've known. Either that or you're psychic.'

'I've had dealings with a few,' Parlabane said. 'Late-night food always makes you their friend.'

'For life,' Sarah added, mumbling with her mouth comfortingly full. 'We're easily bought at this time of night. We even forgive gross invasions of privacy.'

'Yeah, sorry. Didn't want to be hanging around the corridor with a hot pizza. Might get mugged by starving medics.'

Sarah was sated. She had a last gulp of Irn-Bru, wiped her mouth with a paper towel, screwed it up, expertly arced it into the bin and sat back against the ugly plastic headboard.

'So what is it you want to know?' she asked. 'I mean, I think you're a nice guy, Jack, but I can't see you breaking in to deliver late-night pizza just in a bout of spontaneous beneficence. Either you fancy me or you want some information. So which is it?'

He folded up the empty box and placed it by the bin.

'Who wanted Jeremy dead, Sarah? That's what I want to know. The cops found traces of that potassium chloride stuff on a hypodermic in your ex-husband's flat. It's a fair bet the mystery guest intended to kill him with an injection, making it look like sudden death or, as you suggested, suicide. Someone wanted him dead but didn't want anyone to know about it. Someone very dangerous had something to lose if Jeremy kept breathing, and I'm afraid I don't believe you don't have your suspicions.'

Sarah blanched. 'Seriously, Jack. I just went to the flat because . . .'

'I believe that much, Sarah. You didn't specifically go there looking for evidence or even answers. But subconsciously I think you knew something was wrong. Despite your antipathy or even indifference towards Jeremy, I believe you were still aware that there was something suspicious about him, just a vibe that meant nothing at the time but kicked in retroactively when he died. You talked about almost expecting it, you talked about him being self-destructive. What's the deal, Sarah? What was he into?'

She was gently shaking her head and yawning.

'I'm sorry, Jack.'

'Oh come on, there must be something you can give me. What vices did he have, who did he upset apart from you?'

'No, Jack. It's not that I can't tell you anything. It's just that if I start I might tell you everything. It's after two. I'm very tired and that bleeper could go off at any second anyway. Look, I'm free all day tomorrow. How about you meet me somewhere in the afternoon? I'll buy you a drink and you can give me the third degree.'

Parlabane looked closely at her. Her eyes were puffy and bloodshot, her hair tangled and lank, having been stuffed under theatre caps for hours. Her white blouse looked crushed enough for her to have slept in it, and now that she had eaten all that pizza it looked like she was about to do just that at any second.

'Well, to be honest, you don't look capable of sustained rational thinking right now,' he said.

'I'm not,' she groaned.

'And unlike the police I don't find sleep deprivation very conducive to interrogation.'

Sarah's bleeper made its loathsomely familiar sound of peremptory interruption. She closed her eyes and banged her head gently against the wall in rhythm with its electronic notes.

'Told you,' she said, picking it up. She dialled a number on the bedside telephone and exchanged a few quiet words with someone in a ward elsewhere in the complex.

'Emergency caesarian section, nineteen-year-old prim, theatre four. They'd like someone incapable of rational thinking to administer a very rapid general anaesthetic so that they can get the baby out in the next five minutes and hopefully keep the mother alive into the bargain.'

She stood up and, yawning, grabbed her white coat.

'Don't ever get sick, Jack.'

THIRTEEN

'Are you sitting comfortably?'

Parlabane smiled, cradling his tomato juice and leaning back against the wall, one foot pulled up on the bench beside him. They were in one of the more shadowy caverns of Bannerman's in the Cowgate, quite the most conducively conspiratorial drinking establishment Parlabane had ever seen. It was like a rabbit warren beneath the belly of the Old Town, a haphazard network of caves and hollows. They sat alone in their cavern, their words dulled and absorbed by the ancient stone of the walls.

There had been a look of, well, at least acknowledgement in Parlabane's eyes when she appeared, looking a rejuvenated being compared to the pile of damp washing he had seen the night before.

She had undergone a spontaneous self-deconstruction whilst attempting to get dressed and ready to meet him, by which she questioned the motives, semiotics and possible intentions behind every considered article of clothing. It always felt great to get into something attractive after a night on-call, an indulgent glance at herself in the mirror reassuring her that the nocturnal labours hadn't done any permanent or at least visible damage. It was a feeling of bouncing back. But why the black lycra skirt as opposed to the comfortable and even business-like culottes? Why the light – and let's face it, practically see-through – black blouse and not a white cotton one or even a nice T-shirt? And make-up – she didn't wear it very often and certainly never for going out in the afternoon.

She wanted to make a good impression. Nothing wrong with that. And she had every right to look good just for herself and the confidence it gave her. Going to an effort didn't mean anything.

Except that it did.

Whatever she told herself, she still knew that the fact she was meeting him was governing her thoughts. She didn't have any daft, girlish feelings, she just knew that something made her want to look good around him. And *that* didn't have to mean anything, yet.

'It's just that this might be a bit of an epic,' she explained. 'I feel that I have to give you the big picture because what I pick out as highlights might miss something you could consider important. I mean, I could tell you straight out that he had a gambling problem – that's the big juicy bit – but unless you know some more about him . . . I don't know, I'm not sure it should be taken out of context.'

'Well, I've got nowhere else to go.'

'Very well. I did my training here, Edinburgh University. There's a surprise, huh? Firmly established as third choice among England's upper middle classes to educate their off-spring. In my case, as in many, it was the consolation prize for not getting into Oxbridge. No dreaming spires and no punting, but it's got plenty of history and the natives are terribly decent as opposed to that unruly Glasgow place. I think many of them see it as a kind of drifted satellite city of the Home Counties with different architecture, and as many of them stay here for years without going north of Jenners or south of Marchmont, it's probably possible to keep up the pretence. If you drink in the right bars you can even avoid hearing a local accent that would spoil the effect.'

Parlabane blinked slowly in slight incredulity.

'You could be Scottish Watch's first English recruit at this rate. Whatever happened to the *United* Kingdom?'

Sarah sipped at her glass of tonic water and shook her head.

'Just distancing myself from my past. I'm quite good at that. What I'm saying is that I was one of that crowd. Public school boys and jolly hockey sticks girls thinking we were academic geniuses by day and the hell-raising élite by night. We were boorish, arrogant, obnoxious, immature . . . just typical medics, really. I suppose I'm trying to offer some explanation for why I got involved with Jeremy in the first place, give you an idea of what kind of person I was to be impressed by someone like him. Everything I'm about to tell you . . . everything about medics, about doctors . . . that was me, Jack. Fully signed up for all of it until maybe three or four years ago.

'I met him when I was in my fourth year, when he was in his first junior job. He was two years older than me, but he had

80

left school at seventeen to my nineteen, and had taken seven years to my five to complete training because he had done a BSc after second year. It's what you do if you either want to procrastinate or are an incurable academic over-achiever. Jeremy was the latter. He came from one of these Edinburgh medical dynasties – the place is full of them. Generations of doctors, trained here, working here. His father is Professor Ponsonby, head of the cardiac unit at the RVI, his mother's a consultant at the Western, his sister Veronica is an SHO in Livingston, his grandfather was a professor of medicine too . . . The closest thing this family could have had to a black sheep would have been if Jeremy or Veronica had gone into surgery.

'What I'm saying is that Jeremy didn't spend much time staring at the stars and wondering what he would be when he grew up, and medicine is full of people like that. The word vocation is redundant. Hundreds of them, for whom it was just understood that that was where their future would lie. And there isn't much in the way of rebellion or resentment – it's bred far too deep.'

'Plus they know their name will open doors, presumably,' Parlabane offered.

'Well, yes. Their name will also carry responsibility and expectations, but it's still less daunting than venturing into the unknown world outside. And as well as the medical dynasties there's the academics, who consider it a straight choice between medicine and law when they leave school, as everything else is for those less gifted than themselves; with such intelligence and qualifications, any lesser career would be a pointless waste. That was me, by the way.'

Sarah sipped at her drink and looked Parlabane in the eye.

'The point is that medicine is full of people who went into it for all the wrong reasons,' she continued. 'Well, maybe not entirely the *wrong* reasons, as anyone who goes into it to "save lives and cure the sick" is too dangerously naive to be allowed to practice. But still not enough of the right ones. For me it was a career path, an academic route to pursue. For people like Jeremy there isn't even that element of choice. It was simply what he was born to do.

'Anyway, he was impressive, a catch. My whole world was medicine and this guy was on his way to the top of it. Older,

81

more experienced, a known name, and doing the job for real – you spend so much time worrying about whether you're going to make it to that part, and whether you'll be able to handle it if you do, that someone already there commands great respect. So for him to show an interest in me felt all the more complimentary. And with him being from this big Edinburgh medical family, I thought I was really arriving. I wasn't just looking at a career in medicine here, I was *chosen* now, I was on my way to the *inside*. Taken to the right drinks parties, the right social gatherings, the right "at homes". Regular dinners at the Ponsonbys' in Morningside, first-name terms with all the major medical bods before I was even in my first house job.

'We went out for almost two years, and got married a fortnight after my graduation; time for a brief honeymoon before my first Junior House Officer post. We bought a flat in Bruntsfield. It's near the RVI, near the university, and there and Marchmont are where every bloody junior doctor in the city lives. The ones who consider themselves alternative live in Stockbridge along with the lawyers and coke dealers.

'There were two more doctors in our close. You'd bump into colleagues in the supermarket, see them in the street, the restaurants, all a happy wee medical community. There's a couple of hateful wine bars up that way. I doubt you'd ever have call or reason to go into them, but if you do and you feel ill – which is likely – don't ask if there's a doctor in the house, as you'll get crushed to death in the ensuing stampede.'

Sarah laughed bitterly to herself.

'You all live around there as students. You move into a nicer street once you're qualified. And then once you're a consultant you move half a mile down the hill to Morningside.'

She shook her head and gulped at her drink.

'Anyway, married life didn't get off to a great start, as I was working an illegal two-in-five rota for the first six months and a one-in-three the next. Combine that with Jeremy's one-in-four and you're lucky if there's two nights of any week that you're both sleeping in the same bed. Plus Jeremy was constantly studying for the two-part Royal College of Physicians membership exam by this time, which took precedence over spending "quality time" with his new wife. We had all our lives to spend together, for God's sake, whereas the MRCP was urgent.'

82

'Is there a time limit on it, then?' Parlabane asked, pulling his other foot up on to the bench and crossing his other leg beneath his knee.

'There's a limit to the number of attempts you can make to get each part, usually four. They hit you for between two and three hundred quid for each attempt, and there are those malcontents who would suggest that there might be a conflict of interest generated by the fact that first-time passes don't make the Colleges as much money, but I digress. The attempt limit wasn't the reason for Jeremy's urgency. It's a race, you see.'

Parlabane clearly didn't.

'When you're in school you can get As and Bs, even percentages; you can know you got a higher mark than the rest of the class. In university medicine you can get merit certificates, passes with commendation, passes with distinction, even prizes, again letting you know how you shape up against the competition. Once you're into the post-graduate world – things like the MRCP, or the FRCA, or the FRCS – they only tell you whether you passed or failed. You don't find out whether you passed with fifty-one percent or ninety-one percent, and that drives them bloody nuts. So the only way to carry on the academic pee-the-highest, mine's-bigger-than-yours contest is to get the qualifications in the fastest possible time.'

'But don't you need a certain amount of – how would you put it – *clinical* experience to pass these things?'

Sarah laughed. 'One of the first things you learn at medical school, Jack, is that the exams never *ever* test anything you will encounter in a practical context. It's always the periphery, the obscurities that you get asked about. And the result is that the system churns out junior doctors who have paid bugger-all attention to the meat and two veg medicine they will find themselves up to their necks in from day one. The favoured medical cliché – and we love our clichés – is that when they hear hooves they look for zebras instead of horses. However, post-grad, the exams are broken up into parts: two for medicine, three for anaesthetics . . .'

'Why does it have three?'

'It's the new kid on the block, with a chip on its shoulder and a point to prove. It needs to have one more part than the others to demonstrate that it's even more fartily academic than they are. Anyway, you don't sit all the parts then find out you've passed or failed – you need to pass the first before you progress to studying for the second, and so on. The idea, the theory, is that you are indeed supposed to have that parallel degree of clinical experience you mentioned. What's the point of a doctor who got the MRCP in record time but can't spot a sickie if they're dying in front of him?'

'Not much, I would have thought, but I am a lay person.'

'Indeed you are. The theory is fine. The problem is that in practice, the higher echelons are filled with guys like Jeremy a few years down the line; people who are impressed with that sort of obsessive competitiveness, and therefore reward and consequently encourage it. So the theory gets forgotten, and no one cares whether you're a dreadful doctor, as long as you whizzed through the Membership or the Fellowship or whatever. Reciprocally, no-one cares whether you're a great doctor if you struggle with the exams.'

'So did Jeremy win his race?'

'Of course. Passed both parts first time. Made his family very proud.'

'But not you.'

'We had a fight the night he found out he passed part two. He sensed I wasn't knocking him over with congratulations and I told him why. I said I couldn't bring myself to celebrate his achievement unreservedly because I felt it had come at a price. He had paid me so little attention for months because of this exam and I was suddenly supposed to put on my party frock and be full of the joys now that he was ready to come out and play again. I refused to come out that night, sent him off to the pub on his own to celebrate with his chums, whom he presumably told I was on-call.

'I was supposed to have understood the importance of his endeavours and been the supportive wife during those months, then looked on in silent, glowing joy at my wonderful husband's achievement, secretly content with my own, small part in it. And I soon realised that was the template.

'He never forgave me for that night. I think it was the first time he hadn't got his way, got exactly what he wanted; the first time life hadn't served up what he'd ordered. Maybe that's what triggered the self-destructive streak. I've often wanted to ask the Ponsonbys whether Jeremy held his breath as a child when he didn't get his own way. Because although his behaviour was self-destructive, he did it to hurt me.

'The gambling started about then. I used to think it wasn't related, but I came to realise that he was already looking for a way to hurt himself and the gambling just announced itself as a timely candidate. He went to Musselburgh races one day with "the lads", his first time backing horses in his life, got steadily drunk and had a disastrously successful afternoon.'

'Oh dear. How bad?'

'About four hundred quid. He went there with sixty.'

'Ouch.'

'He had started off putting on a tenner on the first race, on the nose, won at fives. Couple of twenty-quid losers, then a twenty-quid winner at eleven to four. By the last race he was by all accounts so arseholed he had to get someone more sober to place his bet because the bookie offering the best odds was too scrupulous and pitying to accept a hundred-pound stake from someone in Jeremy's condition.'

Parlabane reeled. 'Pissed or not, a hundred quid is a lot for a first-timer who started the day on a tenner a throw.'

'Well, don't ask me what was going through his mind. I only married him. Although I suspect it was the risk, because that was what hooked him. Jeremy's life had been such a smooth journey of measured order and control; he had known what to expect in everything he had done. He worked conscientiously for exams but unlike me, he never worried he might fail. He knew what was required, and assessing how much work he had got through, knew what mark he was likely to get.

'And on the practical side, medicine was all cause and effect, problem and solution; percentage chance of survival, percentage chance of complication, patient not for ressus . . . The sense of risk, of a lack of control, would terrify most medics; might even have terrified Jeremy during a less nihilistic phase. Instead it electrified him. He could have lost the hundred quid on that race and it wouldn't have made a tiny bit of difference, I suspect. The rush was enough. The seed was planted.'

FOURTEEN

Parlabane shifted his position and sat forward, placing his empty glass on the table.

'So why did he want to hurt you?' he asked.

Sarah paused, running a hand through her hair and grimacing, thinking uncomfortable thoughts.

'Things between us . . . deteriorated. Slowly at first, a few peaks and troughs, but . . . it was definitely downhill. What confuses it all is that my disillusion with medicine stems from the same period. I don't know whether my disillusionment with medicine accelerated my disillusionment with Jeremy or whether my disillusionment with him made me less tolerant of what I was coming up against in my job, but they certainly had a symbiotic relationship in my mind.

'I had built him up as a figurehead for all of it when I was younger, and . . . I don't know. My attitude to the whole thing was changing and he didn't have a problem with any of it. He never questioned anything in medicine, never thought that how it was wasn't necessarily how it should be.'

'What happened to you? What changed your attitude?'

'Well, after the phony war of medical school, actually working was a rude awakening. You're prepared for the work, the exhaustion, the fear, the mistakes . . . it's not that you're not expecting a hellish time. The first six months as a JHO passes in a sleepless haze of bewilderment and sheer terror. The next six you're used to it, fed-up and vaguely resentful. But by the time you're into your SHO job, your eyes are open that bit wider. You're less concerned about what is happening to you and more able to notice what's happening round about you.

'And to cut a very long story short I didn't like what I saw. I wasn't naive enough to think that I would be saving lives and curing people's ills, but I wasn't prepared for the fact that nothing we did seemed to have much effect. I got the impression that nobody ever got better. There was a soul-destroying feeling of banging my head against a brick wall.

'Looking back, I'll admit that this *was* naive. I should have been ready for the futility as much as I had been ready for all the other pains and torments. Most people were, and they could deal with it. Some developed a cheerful resilience that I admire unconditionally. Sure, it got them down, but unlike me they didn't let it *grind* them down. The word futility had no meaning for them. They knew there was bugger all they could do half the time, but they weren't in the business of lasting solutions. They were in the business of alleviating suffering, slowing effects, combating symptoms. They knew every battle was a losing battle but they could go out there and fight it every day with a commitment I just couldn't give.'

'But presumably Jeremy didn't number among these medical guerrillas,' Parlabane said.

'Not quite. I said some dealt with it with heart and resilience. More time in their company and I might have picked up the example and learnt their admirable attitude. The problem was the other way people dealt with it.'

'Total detachment?'

'Worse. I could have dealt with total detachment. You have to have fucking feelings before detachment becomes a self-defence mechanism. In a nutshell, when I saw a patient with some unusual, bewildering, painful and possibly fatal condition, I just saw a suffering human being that I couldn't do much to help, and it depressed me. Jeremy, and many like him, coming across the same patient, would be bloody delighted. They wouldn't be looking at a person there at all. They'd be looking at a very interesting case. A collection of symptoms. An intriguing study. They'd be looking at a paper in the British Medical Journal with their name and qualifications at the top of it. And if they were really lucky they might get to name what was wrong with the poor bastard after themselves. "Ponsonby's syndrome: a searing, stinging sensation in the rectal region. Other symptoms: sudden disappearance of all your money."

'People like Jeremy – channelled into medicine from day one without being allowed a glimpse of the possibilities in the wider world – they saw medicine as merely a place to excel. They had never considered the patients before they went into the job, why would they now that they were there?

'Anyway, my general dischuffment with the subject wasn't quite the ideal accompaniment to having my own crack at the MRCP, and it was little surprise when I failed part one twice.

It was about a week after I got the letter informing me I'd failed again that Jeremy suggested, basically, that as I wasn't cut out to shine in hospital medicine, I should consider a move into GP training and think about bearing him some children. It wasn't quite as blunt as that, but it was close. I was in a vulnerable and fragile condition at this point, so I just took it along with the other blows, not really thinking about it properly. Then we went to the Ponsonbys' for Sunday dinner and the same suggestion was made by his parents over the fucking roast lamb and mint sauce.'

Parlabane almost choked on his drink.

'What?'

Sarah nodded.

'The message was simple,' she said. 'If you marry a Ponsonby, either you've got to shine dazzlingly in the field, or squeeze out some sprogs to keep the line going and play a quiet, supporting role while he maintains the glorious family reputation. I just said excuse me, walked out and drove home.

'I came to realise that me bearing him kids had always been in Jeremy's plans, even though he hadn't talked much about it. It was as if he had been *expecting* me to screw up in medicine, patiently tolerating this silly pursuit of ambition until I inevitably came to accept reality, then offering me a more appropriate role. So I wondered how far back it went: was I singled out as a good candidate to mother his kids – and therefore someone not likely to go far in medicine – way back when I was in fourth year?'

'So I'd imagine domestic bliss did not ensue after that,' Parlabane offered.

Sarah rolled her eyes. 'Not exactly. That's when he started upping the stakes on the horses. He had been gambling steadily since that day at Musselburgh, but nothing too drastic. He knew I didn't like it, but it wasn't a big deal. He made it a big deal from then on.

'He got sucked in deeper and deeper because he was doing it for dangerous reasons. Doing it as a self-indulgence because things were bad at home, doing it to hurt me . . . But what really nailed him was a combination of the rush he got from risking big stakes and the bizarre confidence he had that he would win in the end. Apart from my refusal to get up the stick, everything had gone Jeremy's way in life, and he thought this must carry through into gambling. If he lost three or four big stakes, he convinced himself that this meant he must be due a really big win. Hundred-pound stakes became two hundred. Two hundred became five hundred.'

'Jesus.'

'And it mounted up over – Christ – a year at least. After a while he was in too deep to be doing it to hurt me any more. He became increasingly secretive about it until one day I tried to pay for the shopping with my Switch card and they wouldn't take it. I visited the bank the next day and found that he had cleared us out. Not only that, but he had run up tabs that were still outstanding, and the bastard sold the car for cash to pay one off because the bookie was threatening to get heavy.

'I kicked him out and we agreed to a divorce. I got the flat, as it was about the only material asset left in the marriage. Ironically, it's me who's still living in Southside Doctorsville, while Jeremy had a place in a more interesting area of town.'

'How did he get that?'

'His father bought it for him. He was a total mess by the end, and was in fact in such a state that he kind of woke up suddenly and looked in horror at what he had wreaked. He wasn't a total bastard, you must understand, just a rather fucked-up individual. I'm only telling you the negative stuff because the good times aren't likely to cast much light on our mystery. He was sorry for what he had done to me, and in fact it was he who first mentioned divorce, saying I deserved better and I should be allowed a clean break from the mess he was in.

'However, it was only once we had agreed to split that he felt able to reveal the true extent of the debt he was in, and it was terrifying. I'd have had to re-mortgage the flat and he wasn't going to let me do that even if I had wanted to.

'I wanted a clean break, but for me that meant I needed to know he would be all right. However, I couldn't do it alone. We had to tell his family, from whom we had kept it all a secret. They just thought our marital problems were down to me being a dope who wouldn't do the right thing by her man.

'He was terrified,' she said, shaking her head again. 'More scared of their reaction than of the bookies who were tapping their feet in the background. But there was no way we could sort it out ourselves. In the end he needn't have worried.'

'Because his family blamed you.'

'He shoots, he scores. But I knew they would anyway. In fact I was banking on it. That way they would pull out all the stops to sort their poor son's life out and get him back on his feet for a new start, free of that dreadful strumpet.'

'So they made good with the big cheque?'

'Not quite. Prof Ponsonby may have blamed me, but he still knew his son had a lesson to learn, and probably feared that if the slate was wiped clean, Jeremy might start all over again. He paid off the bookies' debts, but – using his considerable influence – arranged with the hospital that a large – and I mean painful – slice of Jeremy's monthly wages be paid into his own bank account over two years until the debt was cleared.'

'Why with the hospital? Why not just work out a direct debit?'

'Because Jeremy could stop a direct debit with one phone call. This way there was no opt-out. Jeremy was happy enough with it. I think he had a sense of redemption in paying it off himself, although I didn't burst the bubble by asking when he would be buying me a new car or replacing any of the various domestic appliances and items of jewellery he had flogged.

'Anyway, I was too busy sorting my life out to want to settle scores. I had decided to get out of medicine a good while back, and had got on to an anaesthetics rotation round about the time Jeremy moved out. It wasn't easy; if you get your MRCP then switch to anaesthetics, fine, but they don't like the thought that you're trying your luck there because you couldn't hack it in medicine. I was lucky, I suppose. I think my problems were a badly kept secret in the medical community and my desire for a fresh start was appreciated, but what really clinched it was that most of the interviewing consultant anaesthetists hated Professor Ponsonby's guts.'

'Ah yes,' said Parlabane, eyes twinkling. 'The pungent odour of politics. So how much did you see of Jeremy after that?'

'Occasional encounter in the canteen or a corridor. Less so in recent months as he had been working over at the George Romero a lot.'

'The what?'

'The George Romanes Hospital. It's an attached geriatric

hospital, a granny-dumping site. Some of us call it the George Romero because it's full of the living dead.'

'And how was he when you did see him?'

'In a hurry. Before, he would take time to talk to me, I think because he needed me to be nice to him for conscience-salving reassurance. The few times I saw him over the past four, five months, he tended to dash past and make excuses, and when I did buttonhole him he seemed . . .'

'Nervous? Jumpy?'

'No. Distant, maybe. Guarded. I got the impression he feared – given what we'd been through – that I could see through him, and presumably there was something he didn't want me to see. I suspected he might have been gambling again, but it could as easily have been the fact that he was going out with that nurse.'

'Why should he worry about you knowing that?'

Sarah laughed, the note of albeit mischievous humour like a brief drop of rain on the parched desert of bitterness she had just dragged Parlabane across.

'I was always a bit brutal about doctors going out with nurses. And Jeremy was never done slagging nurses off, so maybe he was afraid of what I would think about him seeing one.'

'But when he was murdered, did you return to the idea that he might have been gambling again?'

'It was there, but it wasn't writ large. I should emphasise that at the time I didn't think he was acting weird at all. I just thought it was symptomatic of our separation, evidence that we were drifting apart. But the reason it stuck in my mind was that while I knew where my life was headed, I was curious as to where Jeremy was drifting to. It was clues to that that I was looking for in his flat, a sense of where his life had been going without me. I suppose I still wanted to know where he would have ended up otherwise.

'But part of me couldn't help suspecting – after the fact – that being murdered *was* where Jeremy was headed, *was* where he was going to end up.'

FIFTEEN

Blast.

The police had released that malnourished local scruff and were maintaining a worrying silence about who they now sought for Ponsonby's murder.

Worry, worry, worry.

Stephen Lime had felt like this before. An ice-walking limbo period, all plans, all hopes, all feelings suspended until further notice. He hated risk, hated the thought that some other factor, some other person could hold the balance of his future.

The time before, it had been stupid. Unlucky, certainly, but still rather stupid. But he had got out of it, come away wiser. A cheap lesson, really, and it had come with the first-time bonus of Darren's seemingly undisposable services.

This time he stood to gain millions if it went right and to lose *everything* if it went wrong, but the risk had been low enough to justify such a high stake. He had endeavoured to minimise that risk, calculated the odds and covered all the bases. What had started as an idle daydream had suddenly become possible when he discovered Ponsonby, and all had run smooth until the final hurdle.

But then that lumbering fool had disobeyed him, tried to deceive him even, by pocketing the cash and carrying out the contract himself. If he had stuck to his instructions, they were covered against all eventualities. By using a private contractor, Lime knew he had the safety net of there being nothing to connect the operator with himself, only with Darren, whom he would only know from a couple of meetings in smoky pubs. And besides, as insurance the hitman was to be told that in the event of getting caught – as he would be going down anyway – his silence would be worth a large sum deposited in a high interest account from the first day of his stretch.

No. You just couldn't rely on anyone but yourself. There was no more vivid illustration of this than the ironic fact that the person who had been the answer to his troubles before was the one who may have dropped him right in it this time.

Back then it had been his ex-wife's fault, Tina, curse the

peroxide slut. She had been a calculating little gold-digger, a predatory secretary in the City, waiting to pounce on the most likely mug to enter her lair, and he had nominated himself. She had been all short skirts, high heels and Wonderbra cleavage, he remembered bitterly. It had become real cleavage some years later, silicone tits he had shelled out for but never even got to touch; he had felt like demanding custody of them in the settlement as he had paid for the bloody things.

She had appeared to be a black-belt prick teaser, a whiff of her perfume and a glimpse of lace-bordered breast as she bent over a desk enough to send himself and many of his boardroom colleagues scurrying off to the toilets for some executive relief. There was a combination of the unattainable and the cheaply tarty about her that had made her the object of his every non-fiscal fantasy.

And fantasy was about as far as he ever imagined he would get, which was why he was so off-guard when some excruciatingly pleasurable flirting – just nod-and-wink suggestive talk in his office one Friday evening – turned into her unzipping his fly and going down on him where he sat.

'See you on Monday morning, sir,' she had said when she finished, then walked out for the night, leaving him in a state of heavenly disbelief.

On the Monday, she acted as if nothing had happened, then at the end of the day came back to his office, locked the door and let him have her right there, bent over the desk.

Women had never looked at him twice before; indeed (although he never told her) that had been his first time, despite being already in his late thirties. And now the girl who was the executive floor's collective wet dream was throwing herself at him.

They were married in a matter of months, throughout which he showered her with gifts and money, while she continued to bestow her exquisite favours upon him, in the office for a fortnight, and after that exclusively in expensive hotel rooms.

Then once they were hitched she seldom let him near her, save for a few isolated fucks in the early years when she wanted a new car or that bloody Jacuzzi when they had the place in Kent. She lounged around the house all day, spent his money and screwed every passing male but him, although to double the frustration he had no way of proving it. She was way too sharp for that.

She had nailed him good and proper, and he knew he couldn't get rid of her without it costing him a slice of every quid he made for the rest of his life. Sometimes he thought it would be worth it, just to be free of her, but he suspected that a lucrative divorce might be the final part of her long-term plan, and he was buggered if he was giving her the satisfaction. Unfortunately, there seemed no hope of her getting fed-up waiting for it to happen, as she was still living the life of bloody Reilly on his money.

He never thought about killing her, no more than spur-of-the-moment fantasies when she was being particularly annoying, or when she was letting fly with that dreadful, whiny laugh she had. He had just resigned himself to being stuck with her, concentrating on getting satisfaction from his business pursuits and writing her off mentally as an immovable overhead.

But there was no relief from the torture of how aroused her eternally tarty behaviour made him feel, still wearing the most revealing outfits, still wandering around the house in her underwear or less, and still not letting him touch her.

An affair was out of the question. Firstly, she was just waiting for him to do something like that. Probably spending *his* money on a private detective to watch *him* every time he was away for the weekend on business or rang to say he'd be home late. Secondly, all evidence had pointed to no woman on the planet wanting to sleep with him except Tina, and she had only done it to get to his wallet.

This line of thinking had led him to consider going to a prostitute. For goodness' sake, he had to do *something*, as he was masturbating so much that he was convinced his right arm was becoming noticeably wider than his left. But the thought of those filthy women on street corners, of disease, and of getting caught – good God, getting caught – always shunted the idea back out of his head.

Then one Friday evening – he had to bloody learn: disasters always start on Friday evenings – he found himself alone in the bar of a hotel in Hornchurch, where the St George's Trust had been having an afternoon meeting after a four-course lunch, paid for by the Trust as it was strictly for business purposes (as were the half-dozen bottles of Bordeaux they had worked through). The board had adjourned briefly to the bar before dispersing, leaving him the last one there, and he had been

94

finishing off a G&T whilst casting an eye over some papers. An attractive, youngish – maybe mid-thirties – woman, dressed neatly, even businesslike, sat down beside him and smiled.

He smiled back.

Then she leaned over and said: 'I'm in business. Are you interested?'

He was rather drunk and slow on the uptake. 'I'm sorry?'

'I'm in business,' she repeated, placing a hand on his thigh.

It took great restraint not to exclaim 'Ah! I see!' as he suddenly realised the situation.

There seemed no reason not to. Tina wouldn't find out as she was staying at her mother's that weekend; the woman looked clean, she looked pretty, and he was also fairly pissed.

He booked a room then and there.

After recovering from the initial bout of panic and fear that followed ejaculation, he arranged a discount rate with her to stay the night.

One night, that was all, just one bloody night. He couldn't believe how unlucky he had been, but it did teach him that the most dangerous risk, however small, is the unknown risk.

The following Tuesday he was walking through Accident and Emergency at St George's, showing the local MP and his entourage around the place, when he saw her – and she saw him. She had broken her arm and was sitting in the crowded waiting room as he passed through at the head of what must too visibly have been a VIP party.

The phone call came two days later. She had checked out who he was, and realised two things. One: he wasn't just the usual travelling sales rep she picked up in hotel bars, but might have a bit of money. Two: he had a public profile and would therefore be keen to protect it. The cheeky bitch even suggested that having to wait for four-and-a-half hours before someone in his 'fucking shitty hospital' had a look at her arm may have been a further factor.

She wanted £50,000 or she would tell the papers, and she assured him that she could remember anatomical details that would make it more than just her word against his.

It was an utter nightmare. Initially he didn't care so much about her telling the papers as about Tina finding out. She would get her blasted divorce and be able to name her

95

terms. Adultery with a prostitute wouldn't score him much sympathy with the judge – at least not in court.

Everything he was ever going to earn was about to be sliced in half and handed to the person he had come to hate most in the world. But even that might not be as much as he had hoped now, as the Party was on the ropes from a volley of sex scandals and would expect him to fall on his sword over his own. He would have to resign from the quango and kiss all his lucrative little schemes goodbye, as well as never getting his real money's worth from the thousands he had pumped into the Party's coffers.

He would have no choice but to pay her, but there was no guarantee she wouldn't hit him for more at a later date, or even go to the papers anyway once she had the money. It wasn't as though she would be handing over any negatives that he could assuredly destroy.

Hopeless.

He could barely sleep a wink the next few nights, and was lying worriedly awake, staring balefully at the augmented boob falling out of Tina's skimpy nightie beside him, when he heard a splintering sound downstairs. Quietly, he got up and crept to the landing, hearing a muffled yelp that sounded like his alsatian, Tebbit. He tiptoed to the hall cupboard and pulled out his shotgun, bought for him a few years back as a memento of a memorable weekend at a hunting lodge in the Scottish highlands. A Surrey catering firm had paid for him to join them up there as they considered the place ideal surroundings to present their bid for the staff canteen contract at the firm he was working for. They had also suggested that a week's golfing in the Algarve might be the best environment in which to dot the 'i's and cross the 't's in the event that they got the job, which, funnily enough, they did.

He popped a couple of shells into the pump-action gun and quietly moved downstairs, then burst into the kitchen where he was sure the noise had come from.

There was an enormous neanderthal standing in front of the sink, behind which the window was broken. He was dressed in a matt black shellsuit and black Adidas trainers with the white stripes blacked out, and at first glance appeared to have a sovereign ring or something equally chunky on every finger. He also had Tebbit's jaws attached to his right forearm, and was holding the dog up above a puddle of blood on the linoleum.

Lime gaped at first, wondering at the stoicism or high pain threshold of this creature who could silently endure such a bite and the massive loss of blood that had ensued. Then he noticed the red-stained blade in the brute's other hand, and the fact that there wasn't much in the way of growling or even movement coming from Tebbit.

'Put your hands up,' he said, nervously and quietly.

The brute obeyed, raising the limp dog as he did so. It hung off his forearm like a hairy scarf, the image reminding Lime briefly and bizarrely of Rod Stewart during one of his more tartan-bedecked phases.

His fear turned to anger as he realised that Tebbit was no more. Not only was his life falling apart, but some bastard had killed his dog.

Expertly killed his dog.

Quickly and with very little sound, killed his vicious attack dog.

Hmmm.

They stood motionless in their respective positions for a while, the ball in Lime's court but him unsure what to do next.

'Look, John,' the brute said eventually. 'You've got the shooter. I'm doin' what you ask. I've got me 'ands up. The weight of this dog's fuckin' killin' me, but I've got me 'ands up. Are you callin' the Ole Bill or what?'

Then he said it before he could think about it. Before he could stop himself, before he could add up the pros and cons, it was out there.

'How would you like to make some real money?'

The brute, Darren Mortlake, was allowed to escape. Lime told Tina and the police that the burglar had fled when he entered the kitchen with the gun, and gave a false description, the principal fib being over the matter of skin colour.

When the prostitute phoned back, he said he would have the money in two days, and the stupid cow – obviously an opportunistic amateur – told him to bring it to her house in Ilford. He said that as he didn't trust her not to set him up somehow, he would be sending a friend with the cash. He also said he wanted assurance that she was in this alone, and that if his friend found anyone else in the flat, the deal was off. She reminded him that she would go to the papers, and he reminded her that the papers would pay about a tenth what she would be getting from him if she cooperated.

He gave Darren five thousand in cash as an advance, another five to be collected upon successful completion of the task. If he got caught, his silence bought twenty. He was to bring along the cash from his advance to her house in a bag, and open it at the front door for her to see, so that she'd let him in.

Darren didn't get caught.

Stephen didn't get caught.

Everyone was happy.

Except Julie Marron, who had her throat cut and bled to death on her living room floor. With no evidence of breaking and entering, it was assumed by the police to have been carried out by a client.

And all Stephen's problems went away.

Stephen was so happy with Darren's work that he paid him a monthly retainer to return his calls and have first shout on his services.

And a bit of lateral thinking helped Stephen apply similar principles to the problem of getting rid of Tina.

He toyed briefly with the idea of paying Darren to kill her too, but decided it was a non-starter. People were always paying to have their spouses bumped off, and they were always getting caught too, because the whole thing was so screamingly obvious. Stephen Lime, Darren Mortlake and Julie Marron were three points on a triangle no one was ever going to draw because there was no apparent connection between even two of them. Stephen Lime, Darren Mortlake and Tina Lime was a different story.

But the thought of employing specialist services led him to an idea that offered an equally effective but even more satisfying result.

He knew his wife was always screwing around on him, he knew she liked young, athletic, well-spoken ('posh') men; he even knew some of their names. He just couldn't prove anything. So he decided he would pay someone to seduce her and tip him the wink as to when he could unexpectedly stumble upon them.

The ideal candidate turned out to be an SHO at St George's, skint because of a recent divorce, divorced because he was fucking anything in a nurse's uniform every night he was on-call. Stephen brought Tina along to a hospital ball and let nature take its course. The over-sexed little bastard insisted on getting to screw her undisturbed for a few days before Stephen was allowed to catch them at it, but what the hell, it was the result that mattered.

And besides, he also chucked in some highly illustrative Polaroids as an added bonus, which helped Lime slaughter her in the divorce without it even getting near a courtroom.

SIXTEEN

Parlabane was steaming around the kitchen, draped in a towel stolen from Le Parc Hotel in West Hollywood, having very recently emerged from a too-warm bath, his white bits pink from the heat. He was about to use his newly-purchased tin opener upon a newly-purchased tin of beans, which he planned to heat in his newly-purchased pot, when the doorbell rang.

He was still too damp to be able to throw some clothes on, so he pulled the front door slightly ajar and leaned his head around it.

Jenny Dalziel was standing there in the unexpectedly simple garb of blue jeans and a self-coloured green T-shirt, a blue denim jacket slung over her shoulder. He hated the word 'strapping' because it seemed to have rather uncomfortable S&M connotations, but there was little other way to describe her. Seeing her divested of her plain-clothes policewoman suits and leisure attire colour schemes that forced Parlabane to avert his eyes, he was able to appreciate Jenny's athletic shape, but was slightly concerned that – as he was only wearing a towel – his appreciation might start to show.

'I was in the neighbourhood,' she said. 'Wondered if you fancied coming out to play. And as I can see you've just washed your hair, it looks like you might be out of excuses.'

Parlabane ushered her into the kitchen and went off to his bedroom in search of another towel and an acceptably clean shirt.

'What did you have in mind?' he shouted through to her.

'Just the usual. Drinks and scintillating conversation.'

'You might have to just make do with the conversation part. I'm still waiting for a money transfer from my bank in LA, and my credit card is beginning to buckle under the strain.'

'Oh, I'm sure I could stand you a couple of beers.'

'It'd have to be a couple of tomato juices.'

'Oh come on, you big poof. A few pints won't hurt you.'

He returned to the kitchen in a pair of black jeans with a sharp fold across both thighs from suitcase imprisonment, and a reddish tartan shirt that his Angelino friends had uniformly found quite horrifying.

Jenny was looking disapprovingly at the constituent parts of his planned evening repast. 'OK. Looks like a change of plan might be called for here. Put on something less embarrassing and I'll buy you a curry.'

'So I see you let your suspect walk,' said Parlabane between mouthfuls of pakora.

'He wasn't *my* suspect, but yes. Had to. Some smart-arse suggested we check the cornicing above the mantelpiece for hairs, and bugger me with a blowtorch if we didn't find a couple. We make our man at least six-five, and he's got brown hair with some truly appalling silver highlights. Suspect was about five-ten and his curly locks were jet black. He was missing the correct finger, though. We do pay attention to these little things. We're not the East Midlands Serious Crime Squad.'

'McGregor given up the burglary theory yet?'

'Getting there fast. I think the needle and the potassium chloride made a big enough hole in his picture to force a change of heart. He's not telling the media that, though. He reckons that the baddies will dig in deeper if they know we've worked out the real story. Unfortunately, as there's nothing else to tell the press, our lengthening silence since letting the burglar go is bound to tip them off eventually.'

'So no new leads? Still no witnesses?'

'Don't take the piss. Nobody pitched up at any of the local A&E departments missing a finger, either. So what about you? Did you speak to the other Dr Ponsonby?'

'It's Dr Slaughter,' Parlabane corrected.

'Patients must bloody love that.'

'Yes, I'm sure the jokes are a daily source of amusement to her. Hearing the same shitey remark for the nine hundredth time must be like a ray of sunshine on a cloudy day.'

'Yeah, well enough of that. What did you get, scoop? And no holding back. Remember who's paying for your Chicken Jalfrezi.'

Parlabane washed down the last of his starter with a gulp of lemonade. Indian cooking hadn't really caught on in LA – confused local connotations were an obstacle – and consequently this was the first curry he had embarked upon in close to two years. His tastebuds were enjoying the hearty reacquaintance.

'Well, the big story is that the late Dr P had a major, wide-screen, full-scale gambling problem,' he said. 'Chucking away two or three hundred a throw at the height of the fun.'

'That what torpedoed the marriage?'

'I'd mark it down as symptom rather than cause, although it certainly speeded up the dénouement. Working at that rate, he had them skint and owing in no time. Around the time of the big split, Daddy – Professor P – paid off the outstandings and arranged for himself to take a direct and large bite of young Jeremy's monthly wage packet to settle the bill. Then they went their separate ways and Jeremy moved into the Maybury Square place, prop: Prof Ponsonby. The Prof also hits him for market-rate rent.'

'But with the debts cleared, Jeremy's gambling problem presumably disappeared overnight,' Jenny said.

'Oh yes, of course. Just like that. They always do.'

'So did you see any bookies?'

'Just two, both names Sarah gave me. There's unlikely to be any more because you have to be a very regular customer before they'll let you run up the kind of credit he did. Naturally, they were both a wee bit broken up about the bad news. I think they'll be sending wreaths.'

'Did he owe them a lot?'

'Not a cent. But his custom was still valued and regular. Not quite laying out five hundred a time, but still plenty of fifties and single tons, and even the occasional couple of hundred. His luck had been marginally better of late, but they were both still making a handsome profit from him.'

'But he really didn't owe them when he died?'

'Ah, that's the interesting bit, Detective. He was laying down only cash bets. His choice, too. They'd have been only too willing to let him run up a tab, but he was sticking with paper. Now, it could be that he had learned his lesson about betting on the never-never, but nonetheless . . . cash doesn't know where it came from, and cash can't tell you where it's been.'

'Whatever are you insinuating?' Jenny asked, dryly mock-innocent.

'Well, I didn't get a long look, and as I remember, things were not at their tidiest, but his flat wasn't exactly threadbare. Looked like a new TV that the hatstand had disembowelled.'

'Widescreen, NICAM digital stereo,' Jenny confirmed. 'As was the video. Tasty Linn Hi-Fi in the other corner too.'

'Not bad for a guy who's having his wages siphoned and is still throwing a lot of money after three-legged donkeys. He had a girlfriend on the go too. I wonder what he spent on her?'

Jenny nodded. 'I interviewed her the other day.'

'What's she like?'

'Young, attractive, but a bit too good-as-gold and frilly-knickered for my taste, to be honest. She was very upset, but then I suppose her ticket to Morningside had just got cancelled.'

'That's most sympathetic of you, Jenny.'

'Oh well, for fuck's sake. It's so pathetic. Have you any idea how many guys end up with that kind of woman? They want some weedy bimbette who'll look up to them because their little dicks go limp at the thought of a relationship with an intellectual equal.'

'Jesus, I should introduce you to Sarah. You'd both have lots to talk about.'

Jenny shook her head and waved dismissively, as if clearing distractingly angry thoughts from her mind.

'Well anyway, she didn't mention anything about bookies, horses or gambling. But she didn't say he was rooked either. Plenty of dinners out at impressively pricey restaurants.'

'But did she say whether he was acting weird, had something on his mind?'

'I'm sorry to put it this way Jack, but my impression was that she was too fucking dippy to notice. Well, possibly that's unfair, but I certainly didn't get the idea that it was a very deep and involved relationship. If he had a problem, she'd have been the last person in the world he'd have let on to about it.'

Parlabane nodded. 'But either way,' he said, 'no evidence from any quarter that the good doctor was enduring an ascetic existence. I'd love to see the bastard's bank statements. There's just no way this guy was clearing enough – after Daddy and the taxman got their slices – to cover what he's been spending. My guess is Jeremy was being paid – in cash – for rendering discreet and very probably illegal services. The questions are what and for who.'

Jenny stared intently, not so much at him as through him,

her mind, like her eyes, looking beyond what was directly in front of her.

'We didn't find any cash in the house, Jack. Is your friend Dr Slaughter working at the hospital tonight?'

'No, she was on last night. Why?'

'There's a phone at the back. Why don't you call and ask her if she'd like to join us on a treasure hunt?'

Sarah stood in the centre of the living room, running a hand through her hair as she looked about her surroundings. Parlabane and Jenny stood back expectantly. Explanations had been brief, introductions barely necessary.

They had shifted the remaining furniture back and forth to expose different floorboards, looking for tell-tale signs of recent and regular lifting, but the only promising marks had been above where a leaking pipe join had been re-soldered. Parlabane had taken some ladders and a torch and checked out the elevated water tank cupboard, but had drawn another blank. Jenny's examination of the cistern and removal of the cover down the side of the bath had proved equally fruitless.

'You know, it is possible that the killer made off with it,' said Jenny. 'That could have been part of the job.'

'Would you tell a contract hitman that there was an unquantified amount of cash – probably in used bills – hidden somewhere in the flat and expect him to recover it for you?' Parlabane asked witheringly. '"Yeah, sorry, man,"' he mimicked, '"there was only a fiver left, honest. Here it is. He must have spent the rest."'

'He could still just have happened upon it. He demolished enough possible hiding places.'

'Well, let's wait until we've definitely struck out before entertaining that helpful idea. Looking for a needle in a haystack is a frustrating task, but the sense of existential angst brought by the possibility that the needle has already been removed doesn't exactly make it a hell of a lot more fun.'

'I think we need to think about who he was hiding it from,' said Sarah, demonstrating why she had been asked along. 'Would it just be from sight, in case his girlie or his parents stumbled upon it in a visit? Or would he want it somewhere that, say, a burglar wouldn't think to look, whether or not the burglar knew there was money to be had? Jeremy was very

104

systematic and liked to anticipate all eventualities. See, he's not going to hide it inside something that someone might think worth stealing, for instance. He'd put it inside something you wouldn't look twice at.'

'He'd also want it somewhere easily accessible, as he would have been dipping into it regularly to pay for those bets,' Parlabane offered.

'The kitchen,' Sarah said, and walked towards it. 'Apart from the bathroom, which we've done, it's the last place a burglar would expect to find something valuable.'

'It was also the only place left undisturbed,' Jenny said, following.

Sarah threw open all the cupboard doors and stood back, looking at what was inside them.

'Pots,' she said, then began pulling them out and removing their lids. Parlabane checked inside an old kettle that had been perched on top of the units, huffily looking down on the more modern model that had usurped its position. Empty.

Sarah knelt down before the cupboard under the sink and removed a bag of rags and wash-cloths, fumbling around inside then dumping it, dismissed, on the floor beside her. She sighed and looked back inside, peeking under the lid of a shoe box that contained some bristle-bare brushes and near-empty tins of Cherry Blossom. Then Parlabane was pleased to notice her brow furrow, and quickly realised what was wrong.

There were two big metal tins of Ariel Ultra sitting one in front of the other on a shelf, and a plastic refill pack beside them.

You didn't buy a second metal tin of something that also came in plastic refill packs.

Sarah pulled out the back-most tin and opened it up, but it was full to the top of blue-speckled white powder. She grabbed the other one and lifted the lid, but that one was merely half-full of what it was supposed to contain.

'Fuck,' she said. 'I just thought . . .'

'Hang on,' said Parlabane, who had dealt with a lot more devious bastards than Sarah ever had to, not least himself, and squatting down, plunged his hand into the fuller tin.

He grinned and looked up.

'So how much are you prepared to pay for me *not* to make a joke about him laundering his money?'

SEVENTEEN

'Well, Jenny, you're the professional,' said Parlabane, holding up a powdery handful of tenners. 'Do you think it's possible Sarah's ex-husband was up to something illegal?'

Jenny sighed. 'You know, scoop, our mutual friend Duncan said you were a moody bastard when an investigation was going nowhere for you. He didn't warn me that you were totally unbearable when it was going well.'

'How much money is there?' Sarah asked.

Parlabane glanced at the pile of cash sitting before them on the kitchen table.

'About two grand. If he had used fabric conditioner, the pile might be higher and more fluffy.'

'So the question is what was he doing for this money,' Sarah muttered.

'Yes,' said Parlabane. 'But the bigger question is who won out of this. Somebody's life got a whole lot easier when Jeremy died. That was the purpose of the exercise.'

'Don't suppose you've any bright ideas on motive, scoop?'

'Well, I don't think it was about money – not Jeremy's money anyway. It remains in doubt whether the hitman was aware of – or interested in – this cash, and therefore it seems unlikely that whoever paid the killer was interested in it. That leaves the two other big favourites: silencing and eliminating competition.

'Now, if Jeremy had competitors for whatever he was doing, he wasn't afraid of them. He was taking no precautions: no baseball bats, no knives, no guns, not even extra locks on the door. He didn't think he was at any risk other than having his cash discovered. There's also the intended method of death to consider: it was supposed to be quiet and unsuspicious, even to look like suicide. As we were saying the other day – and this doesn't just apply to drugs – competitors like everyone to know their rivals were deliberately taken out. So it seems most likely he was murdered to keep him quiet, probably about whatever he was doing for the cash.'

'What about blackmail?' Jenny offered, thinking out loud. 'That could explain the cash and the motive.'

Parlabane shook his head. 'Murdering a blackmailer is something you do *instead* of giving him money. No. I think whoever had Jeremy killed was also the person employing his unknown extra-curricular services.'

Sarah had a look of frustrated incomprehension on her face, which grew into head-shaking and eventually throwing her hands up in front of her.

'I'm sorry, but . . . well, what on earth could he have been doing? I lived with the guy for years, and I never noticed any talents that might have a criminal application. And even if he had – plus the inclination to use them – he wouldn't know who to offer them to. There isn't a crooks' Situations Vacant section in the *Evening Capital*, for God's sake.'

Parlabane smiled. His mouth barely moved, but Jenny could see it in his eyes, that glint that made her want to check her wallet.

'All right, scoop, hit us with the big exclusive,' she said, with demonstrative weariness.

'Someone else noticed Jeremy had talents that had a possible criminal application,' he said quietly. 'An application that suited his needs. It was our bad guy who approached Jeremy with a job offer, not the other way round.'

'Oh come on,' said Sarah, growing impatient with this casual imposition of the idea of underworld activity upon places and people so familiar to her. 'Who's going to ask a respected physician to get involved in something shady when he could very likely just turn round and tell the police about it?'

'Someone who knows he's in trouble,' said Parlabane flatly. 'Someone who knows he's got major money problems and could do with earning some undeclared on the side. Someone who knows his wages are being skimmed at source to pay off a debt.'

Sarah gaped. 'Someone at the hospital,' she breathed.

'Very possibly. So what we need to know first is who knew about the gambling problem.'

'Next to no one. Just Jeremy, me, the bookies and his parents. It's the kind of thing that a family like the Ponsonbys will go a long way to keep under wraps.'

'Fair enough,' said Parlabane. 'They're not going to want it the talk of the wards, but it's still going to be known. The Prof must have mentioned it to someone, particularly when he was sorting out this rather unusual financial arrangement. But even if he confided in his senior colleagues, or even if Jeremy told a couple of pals, the only people who would have known just how *deep* Jeremy was in were the people involved in administrating the wages deal. We need to know who was in on that information, because it looks like one of them acted upon it.'

'And how are you going to find that out without asking the kind of questions that might send the bad guy scurrying for cover?' Jenny asked, then caught Parlabane's eye. 'On second thoughts, don't answer that. In fact, forget I even asked.'

'I suppose you know a little about Jack's less obviously journalistic talents?' asked Sarah.

Jenny indicated right as her car reached the Picardy Place roundabout, nothing else on the road but taxis and discarded chip pokes. She stole a glance at her passenger before advancing, Sarah's determined and handsome profile silhouetted against the orange of the streetlights. Jenny liked her, there was no denying it. Mainly, it was the body language, the way Sarah so assuredly commanded space in a room, instead of waiting to be put or accepting the role she was allotted, something Jenny was constantly disappointed not to see enough of in women. She had an easy purposefulness about her gait and posture, a physical confidence borne perhaps of having more important things to be getting on with than worrying about where she fitted in.

On a less noble level there was also that flowing red hair, but that was another matter.

'I know a lot more about Jack than Jack thinks I do,' Jenny said. 'I've been checking him out a wee bit. I know his pal, Duncan McLean, one of the *Capital*'s football hacks. I also spoke to a cop in London who investigated one of the breaking-and-entering charges Jack faced. They've both got a lot of respect for his abilities, but for appreciably different reasons. Duncan talked admiringly about Jack's "unorthodox" – read illegal – methods, said there was nowhere he couldn't get into if he wanted to badly enough. Said he can pick locks in his sleep and climbs buildings like fucking Spiderman. He does all that indoor rock-wall stuff, and given Jack's small frame, Duncan reckons his fingers probably contain the strongest muscles in his body.

'The cop, who admitted he barely managed to even get this particular charge to court, said he was glad Jack was a journalist and not a career cat burglar. The company that accused him had absolutely no physical evidence that he had been into their building other than the fact that he had acquired a copy of a (later very controversial) document that only the chairman had ever had access to. Even his fellow directors hadn't had their hands on it, so there was no possibility of a leak. In fact, none of his fellow directors were even aware of its existence, which was partly why the said chairman spent much of the next two years as Her Majesty's guest.'

'Do you like him?' Sarah asked shyly.

'I can't professionally say I quite approve of him, but . . . well, he certainly makes things more interesting.'

'No,' said Sarah, 'I meant do you *like* him.'

Jenny laughed quietly to herself, gently shaking her head.

'Jack's not . . . I'm kind of spoken for at the moment. Well, at least I'm hopeful it's going somewhere for a change.'

'God, I know what you mean,' Sarah said. 'I've not had much luck on that front since Jeremy . . . and I suppose that means I've not had much luck full stop.'

'If it wasn't for bad luck you'd have had no luck at all, huh?'

'Yeah,' Sarah laughed. 'So what's his name, this Mr Hopefully?'

Sometimes you had to worry nights about people finding out or having to tell them. Worse when it was someone who was or might be a friend, the possibility of fear or mistrust. Would they think you were only being friendly because . . . Would they be insulted that you didn't trust them enough to . . .

But sometimes you just knew.

'Angela,' Jenny said, then smiled and thought for an absurd second she would giggle.

'So, you want me to stop the car so you can escape?' she added.

'God yes, at once, help help,' mumbled Sarah in a distracted, monosyllabic mutter, staring out of the window as they passed the unnerving spiky splendour of the portrait gallery. 'She know you're a cop?'

'Not yet, but that's the part I'm hopeful about.'

'Good luck.'

'Thanks.'

They pulled up at a red light, the purr of the idling engine emphasising the still quiet of the night.

'You like him, don't you? *Like* him, I mean,' Jenny said.

'He's untypical. I like that.'

'Untypical? Perhaps the witness would care to elaborate.'

'You've obviously not spent a lot of time among medics. The worst thing about typicality is its inexhaustible power to disappoint. *Another* short-arsed surgeon with small-man syndrome, barking orders at everyone because he's got a point to prove. *Another* spineless git who's had a personality bypass marrying a doe-eyed nurse. *Another* academic hot-shot dropping his qualifications into the conversation because you're supposed to be impressed. Oh Jesus,' she giggled, 'there was even one I came across who kept telling everyone he was a distant relative of Oppenheimer.'

Jenny laughed too. 'No, you're making this up now, surely.'

'I swear,' Sarah insisted. 'I've got witnesses.'

Jenny convulsed, swerving the car slightly in her laughter as the pair degenerated into temporary hysterics.

'OK,' Jenny said, eventually recovering. 'But even if what he said was true . . . that still constitutes a new record level in human sadness.'

'Like I said, you've not spent a lot of time among medics.'

'Well, what if I told you Parlabane was a typical hack,' Jenny said.

'I wouldn't believe you. You see, the thing that I most like about Jack is that he gives a fuck, and that's not typical in any profession.'

'Yeah,' said Jenny, 'but that's what worries me about him. I've been told he's a tenacious investigator, and I respect that, but there's more than meets the eye here, girl. Jack Parlabane is working to his own agenda on this, like he's on some kind of crusade. I don't know what it's about, but I'm warning you to be careful.'

'Well I do know what it's about,' Sarah said, in an instantly regretted reaction to feeling she was being patronised. 'And I will be careful.'

Jenny indicated, pulled the car over, switched off the engine and turned to face Sarah.

110

'So what's the story, Doc?' she demanded.

Sarah looked anxiously about herself for a few seconds, then ran her hand through her hair.

'Well, it goes without saying that I'm trusting you not to tell him you heard this. Not just that you heard this from me, but that you heard this at all. Jack's here because he left LA in a big hurry – someone was paid to kill him.'

'How does he know?'

'He didn't say. He just told me someone tried to kill him and he seems very sure it was a professional matter.'

'Well, if he told you that much, there must be more to know. It's a hack's prerogative not to give you the full story. Not in the first edition, at least. But I'll warn you again, Sarah, don't get too close. Whoever's behind all this has had one person killed already. We're dealing with dangerous individuals here, and your safety might not be the first thing on Jack's mind when he gets the scent in his nose.'

'Don't worry about me,' Sarah said flatly. 'I can look after myself.'

I don't doubt it for a second, thought Jenny.

But could she look after Parlabane?

EIGHTEEN

Mike Gorman's secretary, Guadeloupe, didn't put calls through from just anybody. Not only were there less than a dozen names that guaranteed direct transfer, but there were only a few more that she would even ask him for a yes or no on. Her boss was a very busy man, which was one thing, but as Metro editor of the *LA Tribune*, he got hundreds of calls every day from hopeful hacks and hopeless nutcases.

Elvis called a couple of times a week.

A story bigger than Watergate was breaking most Tuesdays.

Jimmy Hoffa frequently rang from somewhere inside the Bermuda Triangle, usually collect.

And Mike was too busy to talk to any of them.

In fact, that afternoon Guadeloupe wasn't putting many calls through at all. She had told him he looked like shit (sir) and should be taking the day off. He was worried-looking, upset, unshaven and tired, and had been growing more so with each of the previous few days.

Mike wouldn't let Guadeloupe fuss over him like that, mainly because he enjoyed it too much, but also because he was precisely the kind of workaholic who, when told he was unwell, worried that he'd have to knuckle under more to make up for not operating at full capacity.

So when Guadeloupe took a call for Mike 'from beyond the grave', she told the person on the other end that he was only taking calls from this world today.

'He's pretty shaken up, then, I'd guess,' the caller said. 'I might be able to put his mind at rest.'

'Who is this?' she asked.

'I can't tell you, but I can assure you Mike will be pleased to find out.'

Mike didn't sound very pleased after Guadeloupe put the call through.

'Where the fuck are you, you miserable Scottish prick? I thought you were dead. In fact after the week I've just been through I was fucking *hoping* you were dead, so that at least all this worry would be worth a goddamn.'

'I'm in Edinburgh,' said the voice after the satellite delay.
'Edinburro Scotland?'

'No, Edinburro Nevada. It's just outside Buttfuck. We're thinking of throwing up a few casinos, getting the town off the ground. Of course I'm in fucking Scotland. I couldn't hang around in LA. I've got a bad allergy to bullets.'

'I guess your hunch was right then. How far did you get?'

'Not very. Dangerous people, Mike. Out of my league, anyway.'

'So what happened to you, Jack? Jesus, your place. You know they found . . .'

'I know what they found, Mike. And what I don't tell you, you don't have to lie about, OK?'

'Roger that.'

'I'm going to be staying here a while, obviously.'

'Bit of hang time might be advisable for a man of your recent history. Go for it.'

"Fraid not. I'm on to something out here.'

'Oh, surprisorama. New town, same story.'

'Something like that. I need a favour, Mike.'

'Jesus, Jack. You were on the telephone for nearly a whole minute before you said that. That makes this like a birthday call or something.'

'Well, after what I put you through. Have you got a pen?'

Clive Medway listened to the unfamiliar ringing tone, halfway across the world, nervously hoping the call would be a waste of time, but knowing it was a check he couldn't afford to omit.

'Hello, *LA Tribune*, Mike Gorman's office,' said a slightly Hispanic American accent.

'Er, yes, hello. This is Clive Medway of the Midlothian NHS Trust in Edinburgh. Could I speak to Mike Gorman please?'

'One moment, sir.'

Click. Purr.

'Hello, Clive. Are we all set?'

'What? Oh yes, of course. I'm just checking . . .'

'We're for real? No, I don't blame you. No, you should see some of the stunts they pull to try and get into my office. You don't have to tell me what devious assholes reporters can be. Hey, I'm surrounded by them. So what time is it out there . . . ?'

*　　*　　*

113

Brilliant. It was no hoax, no set-up. It was an honest-to-God publicity coup, just the sort of thing NHS Trusts needed to counteract the relentless tide of fish stories about overworked doctors and patients dying on trolleys in waiting rooms.

And as Public Relations Director of the Midlothian NHS Trust – 'We've got a heart in the Heart' © – he would be the man who had made it all happen.

It was a no-lose situation. If the article turned out to be a hatchet-job, the only people who would see it would be about 8,000 miles away, and if it was a glowing appraisal, he'd send copies to every paper in Britain and get the pages blown up poster-size for the lobby.

But he was sure the chances of it being yet another negative, one-sided perspective were very remote. He just knew that he and this Mike Gorman chap spoke the same language.

'For God's sakes, this is the Nineties, Clive,' Gorman had said. 'Everybody's had enough of *ER* and white coat mythology. They want to read about how a modern hospital *really* works, what *really* turns the wheels in a place like that. Administration, management, planning. My readers want to touch base with the pro-active chance-takers who pick up the ball and run with it, who make sure that all the pieces are in place before Dr Hot-shot or his patient even come into the equation.

'Now, I got a rough draft of a piece in front of me right here done at OCG – that's Orange County General – looking at twenty-four hours in the life of a hospital. The reporter spent the day finding out a little about the roles of all the administrative staff, then spent the night on-call with one of the doctors, and was able to trace back all the doc's moves to decisions taken at management level. How the doc wouldn't have been able to do such-and-such if the VP in charge of whatever hadn't drafted the right policy directive at an earlier date. And how everything that gets done, right down to stitching up a gang-banger's bullet wound, conforms to the OCG mission statement.'

'Sounds marvellous.'

'It is. The piece could run on its own, we got some great shots to illustrate it. Got a beautiful montage from our art shop of an administrator at a computer, and in the screen, over the account figures he's working on, you can see a reflection of a guy in a surgical mask holding up a scalpel. The whole thing was gonna be primo, Clive. But the guy who wrote it said it would be even better to run it along with a comparative piece on another hospital, somewhere totally different. And I said yeah, you mean like Third World or something, and he says no, like England. He told me – how'd he put it? – "the dinosaur of the health service is finally evolving into something viable in a free enterprise environment", and he said the ideal sidebar piece would be on an English hospital that's changing for the better.

'Of course I said he was nuts if he thought I was paying for him to fly to England just for the sake of filling a couple more pages, but he's from over there and he said he was going out on vacation anyway.

'Unfortunately he isn't going to be in town long, so I'm not giving you much notice, but I'd be real grateful if you could set it up. He won't get in the way – he's the last guy you need to tell about how busy these places are – he'll just watch, ask a few questions, take a few shots.

'His name's Jack Parlabane. I've known him a long time and I really trust this guy's instincts. Believe me, Clive, if he says there's a great story waiting to be found in your hospital, you can be damn sure he'll find it, and you can be damn sure he'll let the whole world know.'

Morag Kinross wasn't a nosy person. She was no curtain-twitcher, like many round here, and despite the torrential flow of other people's business through what was not just her home but *her* business, she had never succumbed to the temptation to poke her snib in where it hadn't been invited. Truth be told, there just wasn't the time. Running the Pilrig Guest House had been work enough to keep her slim and trim into her mid-sixties, and didn't allow much opportunity for playing the spectator upon other people's affairs. Oh, sure, you caught glimpses into the lives of guests as they passed through, but they were like wee adverts for TV programmes you knew you didn't have time to watch. And obviously some of those programmes looked like they might be more exciting than others, but her own show was quite sufficient, thank you.

However, she was a light sleeper. Many was the night she found herself involuntarily tuned into the live radio soap of a couple arguing in one of her rooms, or letting equally heated but less acrimonious passions run their course. The initial outbreak of sound would waken her, but once she had assimilated what it was it would fade into the background and her eyes would close once again.

But with Ruffle missing, just about any wee noise was enough to get her out of bed and looking through the doorway, down into the hall, or out of the window upon the back garden.

A squeaking noise followed by a scraping against the pipes outside drew her to the casement, where she peeped from between a crack in the curtains at the figure of Mr Bond jumping down on to the flagstones. She didn't like Mr Bond one bit. He seemed rough as a crab's backside and wore one of those plastic tracksuit affairs that the wee urchins from Leith used to sport about five years ago, and that she still occasionally spotted on trips to Fife. He was also dreadfully *English* – not nice English, posh English, but like something off that vulgar *EastEnders* programme that the guests sometimes watched in the TV room.

If he had just pitched up looking for B&B, she would have told him the place was fully booked and slammed the door. Wouldn't have been the first time. But the man who had phoned to book the room for 'his business acquaintance' had sounded very posh indeed, and had said the Pilrig was recommended to him by a number of friends at his golf club in Kent. When Mr Bond appeared, looking like he did, she was sure he must be an impostor, but as his first action was to hand her an envelope containing seven nights' advance payment in cash, she decided to wait and see.

She soon regretted it. Comings and goings at all hours of the night. Keeping his room locked all the time. And that horrible smell, like someone had opened a butcher's shop on the landing.

She watched him creep furtively around in the back garden, then climb over into Mr Henderson's. It was dark, and her eyesight wasn't as sharp as it used to be, so as he crept towards the back wall she couldn't quite make out what he was doing. He seemed to crouch down at Mr Henderson's conifers, then to disappear, so she assumed he had gone in behind them. Then he emerged again, stood up and headed quickly back towards the guest house.

As she wasn't a nosy person, she thought no more of it. She had seen many more suspicious things in the back gardens at night – everything from sleepwalking to unmentionable behaviour by that seemingly respectable and middle-aged Italian couple – and knew it was wisest to just turn a blind eye.

But then a couple of days later old Mr Henderson came round with a tear in his eye and told her he had found Ruffle.

She said nothing as he led her, seemingly inevitably, to the conifers, and pointed out the part of the wall from where the stone had fallen, telling her not to look behind the small trees lest the sight upset her. When he apologised and claimed it was his fault for not keeping the dry-stone dike in good order, she told him not to be silly and that she didn't blame him in the least. And when he offered to bury Ruffle there she thanked him for relieving her of an unpleasant task, then silently walked back home, around Mr Henderson's house, along past the front gardens and in through her front door.

There was a large brown envelope sitting behind the storm door in the porch, addressed to Mr J Bond, obviously dropped off by hand, going by the absence of postage stamps. She took the envelope to the kitchen and for the first time in her life opened someone else's mail.

It contained a pair of black leather gloves, a packet of black hair colouring, and a copy of that day's *Evening Capital*. She unfolded it and noticed a faint black ring around part of the main picture on the front page. Opening the paper, she found that the faint mark was the reverse of a harsher ring in heavy felt pen on page two, around a story headlined: *Ponsonby murder: cops seek nine-fingered fiend.*

She put on her glasses and read on: *Police investigating the brutal murder of City doctor Jeremy Ponsonby today stated that they were looking for a nine-fingered man in connection with the crime.*

In a fresh appeal for new information, Inspector Hector McGregor (52), who is leading the investigation, said that the man they were looking for is at least 6'5" tall, has brown hair with silver highlights, and is missing his right index finger, which was lost during the murder.

Mrs Kinross replaced the items and re-sealed the envelope, then put it back where she found it on the porch.

*   *   *

117

'It's fish for dinner, Mr Bond,' she said cheerily, emerging from the kitchen as he came along the hallway, heading for the stairs with the envelope in his arms. 'Would you like batter or breadcrumbs?'

Mr Bond just stared at her for a moment, then muttered 'batter – an' I wannit in me room,' and lumbered up the stairs, where he opened his envelope and cursed that stuck-up cunt who didn't think he'd be smart enough to have already been wearing gloves.

Mrs Kinross went back to the kitchen and prepared Mr Bond's fish, using a special batter enhanced by the powdery contents of several sleeping capsules from the bottle left by that jumpy Austrian woman last year.

NINETEEN

As oily creeps go, Clive Medway was deluxe multigrade. If he had been American, Parlabane decided, he would have had a ponytail, even though he was losing it both at the front and on top. He had the roundest head Parlabane had seen outside of Peanuts, above a shiny blue tie and a designer suit which conclusively proved that shelling out a fortune for your clothes doesn't stop you looking like a complete tit.

He had a whiny, nasal voice which frequently degenerated into a whiny, nasal laugh at his own witticisms, or insincere chuckling at anyone else's. He made Parlabane want to take a shower to wash his presence off, but he felt slightly guilty thinking all these uncomplimentary thoughts, as Clive was introducing him to numerous 'important' people and firmly instructing them to tell Parlabane absolutely anything he wanted to know.

He took Parlabane on a brief tour of the administration block first, explaining which office dealt with which aspect of running the Trust, and allowing him to familiarise himself with the layout of the place.

'Impressive facilities, great decor,' Parlabane said, passing another minor brushland of potted plants. 'It's important to have the right environment for people to work in, I think.'

'Couldn't agree more,' Clive replied. 'You can't expect trained professionals to work in a pig-sty, can you? Ha-ha-ha. You have to show personnel that they are valued and respected if you want them to be team players.'

'I wouldn't imagine all this was cheap, but it's certainly money well spent,' Parlabane offered, reeling him in.

'Well, it couldn't be cheap. This is the corporate face of the Trust, the business image we project to the marketplace. It wouldn't impress anyone out there for us to look impoverished. What the carpers don't understand is that sometimes being what they regard as ostentatious is a pro-active marketing tactic. You have to be seen to be spending money on yourself, on your image, so that the market knows you are in good financial shape.'

Parlabane found the word 'pro-active' enormously useful, as it immediately exposed the speaker as an irredeemable arsehole, whatever previous impression might have been given. Once upon a time, he remembered, people and companies just did things. But that ceased to be impressive enough, and for a while they 'actively' did things. Now they 'pro-actively' did things, but it was still the same bloody things that they were doing when they just plain old did things. Meaningless wank-language. Every time he heard it he imagined George Orwell doing another 360 down below.

Parlabane followed Clive around for a while, shmoozing practisedly, shaking hands, asking questions, having things pointed out to him. The suits needed little prompting from Clive to answer Parlabane's questions, as his very presence was making them feel terribly important. The LA angle was what really opened them up, the thought of all those people out in Hollywoodland reading about their pro-active pro-activeness proving too intoxicating for them to notice that Parlabane wasn't actually listening to anything they were saying.

A sharper eye might have spotted that what Parlabane was actually doing was casing the joint. They saw that his little dictaphone was rolling away on the desk in front of them and seemed to assume that it was linked directly to his brain via his ears. They didn't wonder what a man with a dictaphone was doing scribbling in a notepad as they spoke, or notice that his camera was pointing slightly away from them when he took their pictures.

They all cooperated in standing against one wall for his great idea of taking a shot of a whole office area completely deserted, and then with its staff sitting back at their desks – 'it's for a kind of sequential thing: empty, like first thing in the morning, then busy, with a montage of all you guys at your various duties running alongside it.' Nobody noticed that Parlabane didn't set his camera to flash for the empty shot, or wonder whether it was just for the best angle that he took it from directly underneath the fixed close-circuit video camera. And nobody noticed that he didn't shut the window properly after opening it to take a panoramic shot of the 'wonderful view' enjoyed by RVI staff and patients, or that much of the window concerned was obscured from the aforementioned video camera by a bank of filing cabinets.

Parlabane had anticipated that Clive would introduce him to the happy smile club, presenting the most positive image possible, and was therefore paying attention to who he was specifically not being allowed to meet, as that was who would be most likely to tell him something useful or at least true. The most obvious – and potentially most useful – was the conspicuously pissed-off computer trouble-shooter who was hopping from desk to desk looking stormy and fraught.

'It's a magnificently complex-looking computer system you've got here,' he said to Clive. 'But then I suppose it would really have to be state-of-the-art to run this whole operation.'

'Quite,' Clive agreed. 'It's extremely advanced, and processes everything from budgets and accounts to medical records.'

'Must be some responsibility for the systems manager.'

'Oh yes. He's one of the busiest men in the building, and I'm afraid I daren't interrupt him just now. Can't have the whole Trust at a standstill because the network is down and the systems manager's chatting to a journalist about how great the computers are. Ha-ha-ha. That *would* be embarrassing.'

And so on.

Parlabane bided his time until he was allowed to go walkabout on his own, which came about because Clive had 'an eleven o'clock with the chief exec', followed by 'a twelve-thirty at the Sheraton'. Parlabane figured Clive's day had started with a seven-fifteen on the bog then a seven-twenty-five in the shower, followed by an eight o'clock in the kitchen.

Twat.

He spotted the computer bloke hovering around what looked like an enormous central file server and made directly for him.

'Problems?' he asked.

The guy just shook his head gravely. He looked late thirties, going a bit grey, but maybe it was just the day he was having.

'I don't know a helluva lot about these things,' Parlabane said, 'but that looks like an awful lot of hardware for a place this size.'

'No kidding,' the man replied. 'Everything runs off this file server here – everything. No local facilities whatsoever, so the machines don't get bunged up with personal junk and the terminals can only run what they're here to run. But to be honest, you could run every computer for two square miles off of this rig. It's enormous.'

'Room for expansion?'

The man just laughed, bitterly.

'I've seen a few like this,' Parlabane said, very quietly, touching the seven-foot cabinet full of stacked drives and mini-screens. 'Maybe it's because companies would rather *over*-estimate how much computer they might need. Or maybe it's because the systems manager submitted an accurate spec and the boys upstairs ignored it and bought twice as much because the nice computer company accidentally spilled some money into somebody's bank account. But not here, obviously.'

'Obviously. And that's a very cynical viewpoint, Mr . . .?'

'Parlabane. Jack Parlabane.'

'Parlabane. Very cynical indeed.' He smiled and offered his hand to shake. 'Matt Dempsey. You're a journalist, yeah? You ever seen the system down at the *Evening Capital*?'

'Only very briefly.'

'It's another stoater. The hardware's no bad, but the software? Fuck's sake. Portuguese, it is.'

'Of course,' said Parlabane. 'Think software, think Portugal.'

'I worked at the *Capital* for a wee while a few years back, when they brought that one in,' Dempsey said. 'Nightmare. New DTP system, never been used live by anyone before. The first rule of buying software is *never* buy version 1.1 of *anything*. Let some other clown find out whit's wrang with it and then buy version three when the thing actually fucking works. Not the *Capital*. They volunteer to be guinea pigs on this thing called Dash. The hacks all called it Colon instead, because it's full of shite. When I was there it crashed for a different reason every three hours, half its error messages were in fucking Portuguese and it practically doubled the paper's production times. But I'm sure it was all worth it to the fat bastard in the boardroom who mysteriously acquired a villa on the Algarve and free golf membership for life.'

'But obviously, again, that sort of thing would never happen here,' Parlabane stated flatly.

'Certainly not. All the hardware and software we're running was purchased strictly in accordance with my requests and

122

projections, down to the last floppy disk. That's why we've got a fucking NASA-grade central server and I'm running about daft all day fixing programme crashes and trying to retrieve lost files.'

'And absolutely everything runs off the central server?'

'Aye. Management policy. Means nobody can be farting aboot playing games on their PC or loading up dodgy or even illegal software. It also means the boys upstairs can monitor everything that's going on. The heid bummers can access all levels of the system, so they can spy on the underlings, see what wee messages they're writing to each other. That kind of thing.'

'Yes,' said Parlabane, 'what was the phrase your man Medway used . . . ? Something about showing people that they were valued and respected. So if someone with those privileges wanted to know how much a certain doctor earned, for instance, he could just access the wages files directly?'

'Aye. But that's just the way the hierarchy works. As senior management they've got the right – in fact, I suppose you could say it's their job – to know or to be able to know what's going on down below. The more distasteful aspect is the Loud Labelling.'

'The what?'

'Loud Labelling. It's a wee piece of software. Every type of file gets assigned an automatic label as soon as it's created: accounts, spreadsheets, budget, medical records and all that. But person-to-person messages get assigned a Loud Label. That means it gets noted by the computer that so-and-so sent a memo file to such-and-such, and so the heid bummers can call up a list of who's talking to who. If they see something they fancy a swatch at, they can just call it up. They're at it all the time. Whiling away the hours doing fuck-all work and reading other people's mail.'

'So is it a password system?' Parlabane asked 'Getting into the right access level, I mean.'

Dempsey glared. 'Don't fucking talk about it. The chief exec and a few more in senior management have got passwords that even I'm not allowed to know. How am I supposed to police the system when I don't have access to the whole thing? It's just a power trip. It's not as though there's any information I – or any other bugger – would be remotely interested in. It's only a fucking hospital, for God's sake.

No, it's purely so they can feel more important than everybody else.'

Parlabane looked on with obvious incredulity. 'You're not telling me that you haven't set up a few backdoors for yourself, surely.'

'I'm not a hacker, I'm just a systems manager. And to be honest, I don't have any great curiosity to know what they're up to. I'd just like to have the run of my own network.'

'Does the Loud Labelling have a hierarchy as well? Can the chief exec see what the other big cheeses are saying to each other?'

'Of course. The whole fucking thing was his idea.'

'So if you were able to access at his level, you'd have complete freedom of the system?'

'Apart from the direct programming, which only I can access, aye.'

'So,' Parlabane said, looking Dempsey in the eye with that helplessly untrustworthy glint, 'if someone could provide you with a piece of software that would reveal the chief exec's password, would you be worried about the fact that that person might go poking around your system?'

'Not at all,' Dempsey said quietly, glancing quickly over Parlabane's shoulders to see whether anyone was paying them too much attention. 'Because I'm the only one who could access the direct programming to install that software, and I'd be the only one who could call the software up once it was running.'

Parlabane nodded solemnly.

'Of course,' Dempsey continued, 'that person might not *give* me the software unless I agreed to set him up with a user name – say "Jack P" – and a password – say "hack" – that would allow him to access the system and call up the software at least fifteen minutes after I leave at four o'clock this afternoon.'

With a flick of the wrist Parlabane produced a grey 3.5" disk from his pocket and tapped it absently on the edge of the desk.

Dempsey glanced down and nodded once. 'But before I did that I'd obviously need to know why that person wanted to go poking around my system when he's told everyone he's writing an article about hospital management.'

'Yes,' said Parlabane. 'Chances are you'd feel more public-spirited about it knowing he was actually investigating a

124

murder, but you would feel all the more reassured knowing that if he double-crossed you and raided the files for purposes of profit or espionage, you have his name and about a hundred witnesses that he was here.'

'Yes, that would certainly put me at ease,' Dempsey said. 'So how does it work?'

'Well, the good news is that as you're running everything off the central server, you won't need to install it individually on the machines of the people whose passwords you want. You just need to bung it on the network. The bad news is that it's not a codebreaker and it won't just take a look at the security software then print out the magic words.

'What it *will* do is record every keystroke made on whatever terminal or terminals you tell it to look at, whatever programme they are running, then allow you to get a listing of them at any time. Then you either wait till morning if you're not in a hurry, or shut the system down and ask everyone to re-boot.'

'And the first thing they key in is their name and password,' Dempsey said, grinning. 'Now if you'll excuse me, Mr Parlabane, I think the network might be about to have a problem.'

TWENTY

'I'm a doctor, so I've seen plenty of balls in my time, but this? You asked the systems manager to help you hack his own *system*? He could have had you thrown out then and there. He could have had you *arrested*.'

For appearances' sake, Parlabane had followed Sarah around the wards and theatres for a while after nipping out to the nearest chemist's to pick up his ready-in-one-hour prints, and this was the first time they had been alone together with a chance to talk. He had watched her interview patients who were going to be anaesthetised later, and sat in on a minor operation, at the head end, behind the 'blood/brain barrier'. This consisted of a screen obscuring the surgeon and his 'guddling about', as Sarah described it, from the conscious patient's view. However, from what Parlabane had heard of Sarah and her anaesthetist colleagues discussing their relationships with surgeons, he understood that the brain referred to in the term was not that of the patient, nor of the sawbones.

Parlabane figured that as the intended purpose of the screen was to prevent the patient from seeing parts of his body being abused, then its subsidiary function – of preventing the surgeon from seeing the anaesthetists and ODAs making obscene gestures in response to his arrogant remarks – was merely a useful bonus.

Sarah was leaning against a small chest of drawers, its yellow plastic veneer peeled away from the cheap chipboard on all surfaces. She looked like she would be pacing the floor if there had been enough space in the on-call room to pace in. That utterly remorseless and even vaguely proud look in Parlabane's eye wasn't helping her humour.

'Calculated risk,' he said, standing with his back against the paint-blistered door. 'Computer experts fall into two categories: meticulous, anal-looking bastards with something extremely uncomfortable stuck up their arses, or shambolic, haggard individuals who look like they could use about a fortnight's sleep. The former type will steep the keyboard in disinfectant if you so much as breathe on his computers, while the latter can always do with talking to someone who understands about how he's pissing into the wind trying to run a fucked system against the odds etcetera etcetera, blah blah blah. Also, that Medway prick was very keen for me not to talk to him, which circled him as a possible ally right away.'

'OK, very cute. But what if the systems manager had been one of the anal types?'

'I'd have made out I didn't even know how to switch a computer on, so that he wouldn't be keeping an eye on me. Then I'd have popped my disk into an up-and-running terminal as soon as he was out of sight. I didn't need the systems manager to get it running. I just told him that. The programme is written to automatically load itself into the system and launch immediately. After you've put the disk in, you've got roughly five minutes to access the programme and tell it specifically what machines to look at, otherwise it just goes ahead and records every machine on the network. That slows the network down slightly, which won't be noticed by any of the workers but might make the systems manager jumpy.'

'And where did you get this magic disk? I don't imagine it's on sale next to "Sonic the Hedgehog Meets the Monopolies Commission".'

'I came up with the idea and got a guy in Van Nuys to code it. Two years ago he was just a scuzzball coding freak at a firm in Silicone Valley. Now he's senior VP in charge of something or other. Information is power and all that.'

'So why did you bring Dempsey into it if you didn't need him?'

'Fair exchange. He'd given me some good information. Also, I knew he'd be grateful for what I was giving him, and you never know when a bit of gratitude might come in handy.'

Sarah looked away and shook her head. Then she stared back at Parlabane. 'You know, Jack, I'm beginning to understand why someone tried to kill you.' She walked to the bed, kicked off her shoes and slumped down on it, propping her back up against the headboard with a pook-ridden pillow.

'So what else did you learn?' she asked. 'Did you meet our glorious leader, the big boss?'

'Stephen Lime? But of course. He was the highlight of the tour – as far as Clive was concerned anyway. I got a privileged five minutes with the great one, during which he talked a lot and said nothing, a very valuable talent in both senior management and politics. Lots of press-release jargon, phrases like 'meeting the challenges head-on', plus plenty of mission statements and pro-activity.

'To tell you the truth, I once got caught in gridlock in LA for six hours, day after the last earthquake, and that day was more interesting than this one. I've never had to listen to quite so many suits talking bollocks to me over such a sustained period. I did pick up a few valuable snippets, but the ratio of useful information to corporate wanking was not exactly satisfactory. What about you – did you get to talk to the Prof yet?'

Sarah rolled her eyes. 'Eventually. He wasn't being evasive, it's just you've no idea how hard it can be for two doctors to be free at the same time for even ten minutes. I managed to get someone else to hold my bleep for a while and cornered him in Coronary Care. He told me the whole thing over Jeremy's wages was organised between him and someone called Moira Gallagher in payroll. The only other person who was told anything would have been her boss, as she had to clear it with him. The Prof didn't know his name, but he'll be head of that department, presumably. But Gallagher was the only one he told about the reason for the debt, and he asked her not to divulge it.'

'Was the Prof suspicious?' Parlabane asked.

'Obviously. I didn't lie to him, I just said I needed to know but I couldn't tell him why. I don't think he wants to think about it too much, to be honest – he still looks pretty glazed – so he answered my questions and let it go.'

Parlabane walked over and leaned against the chest of drawers, staring blankly for a second as he processed the information.

'Right, I think that gives us eight people who could have known about it, then. Gallagher, her boss and the six suits with the Loud Labelling crap who could have intercepted a memo from her to the boss about the wages arrangement. Obviously this memo wouldn't mention Jeremy's wee problem with the gee-gees, and it might not have mentioned that he was in debt. But the revelation that a sizable slice of Ponsonby Junior's wages were being transferred to Ponsonby Senior would have been enough on its own to attract some curiosity, and it wouldn't be too difficult after that to work out the young doc owed Daddy money. Now, my guess of there being only eight does discount the possibility of gossip, but I don't imagine the Prof would have approached this particular woman unless he thought he could trust her to keep her mouth shut. She could still have told her husband, for instance, but I'm convinced that this is all within the hospital. Whoever acted on that information had to know enough about doctors to have figured out a way to use a bent one.

'Now, we don't know what that use was, but as we found nearly two K and chances are Jeremy spent Christ knows how much more, then the return for the bad guy must be huge. Especially considering the risk in approaching a doctor to get involved in some kind of scam, however much debt he was in. This has to be big money or big politics, and maybe even both.'

Sarah had a look of concentrated consternation on her face, wincing as she struggled to comprehend something.

'What I don't get, Jack, is why you're so keen to get into the computer system, why you brought that disk along. I mean, if one of these suits or Moira Gallagher's boss or even Moira Gallagher's up to no good, they're not going to write it all down on the office wp, are they?'

Parlabane lifted his feet from the floor, letting the chest of drawers take his full weight. It gave a distraught creak and lurched drunkenly to one side, threatening to collapse completely if he didn't remove himself. He stood off it, righted it and leaned against the wall.

'It's because computers don't understand politics,' he said, trying to thump a wooden bail back into its awl on the teetering construction beside him. 'If you want to know what's going on in a company, an office, get into the computers. They don't always tell you secrets, but they do give you straight answers. From a trawl through the system you can find out what's really going on as opposed to what people will tell you is going on: the power structure, who's working on what, who's likely to know about what, and who's saying what to whom. The computer can be an instrument of politics within an office, but the computer itself is not political. It just calculates, computes, and most importantly, records. I'll find out more in twenty minutes on that network than I did from today's hours of guarded bullshit, where every statement had a motive.

'But most importantly, when you ask a computer a question, it doesn't wonder why you want to know that information and then go and tell the boss that someone is snooping around. I can personally vouch for the advantages of that, with specific regard to the ensuing lack of men with guns – or in this case knives – visiting your house later on.'

'Yes, I can appreciate the benefits of that myself,' Sarah admitted. 'But you said the terminals off the wards were no good, yeah?'

'Afraid not. They're running off the central server, but they're only linked to the medical records database. Even if I booted up with Stephen Lime's user name and password, I couldn't get into the general system.'

'So how are you going to get your twenty minutes on the network?'

'Well, once I've broken into the admin block I'll have all night, if I need it.'

Sarah sighed. 'You know, it worries me that I didn't find that surprising,' she said. 'It means I must be getting used to you, and I don't think that's a good thing.'

She pulled her legs up underneath her on the bed and adjusted the pillows at her back.

'So how are you going to break in? Admin's the one place in the RVI where they've spent money on security.'

'I've already broken in,' Parlabane replied. 'At least, I've done all the difficult bits. All I really need to do now is show up. Their security is abysmal anyway. The only threat they've properly guarded against is someone actually making off with their expensive computers and trendy furniture. And to be honest, apart from one very guilty party, they've very little else to fear from a break-in.'

He reached down and picked up the duffle bag he had given Sarah that morning before going to meet the lovely Clive.

'I've been waiting all day to find out what was in there, but I'm not so sure I want to know now.'

'Just the tools of my trade,' Parlabane said, with a grin of near-satanic misanthropy.

He took off his boring blue tie and unbuttoned the white shirt that he had worn to present a respectable and unsuspicious image to the admin staff, then quickly hopped out of his navy trousers and into a pair of black jeans which he produced from the duffle bag. Then he dipped into the bag again and laid out a number of small items on Sarah's bed.

She looked with minor curiosity at the mysterious pieces of hardware arrayed before her, but her attention was massively distracted by Parlabane's enjoyably prolonged state of partial undress. His skin looked weathered by the sun rather than tanned, muckily dark patches around the neck and shoulders giving way to a more consistent hue about his back and chest, where the hairs appeared blonder than on his head due to their being shorter and finer. She had half-expected to find him rakishly skinny under his clothes, but although he was far from muscular, his arms and torso had a sinewy, taut look of fitness about them.

From the bed he picked up an article of black canvas, punctuated with pockets and sections of elasticated loop, with two sturdy straps situated at equal distances in from each end. He picked up the one item Sarah recognised – the wallet of lock-picking utensils – and shoved it through two of the elasticated loops. Then he repeated the drill with a transparent plastic bag of computer disks and what looked like an extremely compact camera.

'For interesting documents when the people you're visiting haven't been considerate enough to leave the photocopier on overnight,' he explained.

He put his arms through the loops and pulled the strapping around his back and chest like a bra, which he fastened with a plastic clip at the sternum, then attached a neatly folded length of climbing cord across the front. Finally, he reached back into the duffle bag and produced a black polo-neck, which he stuck his neck through and pulled over the whole affair.

'Why can I hear the *Mission Impossible* music in my head?' Sarah remarked. 'Look, Jack, are you sure you know what you're doing?'

'Hey,' he said, opening the window and standing up on the bed, 'Parlabane's back.'

TWENTY-ONE

Parlabane was twelve years old, staying the September weekend at his cousin Moray's in Nairn. All day Saturday they
had been alternately playing and fighting with Heather and
Stephanie, Moray's wee sisters, in the house and round the
garden while their mums drank coffee and blethered in the
kitchen and their dads hit into a force eight on the links.

In the evening, they were packed off to the living room to
watch TV while their parents demolished four courses and
plenty of dry red in the dining room, and hostilities had
inevitably ensued when the girls' choice of *Chitty Chitty
Bang Bang* clashed with Parlabane and Moray's preferred Ian
Fleming adaptation on the other channel. Parental mediation
was sought and produced the kind of compromise that
illustrated why none of them ever got a job with ACAS:
the girls could watch the first half of their film and the boys
the second half of theirs.

The boys elected to back down from this Mexican stand-off
and retreated to Moray's bedroom for the remainder of the
evening, where they played the Escape From Colditz board
game and at some point came up with an idea to even
the score.

Around one in the morning, half-an-hour after the last adult
sound had been heard, they made their way downstairs and
through the house silently. They used two pillows each,
placing them in front of themselves, stepping on to the first
and then taking the one from behind and bringing it to the
front. There were no footfalls, and they could barely hear the
sound of each other's breathing.

Moray opened the girls' bedroom door. They both knew it
squeaked, so it was a very slow and patient process, pushing
it centimetre by centimetre, stopping and pausing awhile after
each hint of a noise, until it was open just wide enough to
squeeze through. Once inside, they stood perfectly still on the
floor for a short while, thrilling to the silence and the sight of
the girls obliviously asleep on the bunk beds. Thrilling to the
feeling of being where they weren't supposed to.

Having steadied their breathing and recovered from the threat of giggling, they went to work. Moray had a rubber skull that glowed in the dark, and he attached it to the bedsprings of the top bunk, so that it dangled in front of Stephanie's face where she lay on the bottom one. Parlabane quietly set about placing every object in the room upside down – apart from, obviously, the goldfish bowl – and arranging all of the girls' dolls doing handstands along the wall.

The next day, the girls quite victoriously got their own back by saying absolutely nothing about it, but that didn't matter.

They had a new game. The best game.

That night he and Moray left their bedroom window open, crept downstairs and out the front door, went around the house and climbed back in via the extension roof and a sturdy black drainpipe. All told it took less than ten minutes, but the excitement kept them awake and talking about it for half the night afterwards.

School disco a few months later, three days before the Christmas holidays. Parlabane had retreated to the first floor toilets to recover from the broken heart and devastating embarrassment of Alison Gifford knocking him back for a dance. All the other cubicles were full of second years drinking Woodpecker and smoking menthols, so he had to settle for the one at the end that no one liked to use because it had a frosted window above the cistern, and 'folk might be able to see in'.

He was hiding, really. Didn't want to talk to anyone, didn't want to be seen. It was stuffy in the gym hall where the disco was, but he didn't want to go out to the playground for air because it was full of lucky bastards getting a snog. With all the illicit smoking going on, the toilets were even more oppressively smelly than usual, and as he wasn't in there to properly use the facilities, he stood on the seat, opened the window and stuck his head out. There was a drainpipe running up the wall just outside, the west wing's flat roof a few feet above.

Guess what.

Parlabane scurried along the roof, looking down through the plastic-domed skylights at the empty desks and chairs in the semi-darkness below. He was in a fairly distressed and nihilistic frame of mind, he would in later years tell himself to explain what he did next. It was as much to do with simply being twelve as being knocked back by Alison Gifford.

He dreeped down backwards, stretching his legs below him and placing his toes at either side of the bottom frame of a window, then pulled himself back up. His trainers scraped along the wood of the frame for a second and then the window came unstuck and slid upwards. He lowered himself back down until his feet were on the sill, then with one instep pulled the window up as far as it would go, and climbed in.

He found himself in the English Base, where all the text-books were kept and where the head of the department, Mrs Innes, had a small office, partitioned off by shelves and cabinets. Parlabane wandered around for a few moments, his heart still racing from the fear of falling, and now dealing with the fear of getting caught.

But there would be no one to catch him. The half-dozen or so teachers mad enough to volunteer to assist with the disco were too busy policing the gym hall to even notice the various illegalities taking place in the toilets, so *nobody* was going to come up here.

He had a seat behind Mrs Innes' desk, just catching his breath, enjoying the silence and the thrill. Then he noticed that the pile of sheets on her desk were the first year pre-Christmas exam papers, with the marks circled on the top-right corners. He flicked through them until he found his own, which had earned him 88%, and a quick scan of the rest revealed him to be top of the year-group.

There were no big secrets, no scandals, no revelations. These papers would be getting handed out the next day anyway. But as he climbed back out of the window, on to the roof, down the drainpipe and into the toilets, he felt invincible, knowing he had been where he should not have been, seen what he should not have seen, and knew something everyone around him didn't.

So upon returning to the disco, the offered consolation from a pal that 'Alison Gifford's got nae tits anyway' was very much redundant.

Parlabane had stayed in shape, retaining a proportionately light frame past adolescence and all throughout his twenties, assisted by an extremely understanding metabolism that was prepared to forgive his appetites for hamburgers and

Guinness. Contrary to his friends' warnings and possibly hopes, his pituitary gland had not packed in and allowed a ten-stone fat backlog to catch up on him. Consequently, he could still support his hanging bodyweight on a few fingers of one hand; he'd rather not if he could possibly avoid it, but it remained reassuring to know it was an option, especially on a rockface or the side of a building.

However, it was not a talent he was going to need on a cakewalk like tonight. The RVI, in its Victorian quasi-gothic austerity, was a helpfully chunky building, designed, it seemed, with the needs of wall-scaling and burglary in mind. Parlabane had first ascended to the slate roof then made his way along the edge of it from above the on-call accommodation to the admin block, via two hundred-yard stretches either side of the entrance to the A&E department, which was at the centre of the main trunk of the building.

He identified the window he had left slightly open two floors below him, and pulled the climbing cord out from under his polo-neck, then secured it to a disused but sturdy chimney pot, and lowered himself down to the wide stone platform of the window ledge. Parlabane had been pleased to see that all of the admin block had been double-glazed – presumably the rest of the hospital would follow in no time – as that meant the frame should slide up quietly and easily, which it did.

Parlabane rolled inside and shut the window, then crawled on his stomach across the carpet to a spot directly underneath the security camera. From a pouch in his 'utility bra' he produced the photograph he had shot from that spot earlier in the day, taken without a flash so that it produced a dark and shadowy image, much like the room looked in the middle of the night with all the lights off. He took out a length of heavy, insulated copper wire and fashioned a small stand for the photo, then attached the whole thing to the bracket below the camera and swung it swiftly around in front of the lens.

The effect on the image appearing on a monitor, somewhere else in the building, would be simply for the picture to suddenly go out of focus, but to still appear to be the same thing. And in the unlikely event that someone was paying enough attention to the monitors to notice that one was out of focus, their first action would be to remote-adjust the camera until the familiar image of the dark, deserted room became clear again.

His activities screened off from prying eyes, Parlabane took a seat in front of the nearest computer and began to lovingly and conscientiously trespass through the system.

He took a deep breath and keyed in the user name 'jackp' and the password 'hack', then breathed out when the alarms didn't start ringing and no message appeared on his screen to the effect that Matt Dempsey had double crossed him and that the cops were already on their way. He accessed the programme menu and launched Hijack, as his friend in Van Nuys had amused himself to call the keystroke application. Dempsey had set it up to record all six of the senior staff's activities, as although Lime's password would grant the highest access privileges, it wouldn't open documents encrypted by the other five, which required individual codes.

Parlabane pulled a scrap of paper from his pocket, on which he had noted down the serial numbers of the machines each exec had been sitting at – Hijack listed these numbers instead of user names, as obviously it would be recording a terminal's keystrokes before it knew the name of the user logging on. Might as well begin at the top, he thought, and pulled up the listings recorded on the terminal in Lime's office.

stephenlime¶tebbit¶1y5→→→ [del] [del] [del] [del] [del] memo to . . . it began.

'Backstage pass,' Parlabane muttered. 'Access all areas. Thank you.'

He shut down and re-started, logging on with Lime's user name and its attendant access privileges, and began looking, familiarly undeterred by the thought that he had no idea what he was specifically looking *for*.

Partly remembering Dempsey and partly just out of habit, he scanned the purchasing records to find out which company the computers had been bought from, then repeated the drill on office furniture, stationery and decor etc, copying the appropriate documents on to one of the disks he had brought along.

Then he launched Loud Labelling and had a look at what the senior suits were pro-actively saying to each other. Nursing 'efficiency' was going to be 'improved' on several wards, by which Parlabane understood that a number of P45s were in the post. Auxiliary staff were going to be 'streamlined', and the number of geriatric beds was going to be 'rationalised'. However, it wasn't all bad news – the Trust's increasingly healthy balance sheet meant big pay rises were in the offing for the people who had worked hardest to achieve that success.

But the biggest buzz was to do with the George Romanes Hospital. Memos referred to how the 'GRH plans are a vital plank in consolidating the Trust's financial stability', by which Parlabane understood it was somehow up for sale, and the 'importance of discretion with regard to the GRH situation', by which he understood that the clinical staff would probably freak if they knew about it.

He reached for the phone and dialled four numbers, then put the receiver down and waited.

After a couple of minutes it rang.

'You said Jeremy was working at the George Romanes Hospital, didn't you?' he asked as soon as he picked it up.

'Yes,' said Sarah. 'In fact he was covering it until his death.'

'Just confirming. That's all. Thank you.'

Now he had an angle. The next task was to find out what the furtive memos were actually referring to, information which he correctly guessed would be held in encrypted files. He called up a list of all documents stored in Lime's personal folders; if anyone knew the full picture about this, it would be the big boss. The list was huge, so he altered the settings to arrange the items by document type. Sure enough, below the vast bank of 'Wordsmith' wp files were a number marked 'Cryptlock document' next to their dates of most recent use.

He double-clicked on the first one and was asked for a password, but 'Tebbit' didn't score. This was one of the problems with encryption systems: they allowed the user to assign a different password to every document; indeed they required the user to assign one every time he or she wished to re-encrypt, rather than encrypting automatically with the same one when the user closed the file. On the bright side, however, there was the practical reality that no one wanted to be juggling too many passwords, and most people tended to stick to the same one or two. Parlabane toggled back into Hijack and looked again at Lime's keystrokes, worrying about the other problem with encryption systems, which was that if Lime hadn't encrypted or decrypted anything that day, Hijack was useless, as no password would have been keyed in.

Fortunately, the word 'thatcher' appeared, sandwiched between a bunch of cursor strokes and function key numbers. Goal.

'I'm Mr Bad Example,' Parlabane sang quietly to himself, scanning the files, 'take a look at me. I'll live to be a hundred and go down in infamy. Oh Mr Lime, you *have* been a busy boy.'

ATTN: Timothy Winton (Eyes only).

It is my consideration that we accept the Capital Properties offer. I believe you are quite right in estimating the value to be nearer the £5m mark than the bid £3m, but I feel that the bird in the hand factor should come into play.

Firstly, having a closed deal on the table at the time of the announcement will go some way towards staving off the inevitable protests. If we merely announce that the GRH is closing and we intend selling the property, we'll be drowning in a sea of placards, as well as having to listen to countless hare-brained suggestions from the Butlins white coats for alternative usage of the site.

Secondly, the immediate injection of £3m in cash would bring the Trust's finances well into the black before the end of our financial year, and I don't need to tell you how useful that would be politically, for us as well as the Scottish Office. The new NHS badly needs success stories and we have the opportunity to be a very big one.

And on an earlier file:

ATTN: Timothy Winton
       Toby Childs
       Cedric Baker
       Penelope Gainsborough
       Elliot Michaels

It has been brought to all of our attention that the bed-usage situation at the George Romanes Hospital has altered, with a steady reduction in the

138

number of long-term patients through placement and natural wastage.

It seems plausible, now, that the GRH's geriatric care facilities could be absorbed by the RVI, albeit with a reduction in the overall number of geriatric beds in the Trust. This would free up the GRH site for alternative and more cost-effective use, suggestions for which I will be welcoming at our meeting this afternoon.

Hmmm, thought Parlabane.

He copied these and several other files on the same subject to his own disk. It was at that point that he came across a file which would not respond to 'thatcher', and saw that the file had not been updated for some months, meaning Hijack could offer no assistance.

Parlabane's eyes narrowed. People changed their favoured password from time to time, sure, but what was suspicious was that there were several earlier files which *had* been encrypted with 'thatcher'.

A one-off, separate password meant top secret, no question. And Parlabane was pretty sure that whatever it contained would be headline news.

He knew the password could be absolutely anything, but figured that if he had a chance it was to follow the pattern and hope Lime had too. He keyed in 'major', and was met with a loud bleep and a screen message: Incorrect password. Attempts remaining: 2. Cancel. Retry.

'Fuck,' he said, angry at his political stupidity. Someone with a hard-on for Tebbit and Thatcher would probably not want to put Major in the same bracket.

He hit C for Cancel, in the hope that if his next attempt was wrong, it would start back at three guesses.

Suddenly remembering who had played the starring role in this fiasco, and who Lime might therefore be grateful to, he keyed in 'bottomley'.

Beep. Incorrect password. Attempts remaining: 1. Cancel. Retry.

'Arse.'

The cancel option was only for getting out of the loop, back into the main network environment. To get three more guesses, he'd have to shut right down and re-boot, but it was a laborious pain in the arse, and could take him all night if he had to make his way through all the cabinet ministers who were 'one of us' until he got lucky. There was also the danger that a third wrong guess might have further security consequences, such as freezing the system or setting off some kind of alarm. He knew he could little afford that, but he could even less afford to remain ignorant of what was in that file.

He paused, took a deep breath and composed his thoughts.

Thatcher. Tebbit. Who would be third in that sequence? Who was equally nauseating, xenophobic, frighteningly right-wing and likely to be lionised by a prick like Lime?

Yes.

'portillo'.

David Forbes
Four-Square Developments
Brewery Road
Romford

Dear David,

All systems go. I can now confidently predict that the site will become available inside a year. However, I must stress that this information is of the utmost secrecy, and must be kept strictly between ourselves at this stage. While a few rumours about the future of the place being in doubt could be trouble enough at my end, the discovery that anyone outside the Trust knew about this would be politically uncomfortable, to say the least . . .

Parlabane had seen enough. He copied the file and closed the machine down, then tucked the disk into his utility bra, removed the photo and its holder from in front of the video camera, and crawled to the window. He wiped his footprints from the sill, nimbly climbed out, shut the window with his foot, got hold of the cord and hauled himself back up to the roof.

No one had seen him, no one had heard him, and he had left no traces.

Except for forgetting to re-encrypt all of Lime's files.

TWENTY-TWO

'And all because, the lady loves . . .' Sarah sighed, watching Parlabane climb back in through the on-call room window.

'Fuck, I forgot the chocolates,' he said, wiping sweat from his forehead with his sleeve. He pulled the polo-neck off and unclipped the utility bra, removing the vital disk from it before folding it in two and stuffing it into his duffle bag.

He wiped at his back and chest with the discarded polo-neck. 'I'm always amazed that I can get this sweaty when it's so fucking cold out there. I'm manky as well. You'd think people would show burglars a wee bit more consideration and give their roofs a wipe down now and again. Don't suppose there's any chance of a shower?'

Sarah pulled a towel out from inside the wounded-looking chest of drawers and threw it to him.

'Follow me,' she said.

'What, you're supposed to use this place?' he asked, surveying the fetidly grotty bathroom. 'I'll need to have a wash after being in here. Not quite in the same class as the executive bathroom facilities over in that nice admin block.'

'You are not telling me they've got showers in there,' Sarah said gravely.

'Of course,' Parlabane continued. 'Possibly for washing Clive off you when he's finished showing you round. Shiny new Royal Doulton stuff. In case you're feeling in need of a freshen-up after strenuously sitting on your arse in a meeting for a few hours.'

He looked at the ceiling above the shower cubicle.

'Jesus. Look at that mould. Another fortnight and that thing'll have evolved into a higher life-form. I'm not sure I'm brave enough to have a shower in here. How do you manage?'

Sarah shrugged. 'It seems the lesser of two evils when you've just been up to your elbows in puke, blood and God knows what else trying to intubate some poor sod. It's still close, though.'

Parlabane looked again at the cubicle's interior, the cracks and lines running through it making it look like an Ordnance Survey map of the Himalayas. 'Well, I suppose it's also the lesser of two evils when you've got those tell-tale "just been up on the roof, breaking into the building" streaks of soot and grime on your face and hair. Have a seat and I'll tell you the latest while I'm at it. And I want you to jump in if the thing on the ceiling goes for me.'

Sarah locked the door then pulled down the lid of the toilet seat and sat down, while Parlabane started the water running and got undressed. She made great play of looking in the other direction while he was facing her, but stole a glance and smiled bashfully to herself when he turned his back to climb into the cubicle before pulling the plastic curtain across.

'So what's the story?' she asked.

'It's your George Romero's place,' he said, over the sound of the water on the ceramic. 'They're closing it.'

'The bastards. The fucking bastards. Well, it's not a huge surprise. They've always wanted to, but I didn't think they'd have the nerve just to go ahead and . . .' She shook her head. 'Bastards.'

'That's only the start. They're not just closing it, either – they're flogging it. They've got a buyer lined up, Capital Properties. I saw a memo from Stephen Lime to Timothy Winton – he's the chairman of the Trust but I think it's kind of a sinecure thing. Lime's the one with all the real clout.

'Anyway, they figure the site is worth about five mill, but Lime's recommending they accept a bid of three. This is because one, a done deal would take the steam out of closure protests, and two, the cash would put the Trust instantly into the black and make heroes out of the suits. And to those I think we can probably add three, Capital Properties will be making it well worth Lime's while to accept their bid. Maybe Winton's too. But it goes without saying that all the suits are being pretty furtive about the whole thing.'

'And well they might,' Sarah said. 'When they were seeking Trust status they gave assurances that they weren't going to close it, but we all knew that they'd find their way round to it soon enough.'

'Why would they want to? Is it always half-empty?'

'Quite the opposite. It's always completely full. Full of expensive geriatrics who can take up beds for months or even years at a time, and whose only financial contribution to this long-term care has been paying tax and National Insurance for the best part of fifty years on the understanding that they'd be looked after in precisely these circumstances.

'You see, Jack, no matter what they get their PR people to say, or whatever slogans they put under their logos, the Trusts don't give a shit about patient care. They only care about pounds, shillings and pence, and that's why they were set up in the first place, and filled with accountants and bankers and a whole legion of grey zeroes in suits. It was illustrated by that arsehole chief exec down south who said a doctor's first duty is to his Trust, then to himself, *then* to his patients. The name "Hippocrates" obviously never meant a great deal to this bloke. They see patients as commodities to be managed. Do it right and you turn them into cash cows. Do it wrong and they're financial liabilities.'

'How so?' asked Parlabane, spitting water.

'Well, ideally, what every trust in the UK would like is to have no geriatric patients, no medical patients, no one suffering from anything chronic and complicated, no one dying very slowly and expensively, no intensive care unit – just wards and wards full of young, fit patients awaiting elective surgery. Varicose vein ops. Palinoidal sinuses. Hernias. Quick, efficient, elective procedures with very little chance of post-op complication; easy to cost, easy to budget for. Elective procedures behave themselves on the balance sheets. Elective procedures make money. Geriatric admissions don't do either. Poor old crumbles with no relatives willing or able to look after them, whose condition is something as incurable as its symptoms are irreversible: old age.

'The more geriatric beds you have, the more of these money drains you must admit to your hospital. So everyone said that the first thing the Trust would do would be to shut the George Romero and open a scaled-down geriatric facility within the RVI. But they were pressed into giving assurances that they weren't going to close geriatric beds "while they remained in demand". Of course, that meant they would be trying out any way imaginable to reduce that demand, or reduce perception of that demand.

'The clinical staff got leaned on to turf patients out to their families or nursing homes as soon as they could stand up, and were basically told not to admit anyone who didn't look like they would drop dead in an economically viable length of time – say, two days. But no matter what they do, the demand will never be reduced. The trouble is that so many beds are taken up by long-term patients, who you just can't put in a home because their problems require proper, full-scale medical care. And not only can you not turf them out, but they reduce the number of beds available for shorter-term admissions. So presumably the Trust is going to sweeten the pill by saying that the money raised will help fund an "improved" geriatric unit within the RVI, which will have fewer beds but will deliver as much patient care "in real terms" as the GRH did. Is that it?'

'Well, not quite,' said Parlabane. 'Ow! Shampoo in my eyes. Can you hand me a towel?'

Sarah got up and lifted the off-white terrycloth sheet, holding it in front of the shower curtain. Parlabane's soggy and soapy hand appeared from round the mouldy, translucent plastic sheet and clawed the air until Sarah placed the towel in it.

'Ta,' he said, whipping it inside then popping it back out. 'They *are* planning to reduce the number of geriatric beds and bring them all within the RVI,' he said, 'but I think the sweetener is more likely to be that the property cash and the consequent saving will be better spent on "other ways of delivering patient care".'

Sarah snorted. 'Yeah. They'll make it sound like it'll all be going on dialysis equipment, when it'll really be buying a few more jobs for managers and some more fucking pot plants.'

'But the thing is, Sarah,' Parlabane continued, 'the memo from Lime said the "bed-usage situation" had changed, and that the number of geriatric patients *had* been reduced.'

The sound of the water stopped, and Parlabane pulled back the curtain, rubbing his face with the long towel, which swung back and forth across his body.

'It said something about . . . what was it? Natural wastage, which I took to mean patients snuffing it, and what was the other thing? I didn't quite follow it. Placing? Something like that?'

'Placement,' Sarah said, shaking her head. 'And that'll be the main thing. "Natural wastage", as he puts it, is negligible. Crumbles never die. Don't believe the hype about frailty. They live forever – and the crazier they are, the longer they live. So the only way to get rid of them is placement. Buff and turf, as the yanks say.'

'?' said Parlabane's look, amidst a flurry of towel and hair.

'Buff them up, make them look healthy-ish. Then turf them into a home and fill the bed with someone less trouble before they can be sent back.'

'Well here's where our suspected villain makes his appearance,' Parlabane said, wrapping the towel around his waist. 'And it looks like the big boss himself. There was a letter from Lime to a property developer down south, telling him the site would become available inside a year. Now, it's dodgy enough that he's noticed the patient levels are falling and he's tipping a property developer the wink about the site before anyone even knows there are plans to close it, but according to the computer, that letter predated all memos about GRH bed-usage by several months.'

'Oh my God,' Sarah said, staring blankly beyond Parlabane with a look that made him fear the mould monster from the ceiling had indeed decided to get territorial.

'What?' he said.

'Jeremy,' she breathed, sitting down helplessly on the toilet with a bump. 'I've just worked out his role in this sordid affair. Jesus.'

She stared into space, Parlabane waiting in excruciating limbo for her to collect her thoughts and elaborate.

'Buffing and turfing on a grand scale,' she said. 'Lime was paying him to declare total crumbles fit enough to go into nursing homes. It wouldn't matter if they collapsed in a gibbering, incontinent heap as soon as they were out the back of the ambulance, because by that time the bed would have been filled with a shorter-term admission, or more probably closed altogether.'

'But wouldn't it damage his professional reputation if patients he'd declared fit turned out to be complete messes?'

'Not necessarily. The thing with crumbles is that they can *genuinely* switch from fitness to decrepitude or vice versa overnight. You'll get some old dear with a few of her pages stuck together, brought in from a nursing home because of a chest infection. She looks like she's at death's door for a week, then one morning you come in and she's drinking her tea and shrieking at imaginary cats. Equally, she might get her strength built up and appear to have made a complete

145

recovery, then cack it the first night she's back in the home. The only damage Jeremy's reputation would suffer would be if he sent a few like that to the same home and they noticed whose name was on the paperwork each time.'

'And what happens to the patient, now that the bed's no longer available?'

'The nursing home has to get on the phone and try to get her a bed somewhere else – in another hospital, and therefore in another Trust. Jeremy reduces the long-term patient levels and they get to close the GRH and sell up to Kickback Properties Inc.

'But why kill him?' she wondered aloud. 'He must have been blackmailing Lime – taking money for clearing the wards *then* threatening to blow the gaffe about the whole thing unless he gave him more.'

'It's more likely he was just killed *in case* he ever said anything,' said Parlabane. 'No blackmail, just covering tracks. Because I feel the stakes for Lime could be a lot higher than putting the Trust in the black and scoring a few K on the side from the property deal. He was talking to that company down south about the site a long time ago, before anyone knew it was remotely likely to become available, and the name of that developer is not the same as the one that's bidding for the GRH. I'd be very surprised if Capital Properties didn't turn out to be a front for a joint venture between Four-Square Developments and a Mr Stephen Lime, which would further explain why he's recommending the Trust sells the site at a knock-down price. Where is this place anyway?'

Sarah unlocked the door. 'Come on back to the room and get dressed. You can see it from there.'

Dawn was thinking about breaking, at the stage where it was rolling about under the sheets after its alarm had gone off, weighing up the pros and cons of getting out of bed. There was a glow of light from beyond the horizon, tinting the city in faint, shadowy hues, like a huge room lit by a lamp with a dimmer switch.

The castle cut the skyline with a tetchy cragginess, ill-tempered elderly resident of the district with a fragile tolerance of the newcomers to its neighbourhood.

And not far beyond the longest spines of its shadow, just past the borders of the Old Town, in the vicinity of law courts, local government, big business and one of Europe's busiest tourist honeypots, sat a crappy wee spread-out collection of prefabricated, low-rise bus shelters posing as a geriatric hospital.

'Ah,' said Parlabane, looking out of the window.

'Get the picture?' Sarah asked, redundantly.

'I'm thinking international class hotel with extensive conference facilities, maybe a shopping complex,' he said. 'Underground parking, centrally located office spaces, *very* exclusive residential development . . . whatever. Except that the deal's off if some wee scrote of a doctor opens his gub.

'Acres of prime site in the centre of one of Europe's most prestigious and historic capital cities for three mill. Now *that's* a bargain worth killing for.'

TWENTY-THREE

'Aw for fuck's sake.'

There was a sharp tutting noise from the staircase behind where McGregor stood in the doorway.

'Oh, sorry. Excuse the language, Mrs eh . . .'

'Kinross.'

'Aye. Sorry. It's not a pretty sight.'

'He's away then,' said the wee woman, peering up to the landing where the policeman and woman stood.

'Afraid so.'

McGregor had instantly regretted releasing the missing digit detail to the press. He had had no idea there could be so many nine-fingered males in the Lothians, and the cooperative public hadn't let the 'at least 6'5" tall' part of the description deter them from reporting every bastarding one of them, never mind the specification that it was the right index finger that was lacking, and not the left pinkie, right thumb or either arm.

The call had come at about ten o'clock that night, after an endlessly irritating day, and he had feared the worst when the switchboard operator told him what it was in connection with and he heard the prim, elderly tones at the other end.

He had listened to the part about the nine-fingered man staying in her guest house with stoic patience, inclining gradually away from professional politeness when she started on about him killing her dog and trying to fake its accidental death in next door's garden. When she said she had him tied to his bed in a room upstairs, McGregor was about to send a car round to pick her up and let her consider the folly of wasting police time at leisure in the surroundings of a particularly smelly cell. But then she told him about the envelope with the newspaper, the hair dye and the gloves inside, and he was on the phone to Dalziel forthwith, telling her to get in her car and meet him at the guest house immediately.

They had sent Callaghan round the back to cover that escape route as they were met at the front door by the betweeded landlady, Mrs Kinross, who had been looking out for them there. Then they had ventured silently up to the first-floor landing, where the old lady's key refused to enter the lock.

'He's jammed something in it,' Dalziel whispered. 'Which does tend to suggest he's not tied up any more.' She advised Mrs Kinross to move back downstairs as there could be trouble.

Then the radio cut in, Callaghan informing them that a first-floor window at the back was both broken and wide open, and that there were what looked very much like blood spots on the flagstones below.

Dalziel received Mrs Kinross's permission to force an entry, and after a nod from McGregor, broke the lock off the door with two crashingly loud kicks, which precipitated pyjama-clad appearances from several of Mrs Kinross's other guests.

Then McGregor had switched on the light and surveyed the scene.

There was a big puddle of fresh spew spread out on the carpet, between the radiator and the foot of the bed. The window was indeed open and broken, with blood smeared greasily over the shards that were still in place. And taking up most of the room was the bed, a big, brass-framed affair with the unusual decoration of lengths of rope attached to each of its four supporting posts. Its quilt lay discarded on the floor to one side, below a heavily bloodstained pillow, to reveal a further and larger streaky mess of damp red on the sheet underneath.

'Do you think it was the man you're after?' asked Mrs Kinross from the stairs.

McGregor hit the smirking Dalziel with a glower like stormclouds coming over the Ochils.

'Don't say a word,' he warned her quietly. 'Not a fucking word.'

Darren was woken from his uncomfortable sleep by the metallic grind of a freight train rolling lumberingly past and slicing his left hand off. His soul-shattered scream of agony and despair was lost to the surrounding buildings amidst the noise of the train's horn and the heavy rumble of its passing.

He looked at the wasted stump, spurting blood like something out of a cheap video, and burst into tears. His livelihood had just disappeared before he was even awake, and there was no facility for disability benefits in his line of work. That was his blade hand, his cutting hand.

With the train slowly slouching its way off ahead of him, he stumbled along the track and found it, lying on a sleeper like Thing, palm down and ragged at the wrist, his sovereign rings glinting up at him from each of the four fingers. He bent down and picked it up with his four-digited right hand, then staggered mournfully back to his bag at the edge of the track, where he sat down with it in his lap and sobbed, bleeding steadily from the truncated forearm.

He ripped the sleeve off the jacket of his shellsuit – his fucking favourite shellsuit – to make a tourniquet, as the blood showed no sign of letting up. He wrapped it as tightly as he could around his forearm and tied a double shoelace knot in it. It was agony, but at least it worked, kind of.

It had been her fault. That old bitch at the B&B.

He thought of the men he'd taken in his time. Big men, hard cunts. Kicked their fucking heads in. Bladed them, cut their throats. He thought of that tart, the one Lime had paid him for. That had been his first pro job, his start. She had been fit. He'd fucked her first. Nice. Mostly men after that. Sometimes fights, sometimes just personal, sometimes jobs, once his rep had got round and the work started to come in from all sorts.

But now it was over because he had been well and truly fucked up by some tiny old Jock granny of a landlady.

He had woken up in the semi-darkness, vaguely aware of someone hauling him about, but too fuzzy to quite work out what was going on. Through the hazy mist of his half-shut eyes he could see her little figure, both her hands clasping his left arm across his chest at the right-hand side of the bed. He felt dizzy and uncoordinated, as if something was trying to force him back into unconsciousness.

The quilt was on the floor and his other limbs were already tied securely to the brass bedposts. His legs had been crossed and his right foot was secured to the left bedpost, his left to the right. His right arm was pulled across him and secured to the left post behind his head, and the old cow had looped some rope round the fourth post and was getting ready to tie his wrist to it.

Ordinarily, he could have swatted her away with one shake of that arm, but his limbs all felt unusually heavy, and even though he got his hand free of her grip, it just swung erratically and slowly around in front of him.

'Amgifackikillyou,' he spluttered, still swinging at the trim figure beside the bed. She bent down, not ducking, but picking something up from the floor.

'Recognise this?' she asked, but he could only make out a grey shape between her hands. He strained his neck but that just made everything in his field of vision swim lurchingly in front of him.

'Why don't you take a closer look?' she said, and biffed him in the face with it, breaking his nose and burying his head back into the pillow. Then she dropped the heavy object around his middle, crushing his balls, which had been sitting on top of his crossed legs inside his underpants. He gave a choked moan as the blood from his nose ran into his mouth.

Mrs Kinross took his hand again, slipped a loop of rope around it and pulled it tight, fastening him completely to the bed.

'It's the stone you placed over my wee Ruffle's head, to cover up the fact that you had *murdered* him,' she hissed at Darren. 'But I know you did it, and I know who you are and what else you did. You're the one who murdered that young Dr Ponsonby. Well that boy's father treated my Hamish, God rest him, and so it's going to give me every pleasure to go down the stairs right this very minute and call the police. You're going to pay the penalty, my boy. Cross a Kinross and it's your loss, as Hamish's father used to say.'

And with that she lifted the stone, went out and locked the door.

He pulled at all four of his bonds, but the knots were strong and efficient. Old cunt must have been in the Girl Guides. Maybe she started the fucking Girl Guides. However, he could get a tiny bit of slack in the ropes securing his arms if he pulled his body up the bed, although it practically cut off the blood supply to his feet.

In his woozy and now pained quasi-consciousness, he remembered his knife, and hoped she hadn't discovered it and removed it from under the pillow. He leaned to one side and strained his neck, trying to edge his head under the cotton-wrapped foam. At first he merely succeeded in squashing it against the brass frame behind him, but eventually it flipped up and landed on his face, from where he was able to wriggle

151

it off his coupon and then use his elbow to nudge it out of the way.

The knife was still there, the tip of the blade pointing towards his face as it lay on the sheet. With an almighty effort he was able to strain close enough to it to get the end of the blade between his teeth, unfortunately sharp side in, gently cutting the corners of his mouth.

He needed to get his teeth into the handle, so he pulled his head back around until the knife was sitting at forty-five degrees to the mattress, blade pointing up, then attempted to gently slide his mouth down the metal to the hilt. However, as soon as he tried to do this, he felt the knife slipping backwards, threatening to fall away from his face and maybe even off the bed, from where it would be impossible to retrieve. Therefore, he had to maintain a grip on it with his lips as he drew his mouth along it, slicing deep slits at both corners until he was able to bite into the handle.

Then he swung his head back around and in a nodding, sawing motion, cut through the rope that bound his left hand to the right bedpost, all the time the strain and friction pulling the cuts wider and deeper at the edges of his mouth. Once his hand was released, he gripped the knife and sliced through the rope securing his other hand in barely a stroke, then bent quickly forward to cut his feet free, a movement that made the room spin sickeningly around him.

He rubbed at his burnt ankles and knelt up on the mattress, at which point the revolving motion of his surroundings caused him to fall forward over the bottom of the bedframe and vomit voluminously on to the floor. The acid content of the puke burnt searingly into his cuts, but he had to stifle a cry of pain in case the old bat was listening.

She must have drugged him. That's what it felt like. Must have been her fucking rotten dinner. He could remember dying his hair – Christ, the smell – then eating his tea, then feeling hellish knackered and deciding on an early night.

Cow.

When he stood up, the room had slowed its rotations, but the hazy, heavy, lethargic feeling was back. He bumped drunkenly against the walls as he put on some clothes and gathered some vital belongings into his plastic satchel, such as his knife, wallet and portable – for fuck's sake don't forget the portable.

152

Then he had staggered erratically to the door and thought about pulling the wardrobe in front of it, but reckoned in this state he'd only pull it down on top of himself. He settled for taking the key from the wardrobe door and jamming it into the lock so that the Filth would have to fuck around outside for that bit longer.

The tiredness came in waves, washing over him and threatening every time to drag him under, but he had to fight it, had to stay awake and on his feet. He trudged sluggishly back across to the window, one foot slipping as another wave crashed into him, and staggered forward, putting his left hand out, palm-up, to steady himself. It crashed through the pane, ripping his shellsuit and the flesh underneath right up to the elbow, and leaving lots of twinkling little splinters sticking out of his palm and his sleeve.

What the fuck. He didn't even have *time* to worry about it.

He climbed out of the window with his bag over one shoulder, and got halfway down the drainpipe before the next wave shook the world just enough for him to lose the grip of his four-fingered right hand and fall painfully to the ground below, putting both knees through the black material of his shellsuit and grazing them on the stone.

Like an animal crazed by an irrational mix of pain and sheer survival instinct, he picked himself up and charged forward, bouncing off a couple of clothes-poles like a pinball until he made it to the wall at the back.

Darren chucked the bag over and hauled himself up behind it, rolling off the top and on to the mercifully soft mud on the other side.

It was comfortable there, despite the cuts and bruises and his aching bollocks and his broken nose and the sting of puke in the corners of his artificially widened mouth. He felt like he could just doze off, maybe just for ten minutes, then he'd be all right to carry on.

But there's no alarm clock can beat the sound of sirens for clearing your head and getting you on your feet, and as he heard the wail from maybe a couple of streets away, he was already grabbing his bag and picking his way through the bushes and trees behind the row of prissy little gardens.

After about a hundred yards he came to a metal railing, which ran for about twelve feet where the muddy, wooded passage came to an end, hitting a pavement at ninety degrees. Directly across the road was a narrow little lane, leading up to some grim and decrepit-looking factories he had seen when he had been walking around trying to find a place to dump Ruffle. There was a gap in the railings where two bars had been bent, probably by kids going through to play on the rope-swings he had passed. Bless 'em. He stuck his head between the bars and made sure there was no one around, then squeezed through the gap and stopped between two parked cars. Another check, then he bent low and scrambled across the street and headed up the lane.

To his enormous disappointment, the decrepit-looking factories turned out to be going concerns, and were securely locked up. One of them didn't have bars on its windows, but even if he broke in, he didn't want to be discovered by some fucker on the early shift in the morning.

The lane wound around between the buildings, and he followed it desperately, breathlessly jogging along, occasionally losing his footing on the loose gravel or bumping into a wall as the tiredness nudged the earth a couple of feet to one side for a second.

The lane bent hard around to the right for about thirty yards, flanked by the kind of huge, round steel bins he remembered from outside school dinners, and up ahead he could see that it was leading out on to another street. The centrifugal effect of running round a bend combined with the endless waves of nausea sent him sprawling to the floor, where he was wretchingly sick again. But then, looking up, he saw that there was a passage leading off the lane to the left, and more railings at the end.

With a low grunt, he struggled back to his feet and meandered half-blindly down to the railings, from where to his grateful relief he could just make out a grassy bank leading down to what looked like a pathway, twenty or so feet below, which led off optimistically into the distance.

Diamond.

He was saved.

With a burst of renewed energy, he climbed on to the top of the railings, then jumped down on the other side, whereupon he lost his footing and fell backwards, rolling at speed down the grass embankment and off the end of a four-foot wall he hadn't noticed was at the bottom of it. By the time he hit the ground and came to a stop he was unconscious, flat out on the gravel at the edge of a council railway, five yards from the mouth of a tunnel, his left wrist resting on the metal line.

TWENTY-FOUR

Parlabane should have been happy as a pig in shit. He was knee-deep in evidence of extremely unpalatable activities and had a porcine appetite for just such matter.

Anna had called back within an hour. She worked at Companies House in London and still owed him a few favours. If Parlabane was being completely honest they were probably all sexual favours, but what the hell, this was payment in kind. She was an excruciatingly petite bluestocking with a fruitily upper-class accent; intelligent, educated, charming and almost irritatingly attractive, but with the inexplicable flaw of a sexual craving for short-arsed Glaswegian investigative journalists who could break into hotel rooms.

Fortunately, she was way too smart to get involved any deeper than the physical with such a social, emotional – bollocks – all-round liability as Parlabane, for which he was fairly glad too. Anna was clever, sussed, streetwise, connected and going places, but he suspected that she was also – in a quaintly English way – completely fucking bonkers not too far beneath her exquisite surface.

He had met her doing some unusually legit research, just checking out who owned what as he mentally assembled the players in his next front-page tragedy-cum-farce. He had been going through a document at a table in the public reading room when she came over to ask for it back. The librarian who had given him it had failed to notice a message on his computer saying that she required it instantly, and she had come down in person to retrieve it. Parlabane was, of course, suspicious as hell, the old conspiracy glands reflexively kicking in, wondering whether someone would be skewering him with a poisoned umbrella on the tube train home. However, his thoughts were totally sidetracked by what happened when their eyes met and stayed met for a few seconds.

Parlabane believed a little in sexual chemistry; there had certainly been plenty of times he had looked at a woman and felt a primal urge that went way beyond mere aesthetic appreciation. When he looked at Anna, however, even aesthetic appreciation was tempered by the feeling that she was not only out of his league but unnervingly scary. What utterly derailed him, though, was the sudden awareness that *she* was feeling the primal urges and he was the object. Or should that have been prey?

She said he could keep the document as long as he returned it to her in an hour. When he asked where she would be she told him the name of a bar two streets away.

He couldn't remember quite how the hotel thing started, even whose idea it was, only that it followed the weirdest conversation of his life and that the first hotel was the one across the road from the bar.

After that they shagged their way around maybe a dozen hotels – different each time – and only got caught twice. Anna would watch at the front desk for people going out for the evening (or afternoon), spotting the room number on the key they handed in. Then she'd go and have a nonchalant drink in the bar while Parlabane nipped upstairs and picked the lock.

The first time they got caught they managed to brass-neck it and convince the astonished elderly American couple that it was *they* who must have mistakenly got off the lift at the wrong floor and intruded on the room above them. Bloody locks must be useless if any key can open them. Watch for your valuables. By the time the oldsters had descended a floor and failed to open the door down there, Parlabane and Anna were in a Covent Garden pub.

The other time was less smooth, and involved a naked sprint down an external fire escape in January and getting dressed in the back of a hackney speeding along Shaftesbury Ave, the lights of Piccadilly Circus briefly illuminating Anna's elegant little breasts before they were covered up by her inside-out silk blouse.

There was no financial reason for it. Just good, clean fetishism. It happened about once a month, though they met for drinks more often. Anna had two separate, 'proper' relationships throughout its duration, about which Parlabane felt vaguely guilty, but as she clearly didn't it wasn't worth getting too upset over. It ended when she decided to make the second of those relationships legally legitimate, but as many hotels had started using card-lock systems, Parlabane had observed that there wasn't much future in it anyway.

157

He got an invite to the wedding, though. He didn't make the actual ceremony as he was in court that afternoon on one of his burglary charges, but he did catch the end of the speeches and most of the reception. He also nipped upstairs and broke into the bridal suite to leave his present on the bed.

She liked that.

He had found her in familiarly buoyant form when he called.

'You only phone when you want something,' she chided him.

'Yeah, well so did you,' he replied.

'Now now.'

He had fed her the names of all the companies who had won large supply contracts from the Midlothian NHS Trust, plus Capital Properties, and the names of Lime and his colleagues on the board.

'Well, Jack darling, I'm sure you'll be shattered as ever to hear that it's another grim picture of sleaze and corruption.'

'Talk dirty to me, baby. It hurts so good.'

'You know I love it too. Anyway, I think I could work out the board's power structure for myself just on the strength of who's been awarded which pickings. At the shallow end you've got Elliot Michaels, poor lamb, who co-owns Evergreen Indoors – pot plant supplies and "maintenance" – through a holding company called Mainstay Ltd.

'Up top you've got Mr Lime and Mr Winton, who both have large stakes in IT Systems, the computer supplier, which appears to have only begun trading shortly before the contract was awarded. Again, both are too smart to have their names listed directly as owners. Winton holds his share through Churchfield Ltd, Lime at two removes, through Greenbank, which owns Infotech, which holds the stake and which was set up very shortly before IT Systems.

'In between you've got Toby Childs, Cedric Baker and Penelope Gainsborough, who indirectly own or have a major share in, respectively, Ladywell Mercedes, Icon Interiors and Red Letter Stationery.

'All rather tawdry, really, and disappointingly familiar. That lot might get you a few inches in *Private Eye* or cause a small stir locally if you flog it to the regional rags, but it's not exactly earth-shattering. It's not even necessarily illegal. I do hope there's more to the tale.'

'Hey. It's me, remember? What about Capital Properties?'

'A merry dance, Jack, a merry dance. Four-Square Developments owns half, run by a chap named David Forbes. That part was simple enough. The other half can be traced back to your Mr Lime, but only through a tortuously complicated maze of ghost firms and front companies. I'd be most interested to see this chap's tax returns, and I'd be rather astonished if he was actually paying any.

'Basically, Jack darling, you can't completely hide the fact that you own something – but you can certainly make sure no one notices it by accident. And there are a few tricks you can do to put people like your nosy self off the scent. Mr Lime has engaged a full repertoire of these, to the extent that if you had only given me his name or the name of Capital Properties, I would not have linked one with the other if I was here all night.

'The other worthies on the board have covered themselves against accidental discovery or speculative angling, but with regard to Capital Properties, Mr Lime is hiding in some very thick undergrowth indeed. I trust you suspect he's up to something truly disgusting?'

'Disgusting enough for him to have had one person murdered so far. Look, can you fax the documentation to Duncan McLean at the Edinburgh *Evening Capital*?'

'Of course. Consider it done. But do be careful, Jack,' she said softly.

'It's me, Anna. I'm always careful.'

'Hmm. Well just think about what it felt like to be barefoot in the snow in a Soho backstreet and remember that your idea of careful isn't always enough.'

The problem was Sarah, and another strange look.

Not like Anna's look, thank Christ, but a moment when their eyes had met that morning over her kitchen table, after he'd made them breakfast. They had returned from the hospital around half-nine, her on-call and his 'research' complete, and Sarah had taken a shower while he brewed some coffee and did his worst for their cholesterol levels with the grill and frying pan.

Sarah had wandered back into the kitchen in a fluffy white dressing gown, patting at her damp red hair with a small towel. When he handed her the plate of good, honest, Scottish

159

heart disease, she had leaned over in her chair, bending down to fetch some salt from a low cupboard. And he simply did not possess the mortal strength not to look as her dressing gown fell open enough to momentarily reveal her right breast. Mercifully, she didn't catch him, as what he had seen had made him too fragile to even attempt to defend himself.

It had caught him off-guard, had its impact before all his policing and defence mechanisms could kick in and neutralise it. Sticking to the task, concentrating on the matter in hand, trying to be professional and trustworthy had made him blank out how attractive he found Sarah, had denied him any real reaction to it. But now there it was, sneaking up on him and shouting 'Boo!'.

Breakfast helped him compose himself. He stole a few glances at her face as she tucked into her eggs, enjoying the strange thrill of seeing someone so familiar in a suddenly different light. And with each glance he felt better, more confident that he could deal with it, that it wasn't going to be a problem.

Aesthetic appreciation.

Huh.

'So is this it for you, Jack?' she had asked. 'Running around, breaking into places, finding out the big secret, catching the villain then disappearing again?'

'You make it sound so irresponsible,' he had replied.

It was a clever joke. It made Sarah laugh politely and it deflected the question. Deferred the question? And acknowledged the question.

Maybe it was even two questions: 'this can't last forever, so where are you going?'; and 'who are you, Jack?'

He had glanced up, suddenly found her looking at him and not looking away when their eyes met. The look was there when she knew he wasn't watching, but she had not desisted when she knew he was. It was a look he had seldom, maybe never seen before. It was a look of interest, concern and affection, but was greater than the sum of these.

Houston we have a problem.

The sudden appreciation that she had feelings for him precipitated the even more dizzying realisation that he had feelings for her. So many other questions had occupied his conscious thoughts all the time they had spent together, but now that most of them were answered, it was as if his brain had backlogged an array of emotions that were now top of the pending pile.

Nestling among them was the feeling of horrified guilt that he had unthinkingly embroiled her in activities that could leave her exposed before some very dangerous men. But what chiefly occupied his mind were re-runs of moments between them, looks, conversation, and meanings he had missed or deferred contemplating. He had known disastrous relationships that had started through some intensity, working together, misinterpreting a close professional relationship for something deeper and discovering the truth in an uncomfortable unravelling later on. This had been the opposite: working so closely on their investigation had obscured what was genuinely developing between them.

It had been a long moment, that look. A moment of many possibilities. He had a great track record for reckless abandon in emotional and sexual matters. He could have walked around the table and kissed her. He could have acknowledged what might lie before them. Instead he talked about evidence and proof and the torture of knowledge and all that bollocks.

Because in that same moment, when he sensed the possible depth of his feelings for Sarah, he realised that those feelings were also the reason why he shouldn't pull her in any closer.

She had offered a potential answer to 'where are you going?', but it was 'who are you, Jack?' that was the obstacle. She had no real idea who he was, and he hadn't spent too much time contemplating that question himself of late.

That was the other thing he had been too busy running around to think about. Or had kept himself too busy running around to think about.

TWENTY-FIVE

What was it, less than a fortnight?

Just a matter of days. And another lifetime.

Another city, half a world away. Remembered not as if in a distant past, not even as if it had happened to someone else, but as a scene in a movie, in that city of movies.

Unfortunately the director seemed to have been Quentin Tarantino rather than, say, Zalman King.

A strange scent in the nostrils, stronger all the time. The feeling of being on to something big but not knowing what it was. A lot of corpses and the broken traces of a connection; like discovering short stretches of an overgrown path through a dense forest, but not yet able to see where those stretches came from or were leading to.

Lieutenant Larry Freeman had been nervous. Larry was about seven feet tall with shoulders 'the size of a Kansas prairie', as his wife put it, a frightening sight in black shades and a black, bald head. And Larry was never nervous.

'Something in the air then, big man?'

'Uh-huh,' he had said slowly in that rumbling burr you could feel in your own diaphragm. 'Remember man, cops like the sound of openin' a fresh can of beer when the case is closed. The sound of openin' a fresh can of worms don't fill their heart with joy, know what I'm sayin'? Now I ain't sayin' there's dirty cops in my precinct, but cops gotta talk to snitches and there's gotta be some give and take. And no news travels faster than a secret.

'You gotta be careful what yo askin' and who yo askin', Scotland. Somebody starts playin' join-the-dots with a bunch of random stiffs and a whole lotta people get trigger-happy. Maybe you ain't even connectin' anythin' to them or to stiffs they got anythin' to do with, but they don't know that and they ain't gonna stop to ask if they get you in their sights.'

'You're saying I should back off? Forget it all?'

'That's up to you, man. Maybe it's too late to back off.

But you better be watchin' your back. I was you, I'd get me a gun.'

Parlabane shook his head.

'You know how I feel about guns. I couldn't carry one of those things around with me, forget about it.'

'Yeah, but I'd have one all the same. Keep it where I could get to it in a hurry. I got a spare one in the john. In a plastic bag taped under the cistern lid. Someone catches me off-guard at home, I got a chance if he lets me take a leak or I can just make it to the bathroom. Mitch Gacy keeps one in his ice box.'

'What, so he's got a chance if the bad guy asks for a beer? You're all fucking crazy.'

'You ain't from LA, Jack.'

In a way, it was the hangover that saved his life.

He had been at Tom and Juan's place along on Melrose, and a few bottles of red with and after dinner had led to a single bottle of Glenfiddich, three glasses and total carnage.

Once upon a time, whisky made him sleep, but not these days. It would set his mind in motion, counteracting the soporific properties of all that full-bodied Californian bottled blood, and he lay awake for a while on the couch after T and J had retired to their bedroom. He popped in a couple of their videos, looking for distractions to stop the room lurching long enough to let him lie back without feeling sick.

Cheers guys, he thought. How unstereotypical. Gay porn and three hours of the fucking Golden Girls.

He figured he must have dozed off some time after four, woken by the sun through the blinds at about eight. It was a chastising, unforgiving sun with a hard-on for Temperance, shaking him awake to face the consequences of his sinful alcoholic excess, and amplifying his headache with its malignantly cheery brightness.

He grabbed his leather jacket and headed delicately out to the car, which he had no intention of attempting to drive. Instead, he retrieved his shades from the glove compartment and placed them gently over his eyes before engaging in the ill-advised, Bradburyesque deviance of walking home. It took about twenty minutes, and every step was a thudding, throbbing, echoing torture.

He wanted water. Not LA's desalinated pish, and not mineral water, but *water* water, freezing cold out a Glasgow

163

tap. Waattur. His joints ached, his hands trembled, his throat stung and his head was undergoing an interior re-fit.

There was a Scotsman, a Mexican, an American and a bottle of whisky.

But it was no joke.

He felt so ill, so delicate, that as he crossed Sweetzer he decided if a car suddenly pulled out he'd just have to let it hit him, as he didn't have the energy or reflexes to get out of the way.

That was what saved him. Not reacting, not acknowledging.

He pulled out his keys and fumbled at the lock, his stomach lurching a little as if suddenly impatient at the thought of the proximity of a familiar toilet-bowl. He shut the door behind him and slouched half-blindly towards the bathroom.

His limbs were too heavy to leap in fright or run, and his neck was so stiff from T and J's couch that it had barely started to turn before he was able to stop it and carry on through the doorway. That was the moment that really saved his life, the real act of nerve and courage, not what happened next.

Because there was a figure in his kitchen, a human shape he had sensed out of the corner of his eye as he passed that doorway on the way to the bathroom. A reaction, an acknowledgement would, he later understood, have killed him.

Parlabane peered terrified through the tiny slit at the hinge and had his fears confirmed. There was a pot-bellied, middle-aged, balding and moustachioed white man in a crumpled dark suit and a sweaty white shirt standing now in the hallway before the bathroom door, looking down and tightening the silencer to the end of an automatic. He was just waiting there, silently and patiently, to kill him when he emerged again after his final piss, dump or whatever.

He felt he might pass out but managed somehow to find some fraction of composure. He needed to work out his options but realised that he was on a rapidly ticking time limit: if the hitman got suspicious he'd shoot the door down or just shoot him through it.

Before he had time to evaluate the wisdom of it, he started to sing to himself, to present the relaxed mood of someone just going to the bog in the comfort of their home, oblivious of the impending death that awaits after that last flush.

'*I was sitting in the Hollywood Hawaiian hotel . . .*'

164

The song had been close to the surface in his mind on the walk home because of the stuff about the angry sun, but as the first line issued from his mouth he was panickedly analysing the remainder of the lyrics in case they contained some kind of give-away Freudian slip. 'Save us from the powder and the finger', for instance, would not have been a wise ditty to render. And 'Thirty years in the bathroom' might also have betrayed his true thoughts.

He cursed the fact that his bathroom had no windows, but then realised that if it did he'd probably be already dead, as the hitman would have checked for possible escape routes beforehand and just shot him through the door rather than risk him getting away.

'All the salty Margaritas in Los Angeles . . .'

He was fucked.

What was the saying? There's no such thing as an atheist in a foxhole? Something like that.

Typical ignorant Christians. As if the non-belief in God was a posture, a luxury, some kind of decadent modern affectation, rather than a completely irreversible understanding. Truth was, you did get atheists in foxholes; they were just even more acutely, agonisingly aware of the inescapable reality of their predicament.

'I predict this motel will be standin' . . .'

And this one knew that if you were down to your last hope and your last hope was God, then there was nothing left. But his last hope wasn't God, not unless God was a seven-foot bald cop named Larry.

'Don't the trees look like crucified thieves?'

That night. That night when Larry had warned him, talking about guns and secrets and snitches. Larry had just shown up at the house, on spec, which he never did. And what had he said as he left, after a couple of beers and some pizza?

'That gun shit, Jack. Forget it. You're right. Just crazy LA cops. You don't need to worry about getting a gun. Hear what I'm sayin'?'

Larry had come round because he was worried, but left telling *him* not to.

'You don't need to worry about getting a gun.'

One last hope.

'Don't you feel like desperadoes under the eaves . . .'

165

He flushed the toilet to cover the sound and lifted the cistern lid, barely daring to breathe, almost unable to look.

Jesus. His future – life or death – was metaphorically in his hands, but literally what was in his hands was part of a cludgie. There was an illustrative image about desperation in there somewhere, but he couldn't really afford to think about that right then.

He turned the lid over to reveal a blue plastic package, sealed firmly air- and watertight, taped to the underside of the vitreous china. He pulled it away and replaced the lid before the cistern began to refill, as that would have made too loud and too odd a sound.

'I was listening to the air conditioner hum . . .'

Parlabane turned on both taps and put the plug down in the wash-hand basin, the splashing sound and his humming covering the noise of him removing the 9mm Beretta automatic from the bag, clicking off the safety and chambering the first round, as Larry had taught him on the couple of occasions he had taken him down to the range.

The water still tinkling and splashing, he delicately returned to the slit and saw that the intruder was still standing there, but now legs apart, gun aimed at the door at head-height.

This was not a time for negotiations, and neither did he fancy his chances in a Mexican stand-off.

There had been no God to save him.

Neither would there be one to forgive him.

He lay face-down on the floor, aimed the gun at an upward angle, closed his eyes and fired five times in a second and a half.

He looked up at the door. There were no holes any further up than those made by his own gun. Remaining understandably cautious, he glimpsed through the slit again. The man was lying bloodstained and motionless on the floor. He couldn't see the gun but he could see an empty hand, and that was good enough.

Parlabane opened the door and emerged, unexpectedly alive, from the bathroom. The hitman, very unexpectedly dead, lay bleeding messily on to the hall carpet from several wounds in the chest area.

Fuck this for a game of soldiers, thought Parlabane.

He packed his essentials and whatever else he could fit into a large suitcase and made some long-distance phone calls.

Then he called a cab, asking it to pick him up in front of the hotel round the corner.

He snuck out the back door, over the fence, down an alley and on to Fountain.

None of the direct flights to the UK left until four or five, flying overnight to arrive around the following lunchtime. He couldn't afford to wait around LA – and certainly not LAX – until then, so he took the first cheap flight east, which was to Newark, and got a connection to London from there.

He could lie low in Edinburgh, get his head together. Maybe work out how he might use his talents to make a living that did not involve the risk of being set up with drugs by bent cops or shot by hired killers.

TWENTY-SIX

Sometimes you could find yourself free-wheeling, coasting in neutral. Not dynamically going after something, no goals, not even striving to avoid a certain outcome. And it was fine for a while. Like free-wheeling, you could just let the wind blow through your hair and watch the view breeze past, relaxing, powered by the momentum of your previous efforts.

Not worrying where you were going.

She took her name back.

Dr Slaughter.

'You can't be Dr Slaughter. What will the patients say? And your superiors certainly won't see the funny side. Interviewing consultants can be nervous about the slightest thing.'

The profession was noted for engendering a dark sense of humour, but the truth was that the laughter stopped if the joke was on medicine. Taking an open delight in the macabre inappropriateness of your name scored only frowns.

She had never been Dr Slaughter. She had listened to Jeremy, she had swallowed it all. The over-riding need for respectability, professional dignity. The sacrilege of flippancy. It was one thing to be born Sarah Slaughter, but to retain the name after marriage would send out bad signals. And to retain the name when the alternative was the revered and door-opening Ponsonby would be an unthinkable perversity. An ingratitude even, for this privileged opportunity.

As she was married before her first house job, she was Dr Ponsonby from the off.

Becoming Dr Slaughter had been like re-starting her career, doing it this time all for herself, on her own terms. She had the flat to herself, no more worries and no distractions, allowing her to concentrate on *her* job, *her* career, and she had the energy of someone eager to make up for lost time.

Her social life wasn't exactly a whirl, as she soon discovered that people she had thought were her and Jeremy's friends were really only Jeremy's friends being polite to the good man's wife. So she made new friends, real friends. But mainly she hit the books. Head down, working her way through the three-part FRCA, while picking up experience and respect on the job.

So that was the career part worked out. It was the life part that would require pedal power when the free-wheeling stopped.

For too many that she knew and had seen, the career was their life. Monastically dedicated to their profession, giving it priority one now and forever. Maybe marrying an obsequious wee nursie somewhere along the line to bear a couple of baby doctors to play with and be proud of when distraction was called for.

For Sarah, there would have to be something else, she always knew. Another relationship, perhaps. What happened with Jeremy hadn't made her forswear men or marriage completely (although medics quite definitely needed not apply); if anything it had often made her yearn for what a good relationship *could* be.

However, it had been a problem she felt she had earned the right to procrastinate over, and for a pleasant time she had. But the pleasure of free-wheeling waned with the growth of her awareness of doing so, and she had found herself unsure of what the future held, insufficiently motivated to attempt to shape it, and suspecting that her inaction was inviting the intervention of fate.

The death of Jeremy should have been an ending, of sorts, whatever questions it left unanswered.

That it should be murder certainly marked the hand of fate, and she knew she had been willing to pick up whatever cards it dealt.

But was aiding and abetting a guy like Jack Parlabane, complicity in the burglary of her employers' offices (and the hacking of their computer system) in the pursuit of a ruthless white-collar crook and his anonymous hired assassin perhaps evidence of a life just the teensy-weensiest bit out of control?

Yes, she thought. And about time too.

She slung her jacket over the back of a chair in the anaesthetics base and sat down at one of its three computer terminals.

Proof, Jack had said that morning, was the word made flesh. However it looks, however it seems, whatever you think

169

you know . . . these were just your own thoughts, fleeting, subjective and insubstantial. You knew nothing until you had proved it to yourself. And unless you could prove it to someone else, knowledge was torture. Jack knew. Jack had been tortured – knowing who the bad guy was and what he had done, and watching him walk away because there was no way of proving it. Or rather no legal way of proving it. That was where the breaking in and 'acquiring' copies of compromising documents had come from.

Proof.

Finally, a practical advantage of the RVI's enormously expensive digital-electronic bureaucrat. Medical records were being transferred on to the computer system, but as it would be a herculean task to input all of them, it was being done on a new-admissions basis. So if you had been admitted since about a year ago, your records would be on-line. Before that, down to the basement. The patients Sarah was interested in would probably have been admitted about the time computer technology involved reel-to-reel tapes and flashing red lights, but no matter. She didn't have any names to call up at this stage anyway.

What the computer did have, though, was a comprehensive record of bed usage, as that was the sort of thing that Trusts liked to pay a lot of attention to. She could find out who was in any given bed, any given ward right now, but more than that, she could find out who had been in each bed before that, right back until when the system was first up and running.

She accessed the bed usage files and selected the GRH. The screen offered her the geriatric hospital's six wards: Abercorn, Boswell, Currie, Dundas, Esk and Fettes.

Start at the beginning, Sarah thought, and hit A.

List by Bed no. or Alphabetical by patient?

She hit B and watched the information scroll down the screen, listing the bed number (GRH.Abe.1), the patient's name, date of birth, the reason for admission and the date of admission. She scanned the right-hand side of the list, looking at the dates. One woman had been admitted three months ago, but most had arrived over the past four weeks.

Sarah selected the first bed on the list, occupied by Theresa Sullivan, 3/5/17, since about a fortnight ago. She pulled down one of the menu bars at the top of the screen, requesting a list of all the bed's previous occupants.

170

The turnover was very healthy, from the Trust's point of view. Plenty of names, longest stay about six weeks before death or discharge. But it was the first occupants of each bed that she was interested in, the long-stay crumbles whose ten-year-plus tenures Jeremy had truncated to free up the beds. She needed names, then she could get their records and investigate the nature of their discharges – and what happened next.

The first bed was a non-starter. Its first occupant was admitted only a month before being discharged, probably pitching up not long before the computer system was rolling. GRH.Abe.2 looked hopeful for the second or so it took her to see a recorded admission date of 2/8/84 and then notice that the patient had died rather than been discharged.

GRH.Abe.3 provided an irritating coincidence, its first recorded occupant also having snuffed it.

GRH.Abe.4's first patient *had* been discharged, but again only a couple of months after being admitted.

GRH.Abe.5 reverted infuriatingly to the pattern of 2 and 3, and for a moment Sarah thought she and Parlabane might be enormously mistaken, and she felt an odd, fleeting feeling of relief at the idea of her ex-husband not being guilty of what she was posthumously accusing him of.

She decided to skip down to the three closed beds listed at the bottom of the main screen. GRH.Abe.20 (DISCONT) had been DISCONTed as soon as its one and only listed occupant curled up her toes back in October. GRH.Abe.21 (DISCONT) likewise, this time November. GRH.Abe.22 (DISCONT) January.

Bollocks.

Sarah looked again at the admission date of that last bed: 24/2/82. Then she recalled the two other DISCONTed beds: 13/6/87 and 6/7/78.

And a frightening thought began to whisper in her mind.

She rattled at the keyboard and called up Boswell ward, selecting GRH.Bos.17 (DISCONT) and GRH.Bos.18 (DISCONT). Both listed only one occupant prior to closure, both listed admission dates of several years back and both listed their patients as having died on the ward.

And the whisper became a voice.

GRH.Cur.22 (DISCONT). Last occupant: McGarrity, Agnes Jean, 3/3/02. Admitted: 26/11/83. Deceased . . .

And the voice became a shout.

171

GRH.Dun.24 (DISCONT). Last occupant: Meikle, Dennis Graeme, 19/8/09. Admitted: 14/1/86. Deceased . . .

And the shout became a scream.

Sarah closed her eyes and took a deep breath, then picked up a pen and with her other hand returned the screen to the Abercorn ward list. Then patiently, systematically, she went through every bed in the hospital and jotted down the names of all the first occupants who were both long-stay and deceased.

There were nearly fifty.

The thought, the answer, the logic was in her mind, but she refused to listen, refused to complete the equation until she had seen the records, though she already knew what she was expecting to find when she got down to the basement.

Stroke, pneumonia and various viral infections accounted for about a dozen, but every other file she picked up told the same story, the words clanging discordantly and relentlessly like a cracked bell chimed by a cracked bell-ringer.

They were all ancient dements. Shrieking crumbles, their minds long gone and their bodies following behind at an excruciatingly slow pace. Incurable. Unturfable.

'Called to see Mrs McGarrity at 07.30a.m. Pupils fixed and dilated. No palpable carotid pulsations. No heart or breath sounds. No response to painful stimuli. Patient confirmed dead at 07.34a.m. Suspect Myocardial Infarction. Charlotte Mooney.'

'Called to inspect Miss Murphy at 07.55a.m. Pupils were fixed and dilated. Patient had no visible pulse and no heart sounds. Patient failed to respond to pain. Declared patient dead at 08.02a.m. Suspect MI. Howard Willis.'

' . . . Suspect MI. Dusan Krivocapic.'

' . . . Suspect Myocardial Infarction. Charlotte Mooney.'

' . . . Suspect MI. Gwyneth Peters.'

And so on.

Glazed-eyed, and with a growing feeling of both emptiness and nausea, she made her way downstairs to Switchboard, where she got a copy of the current six-month rota for Jeremy's firm, and where a quick root through a cupboard produced a dog-eared copy of the sheet for the six months before.

Sarah wandered back to the anaesthetics base and sat

down with the rotas, her diary, last year's calendar and her list of dead patients. A few minutes' work confirmed it. Jeremy had been on-call the night before all but six of the deaths, and ethical arguments notwithstanding, it appeared that her ex-husband was the most prolific serial killer in British history.

TWENTY-SEVEN

Parlabane held Sarah close to him with both arms, his hands pressed against the warmth of her shoulderblades, his face in her hair, breathing in the mingling sweet scents of perfume and shampoo. She had one arm around his waist, the other around his shoulders, and her face was buried in his neck.

Fortunately the recent introduction of the subject of mass murder proved most efficacious in repressing Parlabane's emotions and impulses as Sarah sobbed heavingly against him in his kitchen.

'I don't even know why I'm crying,' she sniffed. 'I didn't even like the bastard. It's just hard to accept that the person you were once married to has outstripped Fred West and Bev Allitt in the murder prolificity stakes. It could be as many as thirty. That would make him the British all-time number one.'

'No, no,' said Parlabane in a gentle whisper. Don't torture yourself. Think of the money you'll make flogging his sexual secrets to the tabloids. Besides, he'd only be number two, behind Margaret Thatcher, unless I'm the only one who thought that winning an election was not ample mitigation for the slaughter of thousands of young Brits and Argentinians.'

'This is not helping,' she said sternly, pulling her blotchy and tearful face up. 'Oh, I need a seat, Jack. Haven't you got any bloody furniture in this place yet?'

'Just the bed, I'm afraid.'

'Good enough,' she muttered, and pulled away, walking trance-like towards the door.

'Do you want a cuppa?'

'Got anything stronger?'

'Just whisky.'

'Serve it up.'

'We need to get this straight,' Parlabane said. 'At this stage I understand just a little more than bugger all. We'll start with the basics. First of all, how?'

Sarah sat with her back against the headboard, sipping

steadily at the medicinally large measure of aqua vitae Parlabane had poured her. She stared dazedly at the wall in front, then closed her stingingly bloodshot eyes for a second and looked more focusedly at her questioner, who was leaning against the casement window.

'It's that ole devil called potassium chloride again,' she said croakily. 'A little injection, myocardial infarction, dead crumble, no traces. Except that no one even goes looking for traces because an old crumble dying of a heart attack is not exactly suspicious.'

'Wouldn't someone – a nurse, say – notice he had been injecting the patient shortly beforehand? How long does this stuff take to work?'

Sarah gave a wry but sad grin. 'About a minute, maybe less. But there would be nothing for the nurses to notice. Jeremy was a clever boy, remember. All but two of the records report the patient being found dead first thing in the morning.'

'So is there no one around then or what?'

'Yes, of course there is. But that's not when he did it. They were *found* dead in the morning, but the poor old duffers would have been lying there all night. Jeremy was on-call for the GRH but as a registrar he wouldn't have been there a hell of a lot. He'd wait till he was asked to come in by the SHO to check out some other patient, or maybe popped in late at night, again, ostensibly to check up on some *other* patient. At that time, the few nurses that are around are having a cup of tea or catching up on the ever-increasing volume of paperwork. No one on the ward, certainly no one in the little side rooms. Jeremy nips in, quick jag to the old soul that's overstayed their welcome, and off again.'

Parlabane retained a look of incomprehension.

'But wouldn't someone notice that a patient was having a heart attack?'

'It's not so spectacular when it's some oldster lying down in their bed, probably asleep. Nothing to see. Trust me, Jack, the first anyone would know there was something wrong would be the next day when the poor soul's cup of morning tea was found going cold. SHO gets called to examine, declares death, times it then and there. And in the one-in-a-million chance of anyone thinking something's suspicious, Jeremy isn't in the equation at all because it was a completely different patient that he was dealing with.'

'But couldn't these be natural deaths? If they're all such ancient old fragile things?'

'Technically, medically, yes. There's no way of proving he was responsible for any specific death, that's why I don't know how many he actually killed. Chances are not everyone who died of a heart attack in the middle of a night that Jeremy was on-call was injected with anything. But not everyone wasn't, either.'

'How can you be sure?'

That bitter, regretful smile.

'Crumbles never die. I told you that. They last forever, unturfable, permanent fixtures. Now and again, one of them is bound to cack it eventually. But not thirty in six months, and not all from MIs, and definitely not all on the nights that the same registrar was on-call.

'Cheers,' she nodded, and had a large swig from the glass.

'Well blinking flip,' Parlabane said, sighing and running a hand perplexedly through his unruly mop. 'That would appear to cover "how did he do it". But I suppose my next question has to be how *could* he do it? A need for ready cash doesn't turn you into a wilfully homicidal maniac.'

Sarah just sat there, shaking her head, staring into space again. Then tears began to form once more in her eyes, but she blinked them away and wiped her face with her sleeve and gave a sad little laugh.

'I'd be surprised if he lost a nanosecond of sleep over any of them. You're forgetting, Jack. Jeremy didn't go into medicine because he had some kind of caring vocation. It was just the family business. To him, patients weren't people. They were conditions, diseases. In this case incurable – and worse, uninteresting – ones.

'These weren't lovable old grannies, either. George Romero's – full of the living dead, remember? Bewildered shells, bereft of all the things that usually let us identify with another human being. The only distinguishing character-istic of each one would be their phrase, their shriek. "Take me out, take me out, take me out." "Come down from there, come down from there, come down from there." "Ming-a-dring, ming-a-dring, ming-a-dring." Most of the language is gone, just some fragment somehow remaining, and that's what they'll scream when they're scared or need some attention, what they'll shout when they're angry or when they're happy, and what they'll just mutter for no apparent reason at all.

'Relatives – if they have any – seldom or never visit. Christ, who's going to come in for that? "How's it going, Uncle Bill?" "Ming-a-dring." "Nice day for it, eh?" "Ming-a-dring." "I see Hearts won on Saturday." "Ming-a-dring." Seeing the person they once knew reduced to a living corpse that doesn't even know they're there, and may not even know he or she's there – who wants to put themselves through that?'

Parlabane nodded. 'So these are people some might say were better off dead?'

'That's a matter of much argument and debate. Certainly, most of them would be marked down as NFR in the event of an arrest.'

'NFR?'

'Not for resuscitation,' Sarah stated. 'We don't go in for euthanasia, but there are times when it is clinically decided to let nature take its course. And these days, with this "living will" business, people are actually requesting such non-intervention for themselves.'

'But these ones didn't.'

'Hardly. The wording of these things has to be a bit less ambiguous than "ming-a-dring". And this wasn't non-intervention.'

'Something a bit more "pro-active", Mr Lime might say?'

'Quite. But Jeremy would still have thought it a fairly logical and even humane course of action. They don't know where they are or what's going on. They don't have anyone who's going to mourn their passing – in fact you could say that in some cases it would allow the relatives to finally properly mourn the loss they've gradually suffered over several years. It's quick and painless. And those beds could well be put to better use.'

She finished off her drink and handed the glass to Parlabane. He placed it on the window-sill and sat down on the edge of the bed.

'Right,' he said. 'That's method and plausibility covered. The tricky part is Lime. It's one thing bribing a hard-up doctor to off-load a few unsuitable patients on an unsuspecting Eventide rest home, but it's quite another to sidle up and offer him a few grand to quietly bump them all off. Unless

Lime paid Jeremy just to free the beds and Jeremy chose his own method of doing so.'

Sarah was shaking her head.

'Lime knew,' she said. 'And I know this for a fact. For a start, he sent his own hitman armed with potassium chloride to kill Jeremy. They must have discussed it, or how else would someone like Lime know about its properties? Even if he did know about potassium chloride independently, it's rather a huge coincidence that he would suggest its use to murder Jeremy, wouldn't you agree?'

'Yes,' he said. 'Also, I suppose Lime would have wanted to know how Jeremy planned to go about it in case he thought it was too risky. But the problem remains: how did Lime know to approach Jeremy? He was in a position to know Jeremy was skint, but how could he know Jeremy would be amenable to administering widescale involuntary euthanasia? And harder still, how could we prove he knew?'

Sarah arched her brow. 'I sat in the anaesthetics base today and asked myself the same question, maybe looking for a way of proving to myself that it wasn't true, that it couldn't be true. How could Lime know Jeremy's views on even voluntary euthanasia? But the answer was literally staring me in the face.'

She reached over to her bag, lying on the bed beside her, and pulled from it a yellowed and dog-eared piece of folded, glossed paper, the corner Parlabane could see dotted with small holes. She unfolded it and held it up for him to read.

'They never clear the noticeboards, so unless someone takes it upon themself to remove something, it can sit there for years, getting stuff pinned in front of it. The bottom half of this was still showing below an ad for last year's Christmas ceilidh.'

It was a poster advertising 'The Great Medical Ethics Debates', organised by Midlothian NHS Trust – 'We've got a heart in the Heart' © – and sponsored, rather unfortunately, by Diarrax, a new drug promising relief from diarrhoea, but not, presumably, of the verbal variety.

There were three scheduled debates, with formal participants listed beneath the subject titles and the promise of an open floor before final summing-ups. 'Jehovah's Witness to the prosecution: religious objections to medical procedures'; 'A doctor's right to choose: moral abstention from terminations'; and of course, scheduled as the start-of-run opening attraction, 'The sanctity of life or dignity in death: euthanasia and policies of non-intervention'. The name Jeremy Ponsonby MBChB MRCP was listed under this last title.

'Don't be confused by the dates,' Sarah said. 'This was donkeys ago. I didn't actually go to any of them. They were all on nights when I was on-call. But the idea was that you had one invited big-noise on each side plus several doctors from within the Trust who particularly had a beef about that ethical question. Obviously Lime could have attended, heard some very radical ideas, and realised a possible solution to his bed-occupancy problems. However, I noticed that there's quite a fair spread of departments and disciplines under the other two, but nearly all these names under the euthanasia title – on both sides – were either covering or would later be covering the GRH. A staggeringly convenient coincidence.'

She handed Parlabane the poster.

'I called that oily little turd, Medway, as he obviously had a big hand in using the debates to present "an outward-looking face of the Trust", as he put it. I told him I was trying to settle an argument, that a colleague said the "Great Ethics Debates" were Diarrax's idea but that I maintained they had been dreamt up by the chief exec. He was delighted to tell me that yes, the whole thing *had* been Stephen Lime's idea, and wasn't it a shame that people didn't always get credit for these things blah blah blah. I asked who had suggested the subjects and he told me Lime had come up with the euthanasia one "to get things off to a rollicking start" but had left it to Medway to seek suggestions from the clinical staff as to the others.

'In enthusiastically blowing – or should that be sucking – Lime's trumpet he told me that the great man had been so enthusiastic about making the first one "a success that would set a high standard of oratory and controversy" that he had specifically encouraged certain doctors to take part, doctors "who were likely to come up against that specific ethical dilemma". He had been less "hands-on" after that.'

'I can imagine,' said Parlabane.

'It wasn't a debate, it was an audition,' Sarah stated flatly. 'Killing off the patients was Lime's idea in the first place, and he came up with "The Great Medical Ethics" crap to see whether there were any likely contenders working at the

179

GRH then or who had a spell at the GRH on their rotation. The other two debates were just cover. He probably didn't even attend them.

'So Lime hears Jeremy and who knows, possibly some others, who sound like they fit the bill. But then he finds out – or maybe he already knows – about Jeremy's financial problems, and suddenly he's got a perfect candidate. And when he speaks to him about it, subtly, gently, he probably talks about how the funds going on those patients could be spent on so many more valuable things. Maybe more Intensive Care beds, or better still, funding for those name-making research projects that Jeremy and his pals are so bloody keen on.

'And perhaps *that's* why he killed him. Maybe Jeremy got shirty when the beds started to close but the money showed no sign of being diverted.'

Now it was Parlabane's turn to shake his head and smile wryly.

'More simple than that,' he said. 'Golden rule of assassination, Dr Slaughter.'

'What's that?'

'Kill the assassin.'

180

TWENTY-EIGHT

The second worst day of Stephen Lime's life had actually started quite well. Lying in his bed, thumbing through the copy of *Asian Babes* he had bought on the way home last night, he had happened across a spread on a little cracker who quite exquisitely reminded him of that young girl who worked in the newsagent's where he bought his cigars.

The ensuing toss was easily the most satisfying sexual experience he had enjoyed in years.

After that he got up and dressed, and made his way downstairs to the kitchen, where he helped himself to a frugal breakfast of six Kellogg's Pop Tarts and a mug of decaff. Sitting at the table, he learned from the radio that overnight, England had won the test match down under with several wickets to spare, and felt that all was well in Heaven and on Earth.

Leaving the dishes for Mrs Branigan, who would be in later on, he picked up his briefcase and his beloved portable and got into his company Mercedes. He popped some Phil Collins into the CD player – God that man could write brilliant songs, especially that lovely, touching one about the homeless – and drove to work.

Things sort of deteriorated after that.

First he had to sit through an incredibly tedious meeting with some consultants, an interminable moan-in about funding and bed availability that just proved his theories about medical staff's inexhaustible capacity for whining. And why weren't these miserable sods on the wards, that's what he really wanted to ask. He didn't pay them to sit in meetings all day, complaining about their lot and trying to tell *him* how to run a hospital.

Then he had found a letter on his desk signed by about two dozen house officers and SHOs, yet another gripe about the state of their on-call accommodation. He really could not believe the sheer temerity of these people. They got these bloody rooms for nothing – what did they expect, the Ritz? And of course it contained the usual digs about the comparative opulence of the administration offices – yawn – where managers were only in nine to five, as opposed to the whole nights and weekends *they* had to spend on-site – snore snore.

So there's a bit of mould on the ceiling. Call the cops. Bloody hell. The lazy bastards were supposed to be on the wards, not snoozing away in their on-call rooms.

He told his secretary to print out the standard reply about how patient care had to be the first priority when it came to budgetary allocation, and therefore the Trust couldn't afford to squander money upgrading accommodation that already met BMA minimum standards (i.e. the rooms had a bed, a table and a telephone).

But the real trouble started with a call from David Forbes.

'David. What the bloody hell are you doing? I've told you never to call me here. Have you forgotten how disastrous it could be if someone found out we knew each other?'

'Here, don't get shirty with me, mate,' came the indignant reply. 'The reason I'm having to call you there is to try and *avert* a fucking disaster. We're looking at a mass bail-out by our proposed investors.'

'What?'

'Maybe you'd like me to call you back at home tonight, when you're not at work and the project's dead in the water.'

'Don't get huffy, David. Tell me what's going on.'

'Nothing's going on. That's the fucking problem. It's the sound of silence, Stephen. It scares the shit out of people.'

'But you told me they were queuing up for a slice of this.'

'They were. But they can only put up with so much nudge-nudge, wink-wink. They appreciate that there's been a need for discretion, but they were hoping for some kind of announcement by now. You know yourself how enthusiastic they were about the project, but the longer this goes on, the longer *nothing* goes on . . . the more they've been thinking I'm talking out of my arsehole.'

This was very bad news indeed.

'And they've been talking to each other, Stephen,' Forbes continued. 'Confidence is low. The whisper is that there's a hotel project in Bristol getting off the ground, and a few of them are thinking of putting their cash into that instead. The potential's not as great, they know that, but it's all out in the open right now. There's even fucking brochures printed – architects' plans, the works. Now you know how these people think. If one or two of them bail out and go for the Bristol deal, they'll *all* fucking bail out.

'They're sitting at their desks, thumbing through glossy brochures and I can't give them a bloody thing other than that we've got an undisclosed city-centre location in Edinburgh. You have to make an announcement. I'm not prepared to watch millions of pounds disappear through you dragging your heels over closing this dump just because you're worried about protests from a few doctors and nurses. Where's your balls? You don't need to announce the land deal, for fuck's sake, just the closure would be enough. Then I can go to them and show them the site, drive it home to them that it's for real.'

Forbes was right, he knew. And he *had* planned to make the announcement. In fact it would have been made by now but for that bloody idiot Mortlake buggering up the Ponsonby thing. His blood was boiling at having to listen to Forbes make that crack about being scared of protests from fucking doctors and nurses. He would happily ride roughshod over the bastards and turn two deaf ears to all complaints, but the delay had nothing to do with them. Forbes had no idea of the dangers he had negotiated – and was still negotiating – to make this thing possible, but that was no consolation.

The truth was, between them they didn't even have the three mill needed to buy the land, never mind the money it would take to develop it, and if the investment didn't materialise, it was all for nothing. The GRH would still close, no question, but there would follow months, maybe years of waiting for a buyer for the site, all the time having to listen to whining about how it could be used for patient care or some other useless crap. Maybe just the consolation of a small kickback from whoever they agreed to sell to. But no money-spinning hotel and conference centre, no cut of the purchase fee, and not even the satisfaction of putting the Trust into the black.

Suddenly the pressure was on, a clock was ticking.

Enough pussyfooting around. The police had signally failed to make any progress on the Ponsonby case and he had waited long enough to see where the cards would fall.

He'd have to set the wheels in motion, force his own hand.

'Tell them,' Lime said firmly. 'Tell them what the site is, show them the maps. And assure them I'm announcing the closure first thing on Monday morning.'

'Good man,' said Forbes. 'Bloody good man.'

Now there was no going back.

His heartbeat was picking up pace from the sudden exhilaration, the feeling of events moving again towards his long-planned success after the temporary limbo of recent days. However, the threat of what could go wrong was now realler than ever, and it was vital that he remained alert and on top of things.

He felt nervous and paranoid. Nervous was a bad thing because it showed, it told tales. He would have to calm himself, present his usual air of assuredness. Paranoia was all right, as he had to remain on-guard against every possibility.

It was this that led him to boot up the computer. He had a feeling there might still be some communication he had sent to Forbes among his files somewhere. It was encrypted, so no one could read it, but now that all systems were go it would be wisest to wipe it from the system altogether. Unfortunately, he couldn't quite remember what its name would have been, so he'd have to open up the likeliest-sounding documents and check them out.

There was something slightly different about the list of files, he was sure; something he just couldn't quite put his finger on but which was not exactly as it should be. Never mind. There was a file called 'FSD-DF' that seemed to ring a bell. He double-clicked on it and reached to gulp a mouthful of tea as he waited for the programme to launch. When he looked up, the document was on-screen, indeed a potentially very embarrassing letter to David Forbes at Four-Square.

He was just about to delete it when it occurred to him that the computer had not asked for his decryption password, just gone ahead and opened the document. He clicked the window closed and looked again at the list of files in his private folder. They were all tagged as 'Wordsmith doc's when the encrypted ones should have been tagged as 'Cryptlock doc's.

It was a bloody nightmare.

Someone had opened his files.

Someone had acquired his password. In fact, all of his passwords.

Someone was snooping on him.

Then in one horrible moment he realised not only who it was, but – in answer to what had been niggling at him since yesterday – where he had seen him before. It was that journalist, that Jack Marylebone or whatever he was called, who was supposed to be giving the Trust a good press in some Yank rag. He had looked distantly, hazily familiar when Medway had introduced them yesterday, but although he couldn't think where from, there was a tone of discomfort about the memory. Medway had said he lived in the States and was just back over on holiday, but the face had bothered him nonetheless.

Now he knew.

It was the bloke in the newspaper, the *Evening Capital*. The picture on the front page the night the Ponsonby story broke, when he had crapped in the bloody bath. He was the neighbour, the man being led away by the cops.

Mother of Christ.

He took some deep breaths, trying to slow his heart and stop himself from trembling.

Right. Damage limitation.

This bloke had been at the files and he would now know about the GRH and the Capital Properties deal. He would also probably have figured out Forbes' and Four-Square's part in it all. However, this Marylebone wouldn't know about his own share, as that was too well hidden and certainly couldn't be gleaned from what was on the computer files. So all Marylebone would really have on him was passing on some inside knowledge, maybe at the outside an accusation of favouritism and impropriety in accepting a low bid for the GRH from a firm he seemed to have a connection with.

But the very reason Marylebone would have been at the files at all was that he had somehow linked him with Ponsonby, and that was what was most dangerous. It was extremely unlikely that the hack could have worked out what the link was, but it was still possible that he had, or that eventually he might.

It didn't bear thinking about. But he *had* to think about it.

The bodies were all long buried, and there was nothing incriminating to be found about them anyway. Ponsonby was dead, so he couldn't squeal, and if he had squealed before he died, the game would be up by now. So the only way anyone would suspect something would be if they noticed that an inordinately large proportion of deaths at the GRH were of long-stay patients.

Again, it was extremely unlikely, but still possible, and therefore couldn't be ignored. And worse, as this bloke had been into the computer system, there was a worst-case scenario that he already knew and even had this stuff on a disk as proof. The medical records of the patients concerned were, mercifully, not computerised, but the bed-usage files could tell Marylebone all he needed to know.

But either way, there was a solution.

You couldn't tamper with the computerised medical records; once you had OKed an entry, it was permanent. You could add but you couldn't take away, to stop clinical staff from ever trying to cover up a mistake. However, the bed-usage files were a different story. He could go in and change them right now, swap names of legit elderly medical discharges from wards on the RVI with the dead GRH long-stay ones. That way, even if on a million-to-one shot, Marylebone had found out – and even if he had copied the files – his information would be useless, as the Trust's own computer system would contradict it.

He called up the bed-usage files and requested the GRH.

The computer beeped a rebuke.

GRH bed-usage files in use. User: sslaughter.

No, he thought.

No no no no no.

Because (no no no no) wasn't that (no no no no) the name of (Jesus Christ no no no) . . . hadn't he heard Jeremy (no no bloody fucking hell no no no) mention the name (no no no no no) . . . joking about it, how the divorce would take her (oh God please no please no) from the illustrious name of (Jesus Jesus Jesus bloody fucking bloody hell) Ponsonby to the ridiculous and embarrassing (aaaaaaaaaarrrrghhhh) Slaughter?

Lime got up and ran to his private chief executive bathroom and was retchingly, convulsively sick, emptying his stomach in three voluminous dispatches and going on to suffer several subsequent spasms of the dry heaves.

He crouched with his arms around the pan, breathing heavily, sweating malodorously and watching the world spin. When the walls eventually returned to a stationary position, he got up and went to the sink, splashing his face with cold water.

He felt very faint, his head a cacophony of hysterical voices. He wandered out of his office and downstairs in a trance-like daze, and headed out to the hospital gardens to get some air. Twenty minutes of pacing and wandering in the cold failed to produce quite the desired effect, so he walked out of the RVI grounds and down the street to the nearest pub, where he ordered and instantly knocked back a straight triple gin.

That was better.

He had to think straight, remain calm, work out all the options and possibilities, and only then decide what action to take.

First of all, he mustn't just accept apparent evidence at face value and imagine the absolute worst. After all, wasn't Ponsonby's ex an anaesthetist? The RVI was a notoriously labyrinthian hospital and the anaesthetists had always been whining about not being able to find half of the patients they were scheduled to be gassing the next day, as they had to discuss the anaesthetic with them in advance. Consequently, when the computers came in, the anaesthetists had requested – and been grudgingly given – access privileges for the bed-usage files to help them keep track of where their patients were.

It was plausible that Dr Slaughter had just coincidentally been accessing the GRH bed-usage files for routine patient location. But he had to know, and there was a way to find out.

He downed another treble and called Medway to ask which doctor this Marylebone character had been shadowing last night as part of this 'twenty-four hours in the life of the Trust' nonsense.

'It was Dr Sarah Slaughter, sir,' Medway told him cheerily. 'In fact by coincidence I'm just off the phone to her. She was wanting confirmation that the "Great Medical Ethics Debates" were your own idea. Sir? Mr Lime? Mr Lime?'

Kneeling on the floor, hugging the pub's single, extremely smelly, stained and pube-encrusted toilet bowl when the agonising dry heaves finally released him from their crushing grip, Stephen Lime realised there was still an escape route.

That idiot Mortlake had been the cause of all of this, but appropriately there was a way that he could get him out of it.

After the lumbering moron's disastrous fuck-up, Lime's first instinct had been to get Darren out of Edinburgh as fast as possible, but when he had calmed down he realised that it was wisest to keep him around as a kind of insurance policy.

Now it was time to cash it in.

TWENTY-NINE

'In the name of Christ, Jenny, would you slow doon for fuck's sake,' gasped McGregor as the rear of the car swung out to the left across the junction, then whipped back into line as Dalziel changed down and floored it, having turned right through the red traffic lights, siren blaring and eyes flashing with malicious delight.

'Sorry, but you have to understand, sir. I'm compensating for my feelings of inadequacy as a female in a male-dominated profession by over-asserting myself in a traditionally macho activity.'

She banked out into the oncoming lane and sped past three cars before lurching joltingly back into the left as the angry lights of a massive Shore Porters lorry blazed before them.

'You're scaring the fucking shite out of me, that's what you're doing,' yelped the Inspector, checking his seatbelt again and gripping harder on the inside door-handle with his left hand.

'Aye, that's the other thing I'm doing. I thought now might be a good time to resume discussions of my controversial haircut.'

'Don't fuckin' push it,' he growled. He heard a furious retort from the engine as the car torpedoed alongside another line of traffic, headlights bearing down upon them from a rapidly decreasing distance ahead. 'Oh, look, would you watch the blood . . . Jesus sufferin' fuck.'

Jenny glared at the image afforded by the grubby rear-view mirror of the inevitably slow Mini Metro – sorry, Rover 100 (she thought with a sneer) – that had caused the tailback.

'What is it, don't those things *have* a fourth gear?' she muttered.

McGregor dared to let go of the underside of the seat with his right hand to wipe sweat from his forehead with a handkerchief.

'You know, we're not actually in automotive pursuit, Detective Constable.'

'Aye, but if we don't get him at his house we might be.

Won't do much good if we get there and he's buggered off.'

'And it won't do much good, wherever he is, if we're married to a fucking skip lorry.'

Parlabane had raised the stakes. There was a bloody surprise. Send the guy to look for a stolen box of fireworks and he'd probably find an international nuclear missile smuggling network.

'Fuck,' she had said, which hadn't really covered it. 'Thirty?'

'About that,' he had replied.

She had been debriefed in Parlabane's bedroom (although she would think twice about putting it like that in any company), Sarah sitting on the edge of the bed, the Glaswegian catastrophe-magnet leaning against the wall beside her.

'There's a chance that two or three might be coincidences,' he went on, 'but I don't think margin of error is likely to be a big plank in the defence's case.'

'No,' she concurred. 'Either way, it's a respectable haul.'

'Yeah. It's all right, we've phoned Guinness,' said Sarah sharply.

'Oh God, I'm sorry,' offered Jenny, remembering Sarah's inextricable link to this diabolical shambles, and noticing the red in her eyes and the puffiness around her face. Explaining it all to Parlabane would have been plenty, but having to go through it all again had obviously been painful.

'It's okay,' said Sarah, shaking her head and waving her hand dismissively. 'I'm dealing with it. To be honest I'm starting to feel more embarrassed than anything else. Thank Christ I changed my name back. Never thought Slaughter would have *less* murderous connotations than the alternative.'

'It's not going to do much for the professor's career, I wouldn't have thought,' Jenny reflected. 'It *was* coronary care you said he was in, wasn't it?'

'Yeah,' Sarah sniffed, managing a small smile. 'Don't imagine he'll be doing any more papers in the BMJ about the relationship between potassium and cardiac dysrhythmia.'

Jenny watched Parlabane place a hand on Sarah's shoulder, caught her glance back up at him. His body language had been unmistakably protective towards Sarah throughout her revelations, hers noticeably less relaxed on the occasions he had moved away or left the room to fetch disks, documents or drinks. It had clearly been a tough and furiously hectic few days for both of them, Jenny thought sympathetically. But as there was definitely no need for any *more* bloody tension, she was sure they would both feel a sight better about a whole lot of things if they stopped fannying about and just got on with shagging each other.

'Look, I don't think we should allow Dr Ponsonby's record-breaking achievements to distract us,' Parlabane said. 'Tabloid shock-horror aside, Jeremy is really just the sad fuck here.' He looked down suddenly at Sarah. 'I mean, eh . . .'

She shrugged.

'No, it's OK. Sad fuck does it for me.'

'Fine. The evil bastard, let's not forget, is Lime.'

'Nae kiddin',' said Jenny. 'I'm not sure if there has ever actually *been* a charge of "conspiracy to mass murder". Under those circumstances I would give him marks for originality, if it wasn't that the whole thing ultimately boils down to another tawdry get-rich-quick scam, albeit with an unprecedentedly high body count. I must say, I'm seldom surprised at how many corpses some people are prepared to climb over to get to the gold, but this guy was going to need Sherpas.'

'He's a bad, bad man,' Parlabane had said. 'Go get him.'

Lime had already left the RVI by the time they got there, and as his secretary explained, he had in fact gone home early that day, complaining of feeling unwell.

'He certainly looked very queasy,' she had said. 'To tell you the truth, he hasn't exactly looked in the pink all this week.'

'Must be something preying on his mind,' Jenny had reflected.

She pulled the car up in sight of Lime's house, McGregor drawing her an unforgiving look as he felt finally able to unplug his seatbelt.

They sat there silently awhile, until they saw Gow and Callaghan approach on foot from the opposite direction.

'I told them to park round the corner, out of sight,' McGregor explained.

'What about the rest of the happy crew?' Jenny inquired.

'There is no rest. Just us wicked.'

'What? This is a mass murder suspect, sir.'

'Aye. And he's a very well-connected mass-murder suspect,' McGregor said, climbing out of the car. 'We can't scream up in about five motors and go steaming in like the Sweeney. This bloke'll have lawyers out the arse. After the shite we've been through on this case, I'm not having the bastard slip the net because we fucked up on some rights technicality. We're just going to knock the door, play it all very calm and above board.'

'And what if his knife-wielding china's in there too?' Jenny inquired, locking the car. 'Are we just going to politely ask him to accompany us down to the station as well?'

'If the hitman's there, all the better. It'll make it a sight simpler to establish their connection in court.'

'Aye,' said Jenny. 'I'm sure a blade through the guts will be much easier to take as long as I know it's going to help secure a conviction.'

'Aw dry your eyes.'

Gow and Callaghan went around to the back of the house as Jenny and McGregor approached the front door and rang the bell, its electronic Big Ben melody chimes sounding from within.

After a couple more tries and a few more minutes, Gow reappeared to confirm that they had seen no one through any of the windows, although Callaghan was staying put in case Lime was lying low and waiting to make a break for it.

'Back door locked, aye?' McGregor asked.

Gow answered with an apologetic nod. The Inspector tutted.

'Hang on,' said Jenny, and walked across the lawn, past the bare-breasted, amphora-carrying fountain statuette in the middle of Lime's pond, to the driveway in front of the garage, which adjoined the house on the right-hand side. She had spotted that there was a slight gap between the bottom of the tip-up door and the concrete below.

'Doesn't appear to be closed properly,' she said. 'Looks like someone might have shut it in a bit of a hurry.'

She wedged her foot into the gap and hauled it back towards herself, the grey metal panel suddenly swinging upwards and open to reveal an empty floor marked by oily tyre-tracks, and in the left-hand wall, a door leading into the house.

'Golly gosh,' she muttered, and walked slowly inside.

'Careful, Jenny,' McGregor said from the garage entrance, as she nudged the unlocked door open from the side, and cautiously climbed the two steps up to it.

The sharp crack of a light-switch being flicked on rever-
berated around the empty space as McGregor and Gow
proceeded into the garage.

'Oh my God,' they heard Jenny gasp, horrified, from within.

The two men looked at each other gravely.

'No again,' muttered McGregor, closing his eyes. 'Please
God, no again.'

Gow was too pale in anticipation to say anything at all.

They both took a deep breath and headed up the steps,
behind where Jenny was standing transfixed in the hall.

'It's just hideous,' she said.

They glanced down reluctantly at their feet, their shoes
almost submerged in a green, savannah-like shag-pile carpet;
then upwards, where a monstrous glass chandelier hung
straining from the hall ceiling above a stretch of the staircase;
then dead ahead, through the glass double-doors into the
lounge, where from above the green-marble mantelpiece, a
huge and screamingly gaudy oil portrait of the great man
smiled down, his insufferably smug visage depicted against
the backdrop of a billowing Union Jack in a work evidencing
all the subtle colour coordination of a goalkeeper's jersey.

'I think I preferred the place with all the puke,' Jenny
observed, before moving forward, perversely entranced, to
meet the gaze of the householder, captured behind a glass
sheet on the wall.

'Oh, yes,' she said with elated disgust. 'Yes indeed.'

She rubbed her hand across the back of Lime's jet-black,
Real Leather sofa, listening to the resultant squeak with a
chuckle, and giggled as she pirouetted with girlish delight
to take in the suite's remaining constituents and the marble-
topped bar built into one corner of the room.

'You have absolutely no idea how much money it takes to
make a place look this cheap,' she said as McGregor entered
the room. 'I can't wait to see the bathroom. There just *has* to
be a Jacuzzi, and I'll bet we find a waterbed in the boudoir.'

'I'd much rather you found a shotgun,' McGregor stated
darkly, throwing her a small, red, empty cardboard box which,
according to its markings, had at one point contained two
dozen shells.

'That was on the kitchen table. Where do you think the
contents are?' he asked. 'More to the point, where do you
think he intends the contents to go?'

193

THIRTY

'Jenny off to the RVI then?' asked Sarah, emerging from the bathroom, gently patting her wet face with a towel. The tears had gone, and although her eyes were still a little bloodshot, her skin had regained a uniform colour.

'Yeah, five, ten minutes,' said Parlabane. 'Thought you'd drowned yourself in the wash-hand basin. You look better for it, though.'

'Thanks. So, what d'you reckon Lime'll get?'

'Fat lady hasn't sung yet, Doc. I'd wait until he's been found guilty before wondering about that. He'll have heavyweight legal representation and we'll get to see some quality squirming before he's nailed. It would sure help if they could find the hitman.'

'Have they made any progress?'

'Well, they reckon they almost got him last night. He was holed up in a boarding house down on Pilrig Street in south Leith. Jenny says the old B&B wifie marked him, but by the time the cavalry arrived he had had it away on his toes. However, as he was at a B&B they figured he would have nowhere to go, so they've been combing the streets all night and all day. There's a police artist's impression in the *Evening Capital*, apparently.'

'So if he was staying at a B&B, that means he's from out of town,' Sarah said.

'Cockney accent, with a nice line in day-glo shellsuits, according to the landlady. From my experience, I'd say Essex. East of Barking, west of Sarfend. Lime's partner in this dodgy Capital Properties carry-on is based in Romford. I wonder, I wonder. Maybe the partner's in on this too. Some kind of Bad Clothing County conspiracy. I wonder what Edinburgh District Council would have said when they submitted plans for an office block with twenty storeys of stone cladding and a used-car lot in the forecourt.'

Sarah poured herself a glass of water from the kitchen tap and gulped it down, then offered Parlabane some, but he declined.

'One question, Jack. If this hitman has been brought in from out of town, what's he doing hanging around so long after the job? Especially as it didn't appear to go very smoothly.'

Parlabane irritatingly changed his mind about the water and cupped a few handfuls from the tap to his mouth.

'At the request of his employer, I'd guess,' he said. 'Either he's being paid to wait around or he's *not* being paid until.'

'Until what?'

'His responsibilities are fully discharged.'

'And what does that mean?'

Parlabane smiled. 'Not what *he* thinks it means. I've told you before. Bad guy psychology one-o-one. Work it out. Actually, come to think of it, I'm surprised Lime hasn't made his move before now. But if his boy's out on the street he'll be forced to pretty soon.'

'I'm sorry, Jack, I don't follow.'

Parlabane walked out to the hall.

'I'd better call the station, make sure Jenny's figured it out too,' he muttered.

As he picked up the receiver, the doorbell rang, sharply and briefly.

'And as if by magic,' he said, putting the receiver back on its cradle and walking to the door. 'That'll be a cop from across the Square now.'

He glanced through the spyhole but there was no one in front of the door. Curious, Parlabane opened it and walked forward, leaning over the banister to look further down the stairs. Then he felt something cold and metallic pressed into the back of his head.

Arse, he thought.

Fuck, fuck, fuck, fuck, fuck.

'Back up. Into the flat,' said a low, nervous voice.

'Why?' Parlabane asked, not moving.

'Because there's a shotgun pointed into the base of your skull.'

'How do I know it's not just a wee length of pipe?'

He heard the unmistakable racking sound of the shotgun being pumped.

'Why don't you just take my word for it?'

'Well, ordinarily I tend not to take the word of fat Tory bastards, but by the law of averages they've got to be telling the truth once in a while.'

Parlabane slowly backed up, turning his head slightly to see Lime staring wildly at him down the shaft of the weapon. He looked tremulous and very pale, his eye twitching and his beard flecked with what looked suspiciously like vomit.

'Hands in the air,' he hissed, giving Parlabane a blast of his breath.

'Jesus,' Parlabane reeled, lifting his arms. 'Breath's worse than the Princess of Wales'. You know, bulimics are supposed to be a bit skinnier than that.'

'Shut up and get inside, you little shit.'

Sarah gaped in horrified disbelief as the pair entered the hallway and Lime kicked the front door shut behind them.

'Impromptu employer courtesy visit,' Parlabane said. 'See, the Trust really does care.'

The look on Parlabane's face puzzled and did not comfort her. It was a livid mixture of apology, rage and – most strangely – tedium, like he had had enough of this crap but had no choice but to tolerate some more.

The look of pale, breathless fear he saw reflected upon Sarah's visage did little to temper Parlabane's emotions either.

'Oh how lovely,' Lime said. 'You're both together. Two birds with one stone and all that. This is very convenient.'

'We aim to please,' Parlabane muttered.

'Very interesting. The snooping journalist is screwing the ex-wife.'

'Chance would be a fine thing,' Parlabane said. 'You know, just because I'm not hairy, fat and ugly doesn't necessarily mean I get the girl, Pork Boy.'

'Watch your mouth, you little prick. Now, down the hallway, the pair of you. Into that room. Slowly. No false moves.'

Parlabane walked delicately and deliberately behind Sarah into the sparsely empty living room.

'Did he actually use the phrase "no false moves"?' he asked.

'Yes,' she said, in a frightened whisper, then cleared her throat. 'I'm afraid so,' she added, louder.

She was trying very hard, Parlabane knew. She was a brave woman, and his anger grew that she was being put through this – and by that sweaty, fat turd.

'What a twat,' he said, shaking his head. 'What a fucking grade-A cock-end.'

'I think you're forgetting who's got the gun here, Mr Marylebone.'

'That's Parlabane,' he spat. 'Jack to my friends. You can call me Mr Nemesis, the end of your sad little wank-in-the-corner world.'

Lime stood in the centre of the room with his back to the close-curtained window, indicating to his captives to take position a few feet apart, two yards in front of him.

'I wouldn't be so sure about that, Mr . . . Parlabane,' he said, trying unconvincingly to sound calm. 'You don't get to be a man of my achievements by being stupid. I've got the situation well under control.'

'No no no no no,' said Parlabane quickly, shaking his head. 'Believe me, tubby. When you're standing in a stranger's living room with two hostages at gunpoint, twitching away like Herbert Lom, then from my experience that means the situation is a considerable fucking distance from being under control.'

Lime's eyes bulged. 'Shut up,' he grunted. 'And you're no one to lecture me about being in control. You're the idiot that raided my computer but forgot to re-encrypt all the documents you were snooping through.'

'Fuck,' whispered Parlabane furiously, trying not to catch Sarah's dismayed glance.

Lime grinned at Parlabane's discomfiture.

'Now. Both of you – on your knees, this second.'

'Afraid we can't, chubster,' Parlabane spat. 'Sarah's got a bucket-handle cartilage and I'm not religious, so I find the kneeling position extremely demeaning. Sorry.'

Lime shook the gun, the veins popping out of the side of his head.

'On your fucking knees or I'll blow them off here and now.'

Sarah knelt down, her eyes rigidly fixed upon the sweating and unhinged figure before them.

Parlabane, infuriatingly, remained standing.

'If you were going to shoot me, wobble-arse, you'd have done it by now. I think we both know that the second that gun goes off, the stop-watch starts counting down to the arrival of the polis, and if all you've done by then is pop a hole in my leg, then you've not really achieved a great deal with this wee expedition, have you? Now, it seems likely to me that the reason you're here is that you think we've rumbled you – we have, by the way – but that you think there might be a way out of it, correct? In which case, the second you blow one of us away, the second you pull that trigger, is the second that your last chance evaporates. So no, Pork Boy, I'm not going to fucking kneel. Why don't you just get on with telling us what you want?'

Lime pointed the shotgun directly at Parlabane's head and clicked off the safety catch.

'What you are forgetting, smart-arse, is that *unless* I can use you two to get out of this, I'm looking at about a dozen life sentences. So if I decide all is lost or you decide not to cooperate, it's not going to make much difference to the judge if I kill you two interfering little cunts as well. Now on your knees.'

Parlabane dropped slowly to the floor and looked over at Sarah, who glanced back glumly at him.

'Interfering little cunts, he said, Sarah,' Parlabane remarked. 'I think he meant "interfering little *kids*", you know, like if it wasn't for us, Scooby and Shaggy, the old haunted amusement park scam would have worked a treat.'

Sarah managed a small laugh.

Herbert Lom, fast becoming Marty Feldman, looked less amused.

'You know, fatso, the cops are on to you,' Parlabane stated matter-of-factly. 'We've told them everything. So you could go ahead and kill us, I suppose, but I think you should maybe just skip to the "killer turned the shotgun on himself" part right now.'

'I'm getting pretty fucking tired of you,' Lime rumbled breathily. 'If the police were on to me, they'd have done it by now. And if they're on their way, if you've already told them everything, then I've got no reason to keep you alive. So, this time the truth: what have you told the police?'

'Nothing,' Sarah said instantly, nervously. 'That's the truth. We've told them nothing.'

Parlabane closed his eyes and nodded. 'She's right. But why don't you just shoot yourself anyway? Go on. Go for the old shotgun blowjob. Make it come in your mouth, big boy.'

'Shut up.'

198

'No. Come on, go out in style. Gargle those pellets, Stevie baby.'

Lime took a step forward, clicked the safety back on and rammed the barrel of the gun into Sarah's head, leaving a large gash on her cheek underneath the right eye.

She squealed and bent over, pressing both hands to her profusely bleeding face. Parlabane began to move towards her.

'FREEZE,' Lime barked, pointing the weapon. 'Now,' he said, breathing heavily. 'Enough of this bluffing nonsense. You're right, Mr Parlabane. Shooting you is my last resort at this stage. But, as I've just demonstrated, there are interim measures to encourage cooperation.'

Parlabane slowly pulled a handkerchief from his pocket – waving it to assure Lime of what it was – and tossed it to Sarah, who dabbingly applied it to her traumatised cheek.

'You know what I hate about guns, Mr Lime,' she said bitterly. 'They make killing too easy. They can put the power of death into the hands of anybody, even a bullied-at-school, sad little wanker like you. All you need to do is pull a trigger and someone dies. It takes no effort.'

Lime patted his mouth in a yawning gesture.

She shook her head gently, staring into his nervous, ugly eyes. 'You fucking arsehole. If you knew what it's like, what it takes to repair someone, to restore their body to working order . . . you'd understand the obscenity in being able to rip it all apart at the flick of a switch. It's too easy. You don't even need to want it that much.'

'It's not the most subtle or elegant of weapons, I know,' he said, suddenly very smug as he realised he finally had them under control. 'But needs must and all that, Dr Slaughter. And you're wrong, you're very wrong. Because if I have to shoot you, it will be because I do want it, a great deal. If you are jeopardising my investment, I'll have *millions* of reasons to want to kill you. You see, we have a saying in business: Do anything you can to protect your investments. Anything you can, Dr Slaughter.'

'You know, we have a saying in Glasgow, too,' growled Parlabane. 'It's you'll get yours, ya bastard.'

'Yes, Mr Parlabane, I'm shaking in my shoes here, really,' Lime said tiredly, glancing at his watch. 'Now, why don't you cut the crap and tell me how much the pair of you know.'

Parlabane glared into Lime's piggy little eyes.

'Why don't *you* cut the crap, fuzzball. You know fine what we know. If you didn't think we knew everything you wouldn't have turned up here with a fucking shotgun. If we *didn't* know what you were up to, that's the kind of behaviour that might make us a wee bit suspicious.

'We know you had Ponsonby murdered, in case anyone ever found out you had paid him to kill long-stay geriatric patients at the GRH, so that you could close the place. We know that you're authorising the underpriced sale of the GRH to Capital Properties. We know you own half of Capital Properties and we know you stand to make a lot of money from building . . . whatever on your fresh, new, city-centre site.'

Lime smiled. 'Hotel. Conference facilities. That sort of thing. Multimillion-pound development.'

Sarah snorted. 'A word of advice,' she said. 'Don't run the hotel like you ran the Trust. If you keep closing beds every day, you won't have anywhere to put the guests. Oh, and if you keep having them all injected with potassium chloride, you might find they have difficulties paying their bills.'

Lime's eyes widened involuntarily, and he glanced at his watch again, more anxiously this time.

'Well, maybe you didn't know we knew *that* much,' Parlabane said, 'but you knew we were on to you. So what do you really want, eh?'

The doorbell rang, shave-and-a-haircut.

Lime blew out a small sigh of relief and smiled.

'I really want . . . you to meet someone.'

THIRTY-ONE

Sod it, Darren had thought.

Bloody fucking sod it.

Lime could keep the money, it wasn't worth this, and it certainly wasn't worth the stir he was looking at. He had to get out of this fucking city as soon as bastarding possible, get out of fucking bloody Scotland and get to a fucking bloody hospital where they weren't on the look-out for nine-fingered men. Or even four-fingered ones.

He had crawled into the railway tunnel out of sight and found a little niche in the wall where he could lie down. He had spent most of the day there, although he had no real idea what time it was. He had slipped in and out of consciousness, as much a result of whatever that old bitch had poisoned him with as the blood loss, and as the niche was about thirty yards inside the tunnel, he was in near-darkness the whole time.

It was usually a train that woke him up when he slipped away again; they had rumbled through every couple of hours, going in either direction. Eventually, one had rolled through when he was already awake, and that was when the idea struck him. They travelled this part of the route grindingly slowly, so he could maybe climb on to one of them and see where it took him. This was the east coast, after all. Fucking thing could be in Newcastle in a couple of hours. Get some Geordie doctor to stitch his hand back on then catch the first bus to London. Convalesce for a while, hit Lime for some sick pay or even disability benefit. And if the cunt wouldn't shell out, wait until he was fit again, come back up north and collect what he felt he was owed – with interest.

In the silence of the tunnel he heard the first tell-tale rattlings of the railway line to signal that there would be a train along soon. He picked himself up and staggered back to the mouth, from where he awaited its approach. It limped along inside the tunnel like an iron worm, a nerve-stretching shriek of metallic protest that horribly reminded him of his most recent personal tragedy.

As the engine emerged, he began jogging alongside, getting

his pace right and picking his spot. With a painful lunge he leapt upon the coupling between two of the huge metal containers and flailed his good hand at the steel bar that ran down the outside of one of them. His hand missed and his foot slipped, causing him to land on one trunk of the heavy steel coupling with the full weight of his impact concentrated on his bollocks. Almost passing out once more with the paralysing pain, he slumped forward and rattled his face off the unforgiving metal of the container carriage in front, and sobbed pathetically to himself.

The train rumbled along for a few minutes with Darren perched where he had fallen, his forehead pressed against the cold, hard surface and his hand gripping the steel bar above to keep himself steady. He was worried about his feet getting caught on something underneath and dragging him below the train, but his crushed testicles would not allow him to attempt to change position. He just had to summon the energy to keep his feet raised rather than merely hanging down.

Then the train began inexorably to slow, and he anticipated the jolt of it finally coming to a standstill just a moment too late to stop himself sliding forward and thumping his tender balls against the base of the car in front.

He rolled over and fell to the ground, where he was not consoled to see that the train had pulled into a depot at a council sewage disposal works, probably only quarter of a mile from where he had boarded.

That was when he realised that the letters EDC, stamped rustily on all of the white containers, did not denote the name of a major rail freight operator.

His life had turned to shit and now he had hitched a ride on the shit train going to the shit disposal depot.

He sat up, buried his head in his hand and stump, and sobbed again.

Then, suddenly, he was startled by a familiar sound from his bag – a sound of unexpected hope, forgotten options – and within minutes, completely out of the blue, the picture had become much, much brighter.

Lime had sounded pissed off, of course. He usually did. You didn't phone a guy like Darren when everything in the garden was rosy. He had been trying to call for ages, but there had been no response – that would have been because he was in the tunnel.

But what the hell. He was back in business, big-time. Lime had found a way to clear everything up and end this fucking nightmare, but he needed Darren's help and was prepared to pay top dollar for it. Lime said he knew it was damn good money he was offering and so he was expecting damn good service, and suddenly Darren felt like a real man again, a man with a job, a man with skills in demand, a man with a life.

Two jobs and out. He had explained that he was in pretty bad shape, but Lime said it didn't matter – they'd already be restrained. He just had to wield the knife. He didn't tell Lime that it was his knife-hand that was lying in the fucking satchel, but the stupid cunt wouldn't know the difference between good bladework and bad – he'd only care that they died. And with thirty grand the total pay-off, he wasn't going to turn down the work, for fuck's sake. Thirty K, then Lime would drive him – *drive him* – to Carlisle, where he could get himself sorted then head for home.

And appropriately, the first job, his redemption job, was at the same address as that fucking Ponsonby fiasco.

It was all turning around, everything.

So often had he cursed the fact that it only seemed to be daylight for about twenty minutes in this cursed northern city. But now, the fast-encroaching darkness – pitch by about tea-time – would cloak his stealthy progress. And those hopeless hours pounding the miserable lanes and sidestreets with that rancid dead dog in his bag now yielded in his mind a map of tree-shadowed back gardens, deserted allotments and derelict waste-grounds that he could invisibly negotiate between here and his salvation.

Maybe it was more a sewage *treatment* works, he thought, stumbling away back down the track with a grin: shit got delivered there, but it got changed into something much better by the time it left.

Hey. That was fucking poetry, man.

'Now,' said Lime, looking relieved but still visibly trembling. 'I am going to answer the door. I'm going to back down that hallway and I am going to keep this gun pointed at you the whole time. Remember: if you try anything, if anything happens that makes me feel the situation's out of control, I start firing. So no funny business and no . . .' he paced forward and burst open Parlabane's cheek with the barrel . . . 'false moves.'

203

Lime was shaking like a Parkinson's sufferer and sweating as if the room was a sauna. He backed away from them very slowly as the doorbell was rung once more, staring wide-eyed at the two of them, side on to him as he edged delicately backwards.

'Well I guess you can scratch that stuff I told you about computers not running off and telling the boss someone's been asking awkward questions,' Parlabane said mournfully. 'Sorry.'

'He's going to kill us, isn't he,' Sarah mumbled, swallowing back tears. 'He doesn't have any other solution, does he?'

Parlabane hadn't been quite sure what Lime might have in mind. At first he had thought the man was just crazy with wild desperation, then begun to realise his actions were a little more calculated. But he wasn't sure Lime was personally up to killing them, or stupid enough to fire off two shotgun rounds in a tenement block in a city centre square and not expect to be seen leaving the scene of the crime. He had thought of Lime's hitman, wondered why – if Lime had decided the solution was to kill the pair of them – he hadn't just got a professional on to it, instead of showing up in person.

He had entertained a strong suspicion that the stupid prick was just playing it by ear, which was why Parlabane had been as obstructive as possible, playing for time in the hope that someone or something might intervene before events came to a final head. So when the doorbell rang he had enjoyed a moment of unexpected hope, then seen it die in Lime's look of relief. The bastard was expecting someone, and it could only be one person.

'Lime's not going to kill us,' Parlabane whispered from the side of his mouth. 'The hitman is going to kill us. Probably a lot more quietly than with a gun.'

'Potassium chloride?'

Parlabane sighed. 'I'm afraid that's not his speciality.'

'Oh Jesus,' she said, and wept.

'Look, I realise that this sounds like the most fatuous thing in the world to say right now, but try and stay calm. No matter how bad it looks, don't panic, don't do anything that'll force Lime's hand. And stay alert. If there's a chance, an opp . . . Jesus Christ alfuckin'mighty. What the fuck is that?'

The creature staggering drunkenly, bow-leggedly down the

204

hallway with Lime was the most revolting vision of bloody carnage Parlabane had ever seen.

He was a leprous gargoyle, shattered and decayed.

He was a giant zombie, slouching lumberingly along, barely sentient, barely conscious.

He was the angel of death in a shellsuit.

His hair was a deep, unnatural black, like it had been coloured in with a magic marker, and was strewn with pieces of twig and tufts of moss and grass. His bloodshot eyes stared unfocusedly ahead, the lids slowly closing then laboriously raising themselves again every few seconds. His nose was spread flat across his cheeks and had bled heavily down over his lips, chin and neck. And his mouth went on forever.

The opening didn't stop at the edges of his lips, but continued on into both cheeks for several centimetres, although it was difficult at first to see where his lips actually stopped and these extrapolatory slits began, because of all the dried blood plastered around them.

His left arm was bare from the sleeve of a grass-stained and (of course) bloody white T-shirt, down to the length of shiny material tied around his forearm in an untidy bow, above a gory stump that appeared to be oozing a variety of unhealthy-looking bodily fluids.

His right hand, Parlabane did well to notice amidst such distraction, was missing its index finger.

'Bloody hell, Darren,' Lime exclaimed when he took his eyes off his hostages long enough to survey his employee. 'What the blazes happened to you?'

'Hannassdent,' Darren mumbled, his pronunciation suffering from the rather flappy action of his widened mouth.

'Christ, did you lose a fight with a combine harvester or something?'

'Thassnofuckifunny.'

'Where's your hand, for Christ's sake?'

'Nnibag.'

'Well, can you still . . .'

'Coursafuckican. Issem?' he nodded towards Parlabane and Sarah.

'No, Darren, these are dinner guests. Who do you fucking think they are?'

'Butafowt . . .'

'Yes, yes. Change of plan. Turned out she was here with

205

him. Both together. Saves us some trouble. See, Darren? Our luck is changing for the better.'

'Yeah,' spat Parlabane. 'You're on a fucking roll. Should have done the fucking lottery this week.'

Darren put his satchel on the floor, swaying woozily as he bent over to open it with his remaining hand. He pulled his knife from it and stood upright again, having to close his eyes for a second as he recovered his balance.

Parlabane glanced at Sarah, who was choking back the tears to concentrate her efforts on staring sheer mortal hatred at Lime. The sight of the knife made her give an involuntary sob, but just the one.

She glanced back with a look that told him she was down to her last hope, and that her last hope was him.

'Do him first,' Lime spat. 'I'm sick of listening to the smart-arsed little bastard.'

Sarah was briefly astonished to see Parlabane wink, and took a deep breath as she remembered what he said about remaining calm.

'There's something important you should know, big man,' he said.

'Wa?' said Darren.

'Your boss never told you why Ponsonby had to be killed, did he?'

'Just get on with it, Darren,' Lime said, agitated.

'No, I think you'll be pretty interested, Darren. This could have a big bearing on your future. You see, Ponsonby was killing for Lime too. Not the same, more specialised.'

'Kill him, Darren. Cut the bastard's throat.'

But Darren was staring at Parlabane, though his eyes couldn't always keep him in focus.

'He killed twenty, maybe thirty geriatrics for blackbeard over there,' Parlabane said. 'And then he had to be killed himself, because once he had outlived his usefulness, he could incriminate little Stephen. Don't you see there could be a wee bit of a pattern emerging here, big yin?'

Lime was going purple.

'Kill him, Darren. Get on with it. If you don't I will.'

But Parlabane knew Lime wouldn't shoot, because Parlabane knew Lime's plan.

'You haven't quite worked out your role in tonight's performance, have you, Dazza?' he said. 'What did Stephen tell you? Kill the two of us and his problems were solved? He'd pay you top whack because he really needed you? Something like that? Then you could go back to Cortinaland with a fat wad in your pocket? What happens when you've outlived *your* usefulness? See, killing us would stop the cops from ever finding out about Stephen's big secret, but it won't stop them investigating Ponsonby's death, and it's you they're after for that. Find you and they'll find him. Even if you don't squeal, they'll know it was a pro job and they'll go looking for who's paying the bill . . .'

'I swear, Darren,' Lime hissed, 'get on with it or I'm halving your money.'

'But if you're found dead along with us, say, with your head blown off and a shotgun lying in your hand . . .'

Darren turned slowly around to look at Lime, who was now shaking so much he could hardly hold the weapon.

'D-Don't listen to him, Darren,' he stammered. 'He'd . . . he'd say anything just now. He's trying to buy time. Just get . . . get on with it.'

'Think about it, big man,' Parlabane said. 'What was the plan tonight? Abduct me, take me to her house, do us both? Think of the story: killer cuts two throats then blows himself away . . . turns out to be the same guy wanted for the recent murder of one of the new victims' *ex-husband*. Cops can play motive roulette until they get something plausible enough to close the case ASAP. You're dead, we're dead and Stephen lives fattily ever after.'

Darren eyed the shotgun, harnessing all his powers of arithmetic to put two and two together.

'Youcun,' he growled.

'No, Darren,' Lime whimpered. 'He's, he's . . .'

'Golden rule of assassination, Darren,' Sarah added throatily. 'Kill the assassin.'

Darren suddenly screamed and lunged erratically at Lime with the knife. The gun went off as they collided and tumbled to the ground, fingers and flesh raining down about them, the blade skidding across the deck.

Lime had blown the remainder of Darren's other hand off, but with the shotgun trapped between their struggling bodies, he couldn't pump it to get another shot in.

They rolled, tangled together on the floor, Darren pinning Lime down with his weight and flailing his head around in a manic attempt to butt his opponent, now that he had nothing left to punch him with.

Parlabane spotted the butt of the shotgun sticking out from between their waists and grabbed it with both hands, Sarah lunging across to wrest Lime's struggling, sweaty fingers from the handle. She got one finger free and bent it back until there was a loud snap and a scream, upon which all the other fingers suddenly relaxed their grip.

Parlabane yanked the shotgun free from the writhing mass of bloody flesh, took a step back and loudly pumped the next shell into the chamber.

'RIGHT!' he bellowed, eyes flashing. 'Enough of this pish.'

The two combatants ceased their struggle and looked up to see him standing over them, the gun aimed in the vicinity of both their heads.

'On your fucking knees,' he barked.

They rolled apart and climbed to a kneeling position.

'Hands in the air.'

Lime complied timidly. Darren gave a whimper, attempted to raise his two stumps, then closed his eyes and collapsed. His face slammed noisily into the floorboards and he remained motionless.

'Right, spunk bubble,' Parlabane said with malicious delight. 'Open your mouth.'

'B-b-but . . .' Lime mumbled fearfully.

'OPEN YOUR FUCKING MOUTH!'

Lime opened his fucking mouth. Parlabane forced the barrel roughly into the hairy aperture, breaking a front tooth in the process and eliciting a muffled yelp from his captive.

Sarah looked on in confusion. The relief at escaping their predicament had barely had time to register before another horrible possibility had presented itself.

Parlabane looked mad as the proverbial bag full of mad things.

'Calm down, Jack,' she stated softly. 'It's over. He's not worth it.'

Parlabane didn't take his eyes off Lime for a moment.

'Don't worry, Sarah,' he said. 'Stephen and I are just talking here, aren't we? Stephen's an important and busy man, so you have to make the most of it when you've got his undivided attention. I do have your undivided attention, don't I, Stephen?'

'Mmm-mm.'

'Good. Because I want to tell you a wee story. I was hoping to get around to telling Sarah this soon, actually, but you interrupted us. Now, are you sitting uncomfortably? Then I'll begin.

'I used to live in Los Angeles, Stephen. Until very recently, in fact. But I had to leave in a hurry, because one morning I came home and there was a man in my house, waiting to shoot me to death with a silenced automatic. A man I had never met, never even seen before. A hired killer, hired to kill me for reasons I didn't even know. I was snooping – that's what I do – and I guess I must have made someone very nervous that I might discover something they'd rather keep under wraps. Can you see where this is going?'

Parlabane stared deep into Lime's eyes, penetrating into a well of confusion, disbelief and growing fear.

'He was outside my bathroom, waiting to murder me when I finished having a piss. I saw him through a wee slit that was under one of the hinges. So it wasn't going to be a surprise. I knew I was about to be killed, a bit like Sarah and I knew we were going to be killed, just a few minutes ago. It's not a nice feeling, Stephen. Don't recommend it.

'Despair. Terror. Anger. Helplessness. No fun emotions in that list, I'm afraid. But as I'm standing here now, I think even you must have deduced that I didn't get killed. How? Well, very fortunately I found a gun in my bathroom, left there by a friend who had tried to warn me my life was in danger. A friend to whom I owe my life. And a friend I can't even phone up to thank because he's a policeman, and it would acknowledge his complicity in what happened next. Can you guess what happened next?'

Lime let out a whimper and tears began to run from his screwed-up little eyes.

Parlabane nodded.

'I shot a number of holes in the bathroom door, and what do you know – when I opened the door, some of those holes were in the hitman too. I killed him, Stephen. Stone dead before nine in the morning. I had no choice. I didn't *want* to kill him. But can you guess who I really, really, really *did* want to kill?'

Parlabane was attracted to some movement below him, and glanced down to see yellow liquid begin to seep from around Lime's knees

'That's right,' he said. 'You got it in one. The smug, arrogant, conceited, worthless piece of dogshit that thought my life was worth no more than a few grand for a contract. The prick who would pay to have people murdered without being around when the screaming started, when the knives went in or the bullets ripped through the flesh. The prick who was maybe kidding himself on that he wasn't a murderer because he wasn't the one pulling the trigger. And the prick who got such a big hard-on at the thought that he could just order someone's death like he was ordering a fucking pizza.

'Now, once I had recovered from the fear and the shock, once I was able to calm down and get my head straight, I wanted to kill him so much my brain ached. I didn't even know who he was, maybe hadn't met him, maybe hadn't even seen him, but I wanted to put a big fucking hole in his world.'

Lime's mouth began quivering around the barrel of the shotgun, his tearful eyes mesmerised, unable to look anywhere but into Parlabane's.

'Unfortunately, I couldn't. For one, I had to get the fuck out of the country. For another, more practically, how could I ever find him? And anyway, this was LA: big-scale. The guy who ordered my death was probably not even the guy my death was intended to protect. The guy my death was intended to protect probably paid a big salary to the guy who ordered my death to make sure that such problems got solved without him even knowing about them. Kids himself that he's not a murderer because he never even gets to hear about the deaths that are necessary to – how might you put it – protect his investments.

'So I could never get the guy who was really responsible, and that was something I was just going to have to live with. But what do you know? Here I am in Edinburgh a little while later, once again moments from being murdered by a hired killer, paid for by another despicable toley who thinks his business plans are more important than the lives of, what, thirty people? Except this time I know who's behind it, this time it's not so big-scale, this time it's just some greedy wee shite with his fingers in the till. And this time, I've got him kneeling on the floor in front of me with a shotgun in his mouth, waiting for me to blow that hole in his world.'

Sarah gently, tremulously put a hand on Parlabane's shoulder.

'Don't do it, Jack. Look,' she implored, indicating the window. 'There's cops swarming across the square. They must have heard something.'

'It's too late,' Parlabane said, in a chilling, breathless hiss that froze Sarah and made Lime crap in his already damp trousers.

Then he pulled the gun out of Lime's mouth and backed away.

'There's already a hole in his world,' he said with that grin, which Sarah was for once comforted and reassured to see. 'It's between your legs, Stephen, and there's going to be a fucking lot of traffic through it when you go to prison. But hey, don't think of it as rape – think of it as their way of "touching base".'

WE ALL SAID GOOD NIGHT

McGregor surveyed the room before him. There wasn't any furniture this time, but that hadn't proven an impediment to generating more inventively wreaked havoc.

There were several fingers – more fucking fingers – scattered about the bare floor, and blood smeared all over the place in what was becoming a familiarly liberal fashion.

Some pathetic, bubbling, bearded nob-end kneeling in a puddle of piss, having his rights read to him. A semi-conscious cro-magnon with a face that looked like someone had been over it with a lawn mower, who they couldn't handcuff because he had no fucking hands.

And that Parlabane bloke again, which was simply the last straw.

He shook his head, turned and walked back down the hall as Dalziel was returning from the close.

'I don't want to know,' he said before she could open her mouth. 'I don't want to fucking know, Jennifer. I'm away hame to get pissed. I don't want to see or hear anything about this case ever, ever again.'

Jenny walked over to where Parlabane and Sarah were standing together against the wall, back from the official activities taking place in the living room. She, McGregor, Gow and Callaghan had arrived about ten or fifteen minutes after the vanguard of cops from Maybury Square.

'You make a lovely couple,' she observed. 'Matching facial wounds – how romantic.'

'Glad you like them,' Parlabane said. 'We were going to get tattoos, but that's so passé.'

Jenny smiled.

'So what kept the cavalry?' Parlabane asked.

'We radioed the station to get some bodies over here as soon as we realised Lime was loose with a gun, but I understand the fun was already over by that time.'

'And what fun it was,' said Sarah dryly.

'Don't knock it,' Jenny replied. 'I think I'd rather be under armed siege than face the paperwork that's waiting for me after this.'

'Well, Jenny,' said Parlabane, 'if we're catching the bad guys for you, you have to be doing something for your money, right?'

She sighed. 'Aye, I suppose. So are you two OK? No offence, but neither of you quite looks peachy.'

'Nothing a shower and half-a-dozen beers wouldn't cure,' Sarah said.

'Well I'll be buying whenever I've finished sorting out this wee pantomime. So I'll see you in the Barony in about August.'

They sat outside on a wall, blankets wrapped around their shoulders, drinking coffee from plastic cups handed to them by the paramedics, as Lime was led handcuffed across the square and Darren was poured into an escorted ambulance.

'So,' started Sarah. 'Where do we go from here?'

'Well,' Parlabane said, touching the Elastoplast on his cheek, 'I was thinking of going to the pub and getting well and truly blootered, then making a pass at you shortly before I collapse.'

Sarah shook her head apologetically.

'I don't think that would be a good idea, Jack. Sorry.'

Parlabane looked like he was trying hard not to appear too crestfallen.

'Well, I could omit the pass bit. It's not obligatory. I was just . . .'

She put a finger to his lips.

'No,' she said. 'I think it would be wiser to go back to my place, go *straight* to bed and then see if there's any pubs still open by the time we've had enough.'

Parlabane nodded.

'Yeah. That probably is a better idea.'

Then they kissed, a moment of memorable tenderness, release, passion and romance, spoiled only partly by their plasters sticking together and Parlabane's coming off completely when they pulled their heads away.

Stephen Lime was given three concurrent life sentences by a judge who was not impressed by his lawyer's attempts to colour his offences as 'white collar crimes'. His brief's plea for early transfer to a low-security or even open prison on the grounds that his client – while having been found guilty of paying assassins – was not himself personally a dangerous or violent man, was summarily rejected, the lawyer reminded by the judge that threatening people with shotguns and blowing people's hands off was still considered – even in these liberal times – dangerous and violent behaviour.

Nonetheless, Lime still took inspiration from his heroes in top-level British management, and is right now attempting to convince anyone who will listen that he has Alzheimer's disease.

The *worst* day of Stephen Lime's life was the first day he and Big Boabby 'touched base' in Saughton.